SO-CEX-531

FAULT LINES

Also by Anna Salter

Shiny Water

FAULT LINES

ANNA SALTER

POCKET BOOKS

New York London Toronto Sydney Tokyo Singapore

POCKET BOOKS, a division of Simon & Schuster Inc.
1230 Avenue of the Americas, New York, NY 10020

Library of Congress Cataloging-in-Publication Data

Salter, Anna C.
    Fault lines / Anna Salter.
      p.   cm.
    ISBN 0-671-00312-7
    1. Child molesters—Fiction.   2. Psychology. Forensic—Fiction.
   I. Title.
   PS3569.A46219F38   1998   97-53084
   813'.54—dc21   CIP

First Pocket Books hardcover printing May 1998

10 9 8 7 6 5 4 3 2 1

POCKET and colophon are registered trademarks of
Simon & Schuster Inc.

Printed in the U.S.A.

For my father,
Theodore Salter, M. D.
1917–1993
He had the gift of healing.

ACKNOWLEDGMENTS

I would first of all like to thank Sandi Gelles-Cole, who edits all my books privately, and who makes an enormous difference in their quality. Sandi has a lot of Michael Stone in her.

I would also like to thank Helen Rees, my wonderful agent, who is warm, humane, and exceedingly competent—a rare combination.

Likewise, I would like to thank Linda Marrow, my editor at Pocket Books, for her vision and her support.

I would like to thank Lt. H. John Wojnaroski III of the Michigan State Police, Polygraph Section, for the use of one of his many superb interrogation techniques.

My appreciation too goes to my colleagues at the Midwest Center for Psychotherapy and Sex Therapy: Dan Brakarsh, Kristi Baker, Harvey Dym, Carol Endicott, Jane James, Pat Patterson, and Lloyd Sinclair. These folks are my professional family.

I would like to thank my long-term mentor and friend, Regina Yando, Ph.D., for her suggestions, her support, and her love.

I would like to thank Minna Alanko for her superb care of my children and for her friendship. Knowing my children are well looked after gives me the ease of mind I need to write.

How can I teach her
some way of being human
that won't destroy her?

I would like to tell her, Love
is enough, I would like to say,
Find shelter in another skin.

I would like to say, Dance
and be happy. Instead I will say
in my crone's voice, Be
ruthless when you have to, tell
the truth when you can, . . .

—Margaret Atwood

1

He's dead. He's dead." The woman on the other end of the phone was sobbing. I tried to shake the sleep off. I looked at the number the emergency service had given me—Clarrington. If the call came from Clarrington, chances were she was standing over him with a gun. Clarrington was a small, industrial town twenty miles from the thriving university community where I worked. Mills were closing in Clarrington; people were more or less constantly being put out of work, and maybe because of that—or maybe because of some esoteric reason I knew nothing about—Clarrington was, I thought, the center of violence in the known universe. Clarrington was like that square mile in Mexico where all the monarch butterflies go, only every antisocial, drug- or alcohol-addicted, violent person in the world seemed to pass through Clarrington.

"Where is he? Is he there?" I wasn't sure what to say. Nothing in my training as a forensic psychologist specializing in child abuse and domestic violence cases covered

1

some of the things I ran into in the real world when I worked emergency for the Department of Psychiatry at Jefferson University Hospital. I was pretty sure "How do you feel about that?" wouldn't cover it, at least not until I figured out if she needed an ambulance.

The sobbing woman ignored me. "He's dead," she repeated. She was crying so hard I could hardly hear her. "I read about it in the paper." I slumped down in the bed. This was another ball game, entirely. I glanced at the clock. Three A.M. Grief time, maybe, for my unknown caller. Still, if she cared that much, odd she had to read about it in the paper.

"I'm sorry to hear that," I said. I wasn't sure what she wanted me to say.

"I didn't know," she said, "I didn't know he was alive."

Wait a minute. Someone she didn't know was alive is dead, and she read about it in the paper. Why is she upset if she already thought he was dead? I sat up straight again and rubbed my eyes. Was I dealing with someone who wasn't playing with a full deck?

"If I'd only known he was alive . . . if I'd only known. . . ." I waited for the list of regrets: the call never made, the apology never delivered, the amends only planned. "If I'd only known," she wailed, "I'd have killed him myself."

I was stumped. Ah, Clarrington. We all have regrets when someone dies, but being deprived of the chance to murder him? I opened my mouth to say something, I'm not sure what, but my unknown caller hung up. It's just as well. I'm sure there was nothing in my training to cover this.

I glanced at the black emergency book on the table beside me. It was passed back and forth from emergency worker to emergency worker. It included all of the chronic callers—the dependent and the hysterical and the entitled folk, not to mention the truly crazy—that made up the vast bulk of calls on emergency. Without a name I couldn't check to see if my unknown caller made a habit of scaring emergency workers. Certainly, her call didn't fit the pattern of any active emergency caller I had been briefed on. It was a strange fact that almost none of the calls that came in on emergency were true emergencies; mostly they were chronic callers who somehow figured out that a voice on the end of the phone pushed back the night.

I had too much adrenaline from the call to go back to sleep. I got up and walked downstairs and crossed the living room of the tiny A-frame and walked out onto the deck. There was just enough moon to see the small stream glistening below. I glanced at the darkness where I knew the trees began, beyond the stream.

I had retreated to the country a few years ago, to a tiny A-frame with no room for guests. The small deck, the stream below, the hot tub tucked around the bend of the L-shaped deck had all brought something I was looking for. But in my line of work I meet violent folk from time to time, and after I had moved, one had stalked me, gotten into my remote cabin, and eventually tried to kill me. Now there were times when I wouldn't go onto the deck at night without my .38 revolver tucked in my pocket.

On impulse I walked back into the house and picked up the phone to call my office answering machine. At least I think that was the impulse. Maybe I just wanted an excuse to get off the deck, where I felt exposed. I was like a drug addict these days, always thinking up excuses when I didn't want to face the real reason I was doing things. It was more than a little silly to be calling my machine. I checked it before I went to bed, and all my clients had the emergency number for anything urgent enough to be calling at night—but to my surprise there was a message that had come in at two A.M.

"Dr. Stone, this is Camille." Camille was a new client coming in today for the first time. "I wondered if it would be okay if I brought my seizure dog to the session today. She's licensed so she's supposed to be able to go anywhere, grocery stores and things like that. Please let me know because I don't think I can come without her." The voice was tiny and had something in it I couldn't identify: not anxiety, not depression, something odd.

A seizure dog. What the heck is a seizure dog? If people can't do anything about someone having a seizure, what's a dog supposed to do? And why is Camille up at two A.M. worrying about this? She was upset enough to be up and calling me, but too polite to call the emergency number I had given her when she made the appointment. That meant the question was important to her and not just an excuse to make contact.

Was she depressed? People who couldn't sleep in the middle of the night were almost always depressed. But maybe I'd be depressed too if I had seizures so often I couldn't go for a fifty-minute therapy session without my seizure dog.

I was still thinking about it on the way into my office the next morning. The drive was fifteen minutes of green, leafy, postcard New England stuff—three quarters of the year. Whoever put together New England decided that it was only fair—given that New England has green, rolling hills dotted with old farmhouses, given that New England has small, winding back roads that meander next to small, curious streams, given that New England has possibly the fewest McDonald's of any place in the nation and, Vermont at least, has people with enough sense to ban highway billboards—given all those gifts, it seemed only fair that New England miss out on something. New England has no spring.

I am a Southerner, born and bred. And while the South has many things that keep me out of it—Mama for one—you have to take your hat off to the South when it comes to spring. Spring starts in February in the South, and the whole world explodes. There is more color in Chapel Hill in February than there is in the entire state of Vermont in May. And the light. In a North Carolina spring there is light—glorious, endless light—light when you wake up and light when you go to bed. But who could go to bed? I remember sitting on my grandmother's porch on the swing in the evening—everybody sat on their porch in the evening—watching the azaleas sway in the breeze off the water.

I glanced at the brown landscape. It was May and the leaves were clearly waiting for mud season to end before they made an appearance. Mud season is the time when the snow melts leaving enough mud that casual visitors assume some sort of flood has gone through. It is also New England's substitute for spring. It looked less like spring and more like a setting for a horror flick.

By 9 A.M. I was sitting in my private practice office waiting for Camille. I had called at eight to let her know I had no problem with her dog. I heard the door to the small waiting room in the old Victorian house open and walked out to meet Camille. A rottweiler roughly the size of my couch walked in, sat down calmly, and looked at me in a decidedly unfriendly way. She had that I've-got-the-distance-to-your-throat-measured look that attack dogs have. She was definitely a working dog. This is a seizure dog? This dog could cause seizures.

I moved forward to shake hands with the woman on the other end of the leash and saw the dog's muscles bunch. Camille was my height but much rounder. She was pale and looked out-of-shape. Her coloring was all wrong, but I was so focused on the dog it took me a moment to realize why. It was the mismatch. Her skin was fair and her eyebrows were blond, but her hair was dark brown, almost black. Very few natural blondes dye their hair an unflattering shade of dark brown, but she had. She had bright eyes, and somehow the body she was living in, her whole appearance, didn't seem to

5

go with those eyes. She was also shaking noticeably, but if she had seizures, maybe she had cerebral palsy too. The shaking didn't explain the dog. You don't need an attack rottweiler just to help with seizures. I know you're supposed to call them protection dogs these days, but somehow when I looked at this one, the term "attack dog" just kept coming to mind.

Camille shook hands with me limply. "I don't know if I can stay," she said as soon as we were seated. "I'm not feeling very well." She was sitting across from me, but she kept glancing at the windows over her shoulder.

"Is there anything that would make you more comfortable?" I asked. She looked extremely uncomfortable.

"Not really," she said, and silence filled the room.

I waited a few moments and then asked, "Where would you like to start?" This was clearly not someone I could just fire questions at. Probably the dog was trained to bite anyone who fired questions at her.

"I . . ." Her voice trailed off, and she looked down. She seemed to be fighting back tears and trying to steady herself.

"Take your time. Say what you can." I considered the options while I waited. Paranoid? No, paranoids are more concerned with what was in the room than what is outside. Paranoids scan the room and inevitably fasten on the couple of videotapes on my bookshelves. Then they look around for a camera. Paranoids keep glancing at the notes I'm writing until I hand them over for inspection.

If not paranoid, what? Battered spouse. Possibly. Battered spouses are often in pretty bad shape, and they are sometimes afraid their husbands will find out they are seeing a therapist. An estranged spouse might be stalking her. But there was something in her level of fear that I had never seen before, not even in a battered spouse. I didn't think it was battering.

"I can't talk about it." She was crying. "But I need to know if I'm ever going to get better. It's been five years. I don't think

I'm going to get better. I can't go outside, and I haven't been alone without Keeter since then. And sometimes I think he's in the house, and I know he's not because Keeter is just sitting there, but it really seems like he's there." She paused and cried for a few minutes.

"I didn't used to be like this," she said. "I was never like this. I was a nurse," she said as though that identity was now light-years away, which it probably was.

Rape? A violent, stranger attack? Maybe. I had seen some people in pretty bad shape from that, but never this bad. Something had shattered her whole sense of identity. She was hiding in the dark hair and the overweight body—which I'd be willing to bet she didn't have before—hiding in the house and behind the rottweiler, but what besides rape would make someone hide like that?

"Most people get better eventually from almost any kind of trauma," I said. I didn't say how much better. Some don't get a whole lot better, but it probably wouldn't help her to hear that right now. "I don't know what happened, and I know you can't tell me right now. But when I learn a little more about what you've been through, maybe I can give you a better idea of time." This woman needed whatever reassurance she could get, even if it was just a vague, most-people type.

"When I talk about it, it makes it worse."

"I'm sure that's true. It kicks off the flashbacks, right?" She nodded. "Tell me about Keeter," I said. She looked up, surprised. She looked at Keeter and then at me. "She won't hurt you," she said. "She's very well trained."

"She looks very well trained," I said. She had to be because it was only her training that was controlling her; this lady sure wasn't emotionally strong enough to control an attack dog right now. "I didn't ask because I was worried," I said gently, which I think was true—although I did know a dog trainer once who was attacked by a rottweiler while she was sitting behind a desk signing its owner up for a class. The rottweiler had gone over the desk straight for her throat without any warning. I glanced at Keeter again.

"I asked because you can probably talk about her without kicking off your flashbacks since she wasn't part of whatever happened to you. You got her, afterward, right? So she's related to what happened, but she wasn't there, and maybe I could learn a little bit about your symptoms without triggering anything if you talk about Keeter and your relationship with Keeter."

She looked at me thoughtfully. I was glad to see she could pull out of herself for a moment. It was a good sign, small, but good. "I've been to counselors before. They always want to talk about what happened."

"But you can't, or you start to fall apart, right?"

"Yeah, but then they just let me talk about anything."

"We'll go at this sideways," I said. "We won't hit it directly at first, and we won't go away from it entirely either. We'll get as close as we can without tearing things up for you. Okay?"

She nodded and sighed, looking ever so very slightly relieved. "I do know a little bit about this problem," I said gently. She was lost and frightened, and she needed to know the person she was asking for directions had a clue which way to go. Otherwise, the anxiety about being lost would make the problem worse.

"What's a seizure dog?"

"Well, she's trained to press a button on the phone, which dials a number for medical help, and also, she takes me home if I'm out somewhere and get confused. I've had seizures all my life, but I didn't get a dog until a few years ago. My first dog was a little terrier, and she was wonderful, but I didn't feel safe afterward. I wanted a dog who could protect me too, and I know Keeter can, it's just . . . I just don't feel safe anymore, even with Keeter."

"So Keeter's a protection dog who's also trained to deal with seizures?" She nodded. It must have been something, trying to train Keeter to let help in instead of keeping people away if Camille was hurt. The two jobs didn't seem all that compatible, and I wondered which way Keeter would go in a pinch.

Camille's shaking had stopped, and I realized it was more likely anxiety than cerebral palsy. This woman was a train wreck, but what kind of train had hit her and how was she ever going to tell me?

"I was never like this," she said. "I was a nurse," she said again. "I was an ICN nurse." She looked up, and I saw her face fill up. That is part of what happens with trauma: People end up grieving their own lost lives. Camille couldn't get used to not being who she had been.

And who she had been was probably a whole lot different than who she was now. The Intensive Care Nursery is one place where nurses never get stuck putting patients in and out of examining rooms. Half the preemies are critically ill at any given moment, and codes are as common as visitors. ICN nurses have a ton of responsibility and do some procedures restricted elsewhere only to doctors.

"Tell me about being a nurse."

Her hands stopped twisting the shredded Kleenex in her lap, and she sighed. "I had a rotating shift. I could have had an escort to the car. I mean, I was on the night shift, and I got out around midnight, and some of the other nurses would call for security to escort them to the parking lot. But I was just never afraid, and security would take twenty minutes, half an hour to come. I just didn't want to sit there. So I always walked down." She stopped abruptly, and when she spoke again all the fluency was gone, and she sounded almost aphasic.

"I just never . . . I didn't expect . . . I *know* I locked the car . . . It was still locked when . . . I still don't know . . . mummy, oh, mummy." Her face had paled, and her eyes were scanning like she was watching something. Keeter stood up, looked at Camille then looked at me. Keeter had a hell of a job. How was she supposed to know whom to attack? I was just sitting there, but Camille was clearly reacting like someone was coming after her with a knife.

Keeter distracted me, and I didn't redirect Camille quickly enough. By the time I opened my mouth to get her back to safer ground she had stood up and was turning to the door. "I have to go," she said.

"Wait," I said urgently. "Don't go yet. Let's pull this together." This was no way for her to leave. I take seriously the idea that therapy shouldn't make people worse. I like to think people leave my office in at least as good shape as they came in. If Camille left now, she would have a dreadful day of flashbacks and fears.

She paused and turned back toward me.

"I want you to imagine a safe place. Sit down for a moment," I said quietly.

She stood a few minutes longer, and I said nothing, just waited. You can't just order trauma victims around; they have to make their own decisions. Finally, she perched hesitantly on the edge of the seat. I guess you'd call that sitting.

I opened my mouth to ask her to shut her eyes and then realized what a stupid idea that was and said instead, "Just imagine any place you'd feel safe—a garden, a fortress, a boat, anything. It doesn't have to be a real place. It can be anything you can imagine." If she could do it, it would bring down her autonomic arousal. Her heart would quit pounding, her palms would quit sweating, the racing thoughts would slow. It would distract her from the threatening imagery and decrease the chances she'd spend the day having flashbacks of whatever had happened to her.

She looked in the distance for a moment and then at the

floor. "There isn't any place that's safe," she said. "There isn't any place he couldn't be."

"Then imagine a place where you would feel a little *less* afraid, however improbable a place. A cloud, sitting at the right of God, surrounded by tanks, whatever." I waited for her to think it through.

"A grave," she said, finally. "Maybe there." I hoped against hope she'd laugh ruefully, but she didn't. Instead, for the first time a fleeting look of peace passed over her face at the thought. I felt my heart drop. When a grave is the only place people feel safe, sooner or later they try to get there.

After she left, I thought it over. It sounded like rape, but it didn't sound like rape. Something more had happened, not that rape wasn't bad enough, but I had always been impressed with people's ability to recover from some pretty terrible traumas. Most women who are raped regain their ability to function more quickly than this lady had. Someone had been waiting in the parking lot that night, and something had happened—something worse than rape—but what?

I was still musing when the phone rang. Carlotta, my longtime best friend despite the fact that she had wasted a six-foot frame on modeling, for God's sake, instead of basketball, was on the line. She was a lawyer now—at least she had come to her senses and gotten a real job. Funny how you can tell if something is good news or bad just by the sound of the voice. I didn't like it when Carlotta's voice sounded like it did now. Once she had given me some very bad news, indeed, and ever since then, I cringed when I heard that sound in her voice.

"What's up?" I said.

She sighed. "Have you seen the papers?"

"No," I said, "What's in them?"

"Why don't you go get one? I'll meet you for lunch. You'll probably be able to talk by then," she said.

I glanced at my watch. It was 10:30. "No," I said evenly. "You're scaring the shit out of me, and I don't want the anxiety of racing around looking for a paper not knowing. What happened?"

There was a pause. "I'm sorry," she said. "Nobody's died." I realized I had been holding my breath as I let it out. "It's just that Willy's out."

"Willy's out? Willy's out? Willy is not out. What? How the hell could he get out?"

Carlotta started to speak, but I kept going. "How could Willy get out? Have you been in a maximum security prison recently? Those things are fortresses. He could not have gotten out. This is a joke, Carlotta. Just the sort of trick that son-of-a-bitch would play. He likes to give me a heart attack."

There was another pause, and I realized this was just what Carlotta had been trying to avoid. I was screaming at her as if she had personally smuggled Willy out of prison. I shut up. After a moment Carlotta spoke.

"He didn't escape, Michael. He won on appeal. The court remanded the case back for a new trial and released him in the meantime."

"What? On what basis?"

"Suggestibility. The court ruled that some of the social worker interviews of the abused children were leading and suggestive."

"I don't believe this." My decibel level was rising again, but what sane person's wouldn't have?

"There's more. I don't think the case will see court again, but look, I don't have time to get into it; I've got a hearing. Go get a paper, and I'll see you at Sweet Tomatoes at noon." Carlotta hung up. How could she leave me hanging like that? Why wouldn't it go back to court?

Carlotta had joined the county prosecutor's staff this year, which meant, even though Willy's case hadn't been in our county, Carlotta could probably get the prosecutors on the case to talk to her. I wondered if she had called them already and that's how she knew it wasn't going back to court.

Alex B. Willy was out of prison. I had never known Alex B. Willy out of prison, and I didn't care to now. When I met him three years ago, he was starting a thirty-year sentence for child molestation. That was long by today's anemic sentencing standards for child molestation, but it had come to light in the sentencing phase of the trial that Willy had had quite a string of victims.

He had turned out to be swimming up to his ears in narcissism, and he had delighted in telling me about all the offenses he hadn't been caught for. As bad as his known track record was, the truth was worse: Willy was not a simple, manipulative, get-the-children-to-trust-him-and-then-molest-them-pillar-of-the-community-dime-a-dozen child molester. Willy was a sexual sadist. What turned him on was hurting people, children, to be specific.

I made it to the corner and stared at the machine holding the *Upper Valley Times* as though it were a mortal enemy. God damn that son-of-a-bitch. No sane person would have put him on the street. I finally came up with the quarters I needed and jerked the paper out. I couldn't wait to get back to the office, so I just stood there and went through the paper until I found it.

MINISTER WINS APPEAL.

Appleton, NH—The New Hampshire Supreme Court ruled today that Alex B. Willy was entitled to a new trial on charges of first degree sexual assault against a minor. In a case that many felt was marked by overzealous prosecution and naive faith in the credibility of chil-

dren's testimony, the court ruled that Mr.
Willy's accusers, a six-year-old boy and a seven-
year-old boy had been subjected to leading and
suggestive questioning by county social workers during their investigation. The Supreme
Court held that the lower Court had erred in
permitting the children's testimony without
first holding a "taint" hearing to determine
whether the children's recollections had been
too influenced by suggestive interviewing to be
reliable.

The ruling stated that a new trial cannot
occur until such a hearing takes place. Prosecutors must prove in the "taint" hearing that the
children's recollections are reliable and were
not unduly influenced by suggestive questioning. If they fail to do so, the state is barred from
seeking a new trial.

Mr. Willy stated that, "I'm just grateful for
the chance to prove my innocence, and I am
confident that a new trial will do just that.
Hopefully, this dreadful ordeal will soon be
over. I hold no malice in my heart toward
anyone. I know the adults involved meant
well, and the children, of course, were just
children and as such were easily swayed by
those around them."

Classic Willy. I could feel the pull of the words even in print.
He sounded exactly like an innocent man, and the average
person reading that statement wouldn't even question his
innocence for a second. In fact, Willy sounded like a *kind*,
innocent man who wasn't even angry about the horrible
things his accusers had put him through.

Willy had a gift. Dealing with Willy was like dealing with an emotional chameleon. He knew, as though he had radar, just what kind of emotional tone people wanted to hear, and he could produce it unfailingly. I had studied Willy for countless hours, but I still didn't know how he did it. Something in me couldn't grasp it.

Slowly, I walked back to the office. Just to reassure myself of my own sanity, I opened the drawer with my Willy-tapes in it. With his permission I had audiotaped some of my interviews with him—getting a sadist to really talk was such a rare thing I had decided to tape so I could go back over them. I could learn a lot from Willy although what he had to teach was pretty depressing.

I thumbed through the cassettes until I found the one I was looking for: the label read "Ways to Con Adults." Willy had signed permission for me to tape his interviews with the written stipulation that I could never share the tapes with anyone else. Just like Willy to tantalize me with something and then make sure I couldn't use it.

I pulled out my tape recorder and popped the tape in. I had left the tape set at the section it seemed to me was the most important. "It's very simple, Dr. Michael," Willy was saying. "Simply find out what people need. What do they need? Do they need money? I'll loan it. Do they need a listening ear? I'll be there. Do they need reassurance? I'll supply it. People are full of needs." He had laughed.

"The only difficult part is figuring out what they need *most*. What do they need badly enough that they will sell their firstborn, so to speak. What do they need badly enough that they will ignore what is right in front of their eyes? I have molested kids in the backseat of a car with their parents in the front seat."

I had been floored by that and hadn't spoken for a moment. Willy had laughed again. "Indeed, I have. I'd simply pull a blanket over a sleepy child and fondle them with their parents in the front seat. They'd wake up, of course, and that trapped look they'd give their parents was *so* satisfying. They knew they wouldn't be believed. Somehow they knew. And they were right. Their parents wouldn't have believed them if they had reported me on the spot.

"There are subtleties, of course, which I can't expect you to grasp. You are really such a *limited* student." Which, I thought every time I heard the tape, was true.

"Like what?"

"What they need. What they hunger for. Ultimately, it's never anything concrete. Oh, sometimes it starts with money, a loan to get them out of debt or something, but it always turns out that the money represents something else—importance or support or something—something that turns out to be much more addictive than money.

"The highest level"—and I could still remember Willy's eyes starting to shine—"is to supply something crucial that the person is not even aware of needing, something completely unseen that they become totally dependent on my providing. Then you can take chances, which of course intensifies the excitement."

"Like what?"

"Oh, you can make the abuse of their child a little more obvious and a little more obvious until they have to work not to see it."

"And what is it that people need badly enough, even unconsciously, to tolerate your molesting their child? Friendship? Self-worth? What is it you supply, Mr. Willy, that is worth so much?"

"Well, Dr. Michael, no good cook shares *all* the ingredients. Really, you don't expect me to do all the work for you, do you?"

And what was it that Willy had supplied *me* with, that kept me coming back to see him? Willy didn't want to talk about that, but then again, neither did I.

I popped the tape, picked up the newspaper, and stared glumly at the article. A taint hearing. The case was over. There wasn't any way to prove something didn't exist. It was like trying to prove a white elephant *wasn't* in the room. Some misguided fool had asked a leading question somewhere along the way, and after that, anything the children said would be considered tainted.

Never mind that the children disclosed abuse *before* the interview with the county social worker—otherwise, there wouldn't have been an interview. Never mind how many symptoms the children had—and Willy had described to me their deterioration in gloating detail.

The bottom line was simple: One thing people surely needed was to believe they could tell who was safe and who wasn't, and a whole lot of people had trusted Willy. He looked good; he talked good; he was a popular minister in his community who had regularly visited the sick and the elderly. A lot of people had been devoted to him. If there was *any* way to explain away the accusations against him, people would take it. And now they had one.

By noon, Sweet Tomatoes was in high gear. Nontraditional pasta dishes are their specialty, and nobody can cook pasta like Sweet Tomatoes. The area is too small for the restaurant to have any serious competition, but it would have held its own anywhere. I have tenure at Sweet Tomatoes.

I was led to the last table by the window, and waved to Harvey, one of the owners, as I sat down. He came over and joined me. "Got a minute?" he said.

"Probably more than a minute," I answered. "I'm waiting for Carlotta to get out of a hearing." Prosecutors don't control when hearings end so Carlotta might or might not show up in the foreseeable future. Harvey sat down, and I resisted the temptation just to close my eyes and listen. He had that kind of deep, snuggle-up, male voice you can't hear without thinking about climbing into bed. He was a teddy bear of a man, a big guy carrying a little extra weight around his middle. You could easily overlook the extra weight. That voice would sound very good about an inch from your ear. But I swore off married men. I did.

"Still making the world safe from child abuse?" he asked.

"Nah, I switched. I testify for the perps now. More money in it."

Harvey looked taken aback. "Just kidding," I said. "I almost got in trouble in court with my sick sense of humor, though. A prosecutor asked me why I was charging so much less than the defense expert, and I almost said, 'Costs more when you sell your soul,' but I didn't."

Harvey laughed. "Why not?"

"Too risky," I answered. "I've already had one judge recluse the jury in the *middle* of my testimony and say to the prosecutor, 'Your witness has come perilously close to calling the defense a flim-flam.'"

"You can't call the defense a flim-flam?"

"Nope. Not even when it is. You're supposed to be respectful. What's up with you?"

"Nothing really. We're going to Italy again. Testing new wines for the restaurant."

"Tough life," I said.

"I wanted to ask you something, about a neighbor of mine. . . ."

"Shoot," I replied. I hated this. People always want me to diagnose their spouses, their children, even their cats. But you have to listen. At least you do if you want the last table by the window.

"I have this neighbor with this vicious-looking dog, and I'm a little worried. . . ." My ears perked up. Could it be? Small areas are like that: You run into all kinds of crossovers—once my dentist turned out to be the battering husband of a new client. But even in small areas, I reminded myself, there is more than one neighbor with a vicious-looking dog.

I didn't get to explore it because at that moment Carlotta walked in. Heads turned discretely. No one actually stares at anybody in New England. Charles Bronson could—and did—walk down the street in the town where he had a vacation home without a single fan drooling on him. But people do notice interesting folks, and Carlotta had been six feet tall and interesting-looking since she was twelve.

Harvey saw her too and stood up. "Never mind," he said. "I'll catch you later."

"Give me a call," I said with, I hoped, nothing in my voice but ordinary friendliness. Sexy men always pull me off center.

Carlotta may have just rushed out of the hearing, but no one in the restaurant would have known. She walked unhurriedly to the table and sat down. She was dressed very simply in black crepe pants, a black matte blouse, and a black blazer. Around her neck she wore a handmade Native American beaded necklace. It was exquisite, and the simple black surrounding it set it off like a frame. If Calvin Klein had walked in, he would have put Carlotta on a runway just as she was. Well, actually, he had, once upon a time.

Carlotta looked worried. "Case go okay?" I asked when she sat down.

"Fine," she said, looking at me carefully. I realized I was the reason she was worried, and it hit me that Carlotta had probably chosen Sweet Tomatoes over my office because she knew I wouldn't yell there. Jesus. I've become someone other people have to manage. Maybe I ought to tone down my temper a bit.

"I'm all right," I said. "I don't like it. I think it's bullshit. I think it's worse than bullshit; I think it's criminal. I think every single judge that voted to put him on the street should be shot, but what can I say, every day somebody gets off who shouldn't."

There was a pause. What was bothering Carlotta? I was calm. Neither of us could do anything about Willy. "Well, what are you going to do?" she asked.

"Do? As in do what? There isn't a whole lot I can do."

"Michael, I don't want to remind you of anything you're trying to deny." Great. Now Carlotta's a psychologist? "But Alex Willy is a very dangerous man."

"So?"

"So, if I understand this right, he has told you things that no one else knows about him."

"So?"

"So, maybe I'm missing something, but isn't that likely to worry him?"

"Maybe," I admitted. "But how much harm can I do him? Obviously I can't put it in the paper. What's he got to worry about?"

"Is he going to quit molesting children?" Carlotta asked me directly.

"No, he isn't."

"What are the chances he'll get caught again?" she pressed.

"Eventually it's likely," I said. "But probably not soon. Willy controls kids with a combination of getting the kids to fear him and the parents to trust him, and the things he does to the kids are so extreme. The kind of abuse he inflicts doesn't sound plausible to most parents."

"So why is he going to get caught again?"

"He's too active," I answered. "He just molests too many kids, and he loves to take chances. He'll push the envelop until eventually he's caught."

"And when he is, what about you?"

"Carlotta, what do you mean what about me? What about me nothing."

"Are you or are you not a threat to Willy?" Carlotta said as though she were cross-examining a hostile witness, which she was, sort of. "Given how much you know, wouldn't you be a *very* effective witness for the prosecution?"

"You forget, counselor. Everything Willy has told me is considered 'hearsay' by the courts, and it is not admissible."

"There are twenty-four exceptions to hearsay. I won't bore you with the details, but the bottom line is I've gone over this carefully and checked it out with my boss—without any names, of course," she added hastily, "and I think the stuff he's told you would be admissible."

"Jesus." Willy wouldn't like that. And he would surely check it out. Willy counted on the fact that any abused child who reported him would not have any corroboration of what he was saying. And regardless of what happened to the current case, there would surely be abused children reporting him in the future.

"Patient/doctor confidentiality?" Carlotta asked. "What about that?"

"I don't think so," I had to answer. "He was never a client of mine. I never provided any services."

We were both quiet for a moment. "Michael, anything he's confided in you might even be admissible if he's ever tried again for the *current* offense."

"He won't be."

"True."

Silence fell. This conversation was not going anywhere I wanted to go. I picked up my menu and got very involved in the choices.

"Michael, you're going to have to deal with this."

I put the menu down. From her artful makeup to her tastefully streaked hair, Carlotta looked like a woman whose chief concern in life was not breaking a nail. Not exactly. I knew Carlotta well enough to know once she got her teeth in something, there wasn't going to be any way to ignore it.

"Deal with what, Carlotta? Look. He's not really interested in adults sexually, so he wouldn't go after me just as a straight victim. And remember he's been away from kids for years now, and he's built up a lot of fantasies. He's going to set himself up somewhere and start ingratiating himself in the community.

"I don't think he'll want to take a detour to come after me just to keep me quiet. He can solve his problem with me by moving as far away as possible. I'll never know if he gets caught for something new. And the old case isn't going back to trial. You know that."

We sat in silence again. I went back to the menu, although not very hopefully. "Is it likely?" Carlotta asked. "Would he just move away? And could *you* live with it if he did? Knowing that he would still be out there molesting kids?"

"No" to everything, I thought. In my heart of heart I knew Willy was too thorough to leave loose ends. And part of it was he'd know that even if he left me alone, I wouldn't leave him alone.

"Sure," I lied. "Why not? Look, do you know how many people there are out there molesting kids? I can't make myself crazy with it. I do what I can do." And, I thought, Carlotta was right. I needed to *do* something about Alex B. Willy.

But there was no way I'd tell Carlotta that. She would hover and scold and act like a mother hen. Worse, she'd tell Adam, the town's full-time police chief and my part-time lover, who would get protective and make me crazy with it, and then I'd lose the relationship with him and the friendship with Carlotta, and it would all be because I had told Carlotta the truth. So, really, I was just protecting my relationships with both of them by lying, through my teeth, to Carlotta.

Mama wouldn't have done it. Mama likes to let the chips fall where they may. Sometimes Mama throws the chips. But I wasn't Mama. Definitely, I wasn't Mama.

"Ummmm," Carlotta said, and I saw the indecision in her eyes. She should know better than to believe me. And then a chill went up my spine. I was selling Carlotta safety. She wanted to believe I was safe so she didn't have to worry about me, and she'd go against her own best judgment to believe it. Maybe, I had learned something from Willy after all.

3

I am not good at waiting, and I am not a procrastinator. I'm the kind that speeds up at intersections. When I jump horses cross-country I sometimes—well, frequently to be honest—have horses taking jumps too fast and too strung out, but I rarely have a horse balk. We are going over that jump if it kills us. It's a genetic thing, the price of being related to Mama.

I could have asked Carlotta to use her connections in the prosecutor's office to find out where Willy had gone once he was released. She was a Vermont prosecutor, and Willy's case was in New Hampshire, but one prosecutor would talk to another regardless. But looking at her, I didn't think it was a good idea. There wouldn't be any way I could ask her without tipping her off.

We got off Willy, finally, and onto the backlash against victims of child sexual abuse and "taint" hearings and legal issues and the way the media gobbles up any perp's version of events regardless of how bizarre, but underneath it all I kept thinking about Willy. Carlotta had kicked off something. I had been so furious that some fool judge had released him that I hadn't yet thought about where his release put me. By the time lunch was over I was facing the fact that if Willy didn't go after me, I'd have to find a way to go after him. I couldn't just walk away knowing he was going to sadistically abuse eighteen million kids.

I walked back to my office thinking about the problems that come when you start on a life of deception. If I was going after Willy it would have been safer to have somebody know exactly where I was and what I was doing at all times, but it wasn't worth the hassle.

This was Carlotta's fault, I rationalized. If she weren't being so controlling I could have told her. I *would* have told her if I had trusted her to stay out of it and not blab to Adam. I, of course, would stay completely out of it when dealing with a friend who was doing something stupid beyond belief. Right.

In my defense, it had always felt better to be in the driver's seat than the passenger's seat. Willy would look me up even if I didn't look him up, and I couldn't see just sitting around waiting to be surprised. Neither of us had counted on his getting out of prison when he waxed eloquent about his various techniques for entrapping children—after all, he'd been in his sixties and starting a thirty-year prison sentence.

But the real problem—which was so formidable I didn't even want to think about it—was what the hell was I supposed to do once I found him? I couldn't just shoot him—despite my unfortunate, politically incorrect fondness for guns and the fact that I had a fair amount of expertise with them. I couldn't imagine shooting anyone in cold blood.

I wasn't going to talk him out of anything. I could see it now: "Willy, did you know molesting kids was *wrong?*"

"Gee," he'd say, "I never thought of that. "I'll quit right away."

26

Threatening him would just put me in more jeopardy. The more Willy was sure I would try to harm him, the more he'd go after me.

Could I warn people in his community? Put it in the newspaper? Without a doubt no one would believe me. Willy was too glib and too charming.

I'd end up with a major lawsuit against me for slander plus get labeled as a crazy whose word was worthless. People have a way of ignoring evidence if they really like someone. A few months before, a teacher at a private school had been caught with mega-amounts of child porn. His colleagues had claimed it didn't mean he was a pedophile. Right. Like people who own two hundred cookbooks don't cook.

I had to smile thinking about Willy's defense. I would say truthfully that I had visited Willy in prison to learn about sadistic offenders. Willy would no doubt use the visits against me. He would portray me as a paranoid who had been harassing him for years and was now making up stories about him.

But if he did sue me, the audiotapes might be admissible under the rules of discovery. I brightened a little thinking I had one option, even though professional self-immolation would not be my first choice.

I walked back to my private practice office a few blocks from Sweet Tomatoes. My private practice was in a house I had once shared with Carlotta. I was only there one day a week. I spent the rest of my time in the Department of Psychiatry at Jefferson Medical School, where I taught, super-vised residents, sat on stupid committees, and endlessly annoyed the chairman, who thought tact was an art form and that I knew less about it than anyone he had ever met.

That wasn't exactly true. I knew about tact. I just thought it was a character flaw. So what if he had had a few dozen complaints about me over the years. Nobody ever complained that what I had said was actually *wrong*. They just seemed to think I didn't need to say it exactly that way at exactly that time, if at all. Details.

I had a half hour before my next client, and I started to pick up the phone to track down Willy. The absence of a plan was definitely a problem, but why worry about it now. First I had to find him. But the phone rang before I could pick it up.

"This is Dr. Stone," I said.

"Michael," the voice on the other end said simply.

My heart rate went up a notch, which annoyed me exceedingly. I could never seem to control the effect Adam had on me. "Good afternoon, Chief Bowman. Caught any crooks today?"

"Half a dozen before sunrise," Adam replied. He paused. "I'd like to come over this evening," he said. Adam could be more direct than I was.

"Why?" I said, suddenly suspicious. "Did Carlotta call you?"

"What's with the third degree?" Adam asked. "Why would Carlotta call me?"

I had blown it. Now he'd call her if she didn't call him.

"Nothing," I said. "Really, it's nothing. She's just on the rampage about me, as usual. I thought you were coming over to lecture me—which I would not have liked," I added sternly just in case he did call her.

"No," he said slowly, "that wasn't exactly what I had in mind."

Adam could say fewer words and get a bigger reaction from me than anyone I had ever known. I found my mouth was dry.

"Sounds fine," I said trying and miserably failing at keeping my voice even. "Dinner?"

"Sure," Adam said, and we got off on the when and where stuff, which allowed me to get my heart rate a tad short of tachycardia.

There was nothing I could do about the estrogen vote. I

liked living alone. I didn't want a steady boyfriend. But every time Adam came around, the estrogen just started swimming in my ears.

Once Adam and I had gone to Hawaii. Well, actually I had gone, and he met me there. I wasn't even sure he was coming, and I had been walking on the beach when I realized the barefoot guy in shorts walking toward me was Adam.

The whole time we spent there had been a world apart. Like ghosts of the Aaragone, we never spoke of home. We never talked about his job or mine or sex offenders or my prickliness about independence or anything to do with the real world. I had worn long cotton dresses on the beach at night with nothing underneath, and the wind had whipped my dress around and lifted my skirts. I had felt like Marilyn Monroe standing on that grating, and I have never felt like Marilyn Monroe before or since. I could still remember the feeling of the wind on my bare thighs and bottom. I could remember the feel of other things too. Sitting in my office a million miles from Hawaii, it still made me smile.

On the way back to the mainland we had both been glum. The real world was rushing toward us with every mile, and we both knew it wouldn't be the same. It hadn't been.

I picked up Chinese on the way home. The best thing about being in my forties was making my peace with who I was and who I wasn't, and I wasn't Julia Child.

I was, however, happy to see Adam when he walked in. It was still light out, and mercifully, mud season seemed to be warming up so we agreed to dinner on the deck. I was busy unpacking cartons and didn't notice how still Adam was.

"I've been thinking," he said, finally. "How would you feel about moving in with me for a while?"

"Why?" I asked. "What's wrong with the way things are now?" I am never very smart when estrogen is roaring in my ears. I should have seen what was coming, but I didn't.

"The commute's too long from my house to yours," he said lightly.

"Fifteen minutes? Boy, you've been living in the country too long. Fifteen minutes would buy you a block in Boston at rush hour."

Adam didn't say anything, so I went on, "Look, why spoil a good thing? I am not the easiest person to live with." Actually I am impossible to live with.

Adam persisted. "Then why not move back into town with Carlotta? You and she got along when you were living there before."

I knew, then, where this was going. He had called Carlotta. "I can't move in with Carlotta," I said sitting down to face him. "If there is any risk, and I'm not saying there is, I don't want to put her in the middle of it. You know Carlotta. She doesn't know zip about self-defense. She used to hate it when I had guns in the house."

"You can't stay here now, not with Willy out. You're a quarter mile from the nearest neighbor."

"Why not?" As if I didn't know.

"Michael, have you ever been to the scene of a homicide?"

"No," I said. "What's that got to do with anything?"

"Because I'm not sure you realize what you're getting into."

"I'm not getting into anything."

"Buy that and I've got a bridge to sell you."

"Adam, there's no point to this."

"Look, I do not want to find your bruised and broken body with needles under your fingernails."

"Cut it out, Adam. Isn't that a little baroque?" It was kind of a weak comeback, but I didn't seem to have anything convincing to say. Adam was way ahead of me. He had a full head of steam about this, and I was still flapping around on a beach in Hawaii. So much for letting your guard down.

"Not if you have found bodies like that before." Well, he

hadn't, at least not in Vermont. Well, actually, maybe he had. Like most of the country, Vermont had had at least one serial killer, I remembered. He had operated for a couple of years a while back, leaving a body every six months. All right, so that kind of thing could happen here.

"He will kill you," Adam said quietly.

"You could at least say 'could.'"

"He will kill you," Adam said a little more strongly, "and then I will kill him."

"Come on, Adam. For Christ's sake. You will not. You're a cop, a good cop. You don't go around killing people."

"I will kill him," Adam said again, firmly. "But it will do no good because you will be just as dead. And then I will miss you," he said gently, "every day for the rest of my life."

I froze. He was repeating back to me something I had said to him about my daughter who had died of SIDS a few years back. Jordan was absolutely my Achilles' heel. I had had no warning he was going to raise her, and her death rose from whatever pool of misery I kept it trapped in and flooded through every pore. Suddenly I had the metallic taste in my mouth I had had for weeks after she died—grief has effects no one can seem to explain. I got very cold and knew if I wasn't lucky I would start shaking soon from the cold. I looked up. Surely, the reference had been inadvertent. Surely, he had not meant to invoke Jordan. I saw in his eyes that he had, and I stood up.

My voice was dead calm, but to say it had ice in it was to say the Arctic Circle had a couple of cubes. It also had a sound in it a rattler makes when you step on it. "Don't you ever, ever in your lifetime or mine use Jordan against me again. Not for any reason. Not to save my life. Not to save the lives of all the starving children in the known universe. Not one time. Not ever."

I was dizzy and cold. I went over and picked up my car keys

and my coat. Adam had gone stock-still. Wisely, he didn't speak. "Be out of here by the time I get back," I said. I knew he would. He had not heard that tone in my voice before. But then again, neither had I.

It took enormous effort, but I made myself stop at the door on the way out. I put one hand on the frame to steady myself and turned back. "I can't do it your way. I can't hide behind your coattails and live in your shadow. I can't run home to big daddy when the going gets rough. I know exactly how dangerous Willy is, far more than you do, and yes, he probably will kill me if I'm stupid or careless enough to give him the chance. But if I run and hide, I'll lose who I am anyway, and it isn't worth it, so stay out of it. I'll make it or I won't. All you will do is destroy what's between us." Adam didn't speak again, and I waited for a moment, then left.

I drove around for a while, but it was difficult remembering where I was. Jordan was back in full force. Grief and depression are not even on the same planet. Depression is like a slow-onset paralysis. After a while it's too much effort to lift your arm, to get out of bed. Grief is more like being beaten up. It's a spasm. You feel like curling up in a ball to ward off the blows.

Finally, I realized the car was near Marv's house, and I headed over. I was coming up enough to realize I wasn't competent to drive. I needed to get off the road, and I wasn't ready to go home. I'd be damned before I went to Carlotta's.

Marv had a condominium in town. It wasn't fair to say he lived alone, although there weren't any other people living there. He lived with his paintings and his sculptures — folk art he had collected from all over the world. It was a soothing place, even for me, who knew diddly-squat about art. Marv was a very good psychiatrist and a bad witness in court. He was the person that I called when I needed a consult on a case if he didn't have to testify. I didn't need a consult tonight.

Maybe I just needed to sit around the paintings for a while. Was that because I got something from the art, I wondered, or from the fact he loved them so?

I knocked on the door and heard the padding of Marv's slippers as he came to it. Marv's purple slippers. He always wore them at home, and they were ugly beyond belief. Marv opened the door. He was wearing his usual mismatched thrown-together colors. He was short and partly bald with a potbelly. I was never troubled by the estrogen vote around Marv, and tonight that seemed nothing but comforting.

He looked startled and began to speak. He checked himself and looked more closely. He had told me once he had counseled a cross-dressing client who had determined not to go to any therapist who didn't realize he was male. The guy had interviewed six previous therapists before he found Marv. Marv spotted him immediately by the size of his wrists. I couldn't have hidden what shape I was in from Marv if I tried.

"I was wondering . . . ," I started in lamely.

"Wondering, nothing," Marv said, putting his arm around me. "Come on in."

"Have a seat," he said pointing to the couch. "Let me stoke up the fire a bit and put on some hot tea." I didn't even drink hot tea, but I knew he was right. "Now," he said, when he finished with the fire, thinking out loud. "Before the tea, a blanket—how about an afghan from Albania?"

It was the first thing all night that had made me smile. Somehow you just knew Marv wouldn't come out with an army surplus blanket. I must be getting punchy. I had an image of some natural disaster—a hurricane maybe—and Marv running around putting Albanian and Russian and Spanish afghans around the survivors.

Marv fetched the blanket and the tea and just sat down on the couch and drank his tea quietly staring into the fire. He didn't say anything at all.

"You can go on with whatever you were doing," I said. "I just want to hang out for a while."

"I'm fine," he said. "Am I bothering you?"

"No," I said honestly. "On the contrary."

That was it. He never asked a question. I never volunteered anything. I shook for a while, despite the fire and the blanket and the tea, and then slowly I drifted off. I knew what would happen. It happened every time. I'd wake up thinking she was alive for a second and then realize she wasn't. I hated that fall more than anything in the whole world, but there wasn't anything I could do about it. Marv's was a better place than most to ride it out.

Circle of life bullshit. Death was an ugly business. The New Age philosophers chirping that everything happened for a reason made me want to vomit. Jordan's death had pretty much eviscerated me just like a child's death eviscerated every parent I had ever met who had lost one. It didn't make us wise or deep and appreciative of life; it made us hurt.

Adam didn't have a clue what I was really afraid of. It wasn't that Willy would torture me to death. That was flat-out horrible, even though I wasn't all that afraid of dying—people who had lost children never were. But what I was really afraid of was that Willy would know enough to use Jordan against me somehow. But irony of irony, it was Adam who did that. Serves you right, I said to myself as I drifted off. Serves you right for letting the son-of-a-bitch get under your skin.

4

When I awoke there was a fresh fire burning in the fireplace and a small coffeemaker set up on the end table beside the couch. All I had to do to get fresh coffee was to flip a switch. There was a cup with milk in it next to the coffeemaker and a single crocus in a small vase next to the cup. It was still early. What time did Marv get up to do all this?

I looked at the crocus. I'd have bitten off Marv's head if he'd told me that things would get better or the darkest day was just before dawn or any other such drivel. He hadn't said anything. He just left a crocus—the first flower in the spring and the only one that will stick its head up through the snow. Hard to argue with a crocus, even for me.

I thought about it. I was more on the Carlotta and Adam side of things than I cared to admit. If I had a friend who was on some kind of stupid collision course, I'd have ranted and raved, cajoled and persuaded, probably with less art than either of them. I wouldn't have handled things the way Marv did last night. Yet what could anybody have done for me that was better? I thought guiltily of my battered women clients. Maybe I ought to argue less and put out a few more crocuses.

Of course, I wouldn't have been stupid enough to use a dead child against anyone. The day after, I still felt emotionally stiff and sore—as though I'd taken a bad beating, which I guess I had.

I had woken with my worst nightmare, as I knew I would: a comfortable sense that Jordan was in the next room and I just needed to get up and check on her because she was sleeping so late. Then the crash—all of which happened, as usual, while I was still in a twilight state. By the time I was fully awake I was pretty much through it.

I got up and padded into the kitchen looking for Marv. He was gone, but there was a note on the table. "I'm off to the jail to do a consult. Suicide attempt last night. Stay as long as you like. The place is yours. Love."

If Marv ever came to my door, not a single question, I admonished myself. Not one. But would anyone come to my door who didn't want a single question? The whole thing was a little uneasy-making. I was like a surgeon whose answer to every problem had been to cut it out. Only now I was the patient, and I had developed something that couldn't be cut out.

The only person who could help turned out not to be a surgeon at all, but a chronic disease doc who knew how to manage the kind of things that didn't kill you and didn't go away. I had learned something from Marv, but I doubted I could use it. Surgeons make bad chronic disease docs and vice versa.

I went out to the car to get my travel bag. I had a habit of traveling impulsively, and a packed bag, as always, was in the car. I don't own a lot. I make a point of never owning more than two hundred and fifty things total in my life, but one thing I never skimped on was the travel bag. It had everything I need in it to stay a weekend or even six.

What do you really need to travel: two pairs of shorts, three T-shirts, one bathing suit, two pairs of long pants (one of which you wear), two shirts with collars, one dress, one sweater—if you needed a coat you shouldn't go there—five pairs of underwear, and two bras. A few toiletries, and that was it. Everything was wrinkle-free, everything went together, and everything washed out in the sink and dried before morning. What else do you have to have? I was never trapped as long as I had my travel bag and a credit card, which I also kept in the bag.

I retrieved my toothbrush from the bag and the only dress: a generic stretch-velvet, long-sleeved, black turtleneck that came down to mid-calf. It was modest enough to wear in the Vatican or the Middle East, shiny enough to wear to a symphony, and plain enough to wear in the daytime. I don't believe in single-purpose items.

I had no sooner arrived at the Department of Psychiatry, where Marv and I both worked, when Judy, Marv's secretary, sought me out. "Do you know where Marv is?" she said.

"Actually," I said, "I do. He's at the jail. Someone made a suicide attempt last night."

"Oh, dear," she said.

"Why, what's wrong?"

"There's a woman here who thinks she has an appointment to be screened for his new group." Marv was starting a new interpersonal therapy group, and like most therapists, he screened people in individual interviews first. Otherwise, someone could join who was far too ill for a group and who might attempt suicide the first time someone confronted her. Or he could end up with a stalker in the group who would immediately pick up on the most submissive female and make her life hell. Groups worked when the people in them were reasonably well-functioning. Even in a single screening interview a therapist could weed out the folks who were wildly inappropriate.

"So? Can't you reschedule her?"

"I could. I guess I will. I just don't think she'll come back. She seems pretty nervous."

Clearly, I owed Marv, and while Marv's ability to calm down a nervous client was probably far better than mine, it was probably better for her to see me than be rebuffed and told to come back later. "Okay, I'll screen her for him," I said.

"I put her in his office," Judy said. "Ginger's in the waiting room again, and she freaks new clients."

I almost changed my mind. I didn't want to see Ginger. Ginger wasn't my client anymore, and my plan was never to see Ginger again in my lifetime. Unfortunately, Marv's office was down the hall on the other side of the waiting room, and if I saw his new client, I would have to cross the waiting room and go past Ginger. I started to tell Judy that hell would freeze before I voluntarily walked into a room with Ginger, but I stopped.

What cowardice. After all, I was the reason Marv had to deal with Ginger in the first place. She had walked into my office a couple of years ago saying she didn't have any huge problems, she just wanted a little help with some issues on the job. This is called telling the big lie. She had immediately locked into a symbiotic, fused, hang-on-me thing that had nearly suffocated me.

Ginger was relentless. She came to my office when I was seeing other patients just to be near me. She called my answering machine to hear my voice. She showed up hours early for her appointment and slept in the waiting room. She refused to leave after her appointment. She called every day and demanded callbacks. If I couldn't or didn't get back to her she threatened suicide. If I went away, she tried it and then blamed it on me for abandoning her.

If it had gone on, I think I would have ended up on the inpatient unit myself—committed, no doubt, for killing her. Finally, when I found myself dreading to go to work every single day, I had transferred her to Marv. I had consulted him regularly on the case already, and both of us had hoped it would be different with a male therapist. It hadn't been, but I hadn't offered to take her back.

Ginger was sitting in the waiting room, dressed entirely in black. She was in her thirties, but her face was so angular and lined she looked older. She was small with dark hair cut severely short, and she was curled up in a fetal position on the couch. There was no peace in Ginger, and everything about her reflected it.

What she lacked was an ability to self-soothe. She felt at peace only when she was around whoever she was attached to at the moment. Outside that person's presence she fell into the abyss. Marv was better than anyone I knew at teaching people to self-soothe, but it looked like he wasn't getting too far with Ginger.

I don't believe in diagnosing people by what colors they wear, but in Ginger's case you could always tell what her mood was by what she had on. When she felt neglected by her therapist—which was frequently—she always wore black.

Ginger looked up when I came in, and I stopped. I had to. "How are you, Ginger?" I asked.

"Well, things aren't going too well right now."

"I'm sorry to hear that. Are you waiting for Marv? I don't think he'll be in for a while. He had an emergency. What time is your appointment?"

"Oh. I don't have an appointment until one. I just thought I'd come a little early. Do you have time to see me? You know, I really think I did better seeing a woman therapist." Whoever

39

Ginger's therapist was at the time, he or she was always failing her, and whoever her last therapist was, that person always walked on water.

There was a major unempathic part of me that wanted to scream, "NOT ON YOUR LIFE. NOT UNTIL THE BULLS TRADE MICHAEL JORDAN. NOT UNTIL THE CELTICS OFFER ME A SPOT. NOT UNTIL THERE'S PEACE IN THE MIDDLE EAST. NOT UNTIL THE FALSE-MEMORY HIRED GUNS TELL THE TRUTH IN COURT. THEN I'LL SEE YOU— THAT IS, IF I'VE HAD A LOBOTOMY IN THE INTERIM." I had paused too long, and Ginger looked up hopefully. Maybe she could even see two therapists at once.

"I don't, Ginger," I responded calmly. "And I don't really think it would help you to go back and forth between therapists, anyway. Why don't you talk things over with Marv and see what he thinks? I have to go, but I hope things get better for you."

And all of the screaming in my head aside, I truly did hope she'd get better, but it didn't seem likely. Ginger had no clue how to feel good without sucking the breath out of somebody else's life, and I doubted she'd ever figure it out. And worse, almost, she had no idea how hostile her leechlike behavior was. She just felt entitled.

I felt like a criminal escaping the scene of a crime, which was a big part of the problem. No matter what you did with Ginger, you never escaped the guilt trip she soaked you with.

I closed the door to Marv's office and tried to put Ginger behind me. The woman Judy brought in didn't look like the type who usually showed up for interpersonal growth groups. She had a tiny, sharp chin—far too small for her face—and it spoke not just to malnutrition in her childhood but to generations of her ancestors never having enough. Her shoulders were thin and hunched over. When she smiled nervously at me I could see several missing teeth and several darkly stained ones. She was wearing the kind of cheap polyester that mimicked the latest style but was so poorly made it seemed more mockery than mimicry. Far better, I thought, would be an honest pair of jeans and a workshirt.

It was simple: She was poor, and the teeth and the chin said she and her kin had been poor for eons. I couldn't tell how old she was: Poverty ages people so badly they are always younger than they look. I'd have said mid-fifties, so probably she was in her early forties.

My lawyer Daddy had come from people who had a little money, but my intrepid Mama had come from people who made their living from the sea. Some of them had been as poor as church mice all their lives. I had been too young to remember any of them clearly, but I had heard stories that made the Depression sound pretty watered-down in comparison. When you live off the sea, and the sea doesn't produce, and there are no societal safety nets, and your neighbors are in as bad shape as you are, you just go hungry, and some of them had.

Dresses had been made from the feedbags for the animals, which wasn't as bad as it sounds. Actually they looked a lot better than the polyester in front of me. The feedbags came in soft floral print cotton, and I had vague memories of those small floral print dresses on elderly ladies sitting on porch swings. Somewhere in my genes I knew poverty, even though I'd never seen it in my lifetime, and the woman in front of me felt like some kind of relative.

"Hello, I'm Michael Stone," I said and extended my hand. She stood up and held out her hand awkwardly, but when she took mine she surprised me with the firmness of her grasp.

"I'm Katy," she said.

"I know you're here to see Dr. Gleason, but he got called out on emergency, and I thought maybe I could help. Have a seat. You're here about his group?"

"Well, I think so," she said sitting down on the far end of the couch. "Although sometimes I have to work nights, and I don't think I can get off, so I don't know if I can do it, but I thought I'd come and ask about it, anyways. The kids are gone now, and I think maybe it's time I got out some. I haven't gotten out much for a while—well, quite a while really, but now they're all grown up and gone. The last one moved in with her boyfriend the day she turned eighteen last Tuesday, and I thought I just got to get out and do something more than just go to work and come home and sit in front of the television." She was nervous and running on, which wasn't surprising if she had gotten out as little as she said.

I started to say something, but she went on. "I just was never one of those mothers who run around all the time. I don't know why some folks have kids. They never stay home with them. Even my sister—I love her the best—but she's out at Bingo five nights a week, and her youngest isn't any more 'n ten."

"What made you choose this particular group?" I asked. I wanted to ask her about her goals for joining the group, but I didn't know how to phrase it in a way that wouldn't sound pretentious or threatening.

"Well, my friend saw the ad, but it didn't say nothing about how much it cost so that's another thing."

"It's a sliding scale," I said. Actually, I didn't have a clue what Marv was charging, but I knew he was a softer touch than I was. "It's whatever you can afford."

"Not very much right now, I'll tell you that, although I might be able to get more work in the summer. Lots of people take time off in the summer, and they're short on some of the shifts."

"What about the group interested you?" I persisted. It was hard to see her in a process, obsessing-over-your-naval, interpersonal growth group.

"I just haven't done much social," she said, "so when Tanya said it was a social group, I thought, well, what have I got to lose? I haven't met any decent men, and I figured a dating thing like this was a lot better place to look than going to a bar. I just don't hold with bars. I've seen too much drinking and carrying on."

Uh-oh, her friend had thought "interpersonal" had something to do with dating, which wasn't a bad guess but made this awkward. "Well, it's not really a dating kind of thing. It's a group for talking about problems. And mostly, these groups are made up of women. A few men might come, but they're likely to be married. It's not really set up for dating."

"It isn't? . . . Oh."

"No, although I can see where the ad might make it look that way, but it's really for talking about problems."

"I've had my share of those, I tell you, but I thought it was a group to meet people."

"No," I said. "What kind of problems have you had?" I don't know what made me ask. I could have just let her go. Maybe I asked out of curiosity because of her handshake. Maybe I just didn't want to go back into the waiting room. Maybe it was because people sometimes lose their nerve at the last minute when they come to see a counselor and pretend they came to the wrong place.

I was a little more rabid than most about that since the day a woman came to my office and asked if it was the social security office. I said "no" and gave her directions. Three days later she attempted suicide. I saw her right after that, and only then did I begin to learn about her fears of poverty.

"Well," she said. "I seen hard times, though not as hard as some. My husband was a drinker. I didn't mind that so much, and he used to hit me too, but I could take that, and then one night he tore my little Billy up, and he weren't no more 'n five. I tell you he could do anything he wanted to me, but he hadn't never hit one of my children before, and I said right then and there that he wouldn't never hit one again.

"I tried to stop him when he started in on Billy a'course, but he was a big man, and when he set his mind to beating something, he beat it. He went out drinking, and I cleaned Billy up as best I could. He kept asking me what he done wrong, and I told him nothing, but a little child don't understand.

"I waited up for him. I knew he'd be liquored up when he came back, and sure enough, along about five o'clock he came in drunker than a skunk, and I hid behind the stairs. When he started up, I just stepped out and hit him as hard as I could right in the face with one of those big iron frying pans. I hit him square in the face, and he stumbled out and never came back no more."

"Never?" I was mesmerized. She had come for something more than the group, but I wasn't sure what. Maybe just to tell someone her story.

"Never. We did all right, although it was a hard time that first winter. We got ourselves a house for five hundred dollars." I must have looked surprised because she quickly added, "well a chicken coop, really, but me and the kids fixed it up. And we dug ourselves a well, got it down to close to twenty feet. It was hard going, but the kids helped me. I took in ironing, made twenty-five dollars every other week.

"But that first winter the day came when I didn't have any money, and the kids were hungry, and there wasn't a thing in the house to feed 'em. I heard he was up at his mother's, and I hadn't asked him for a cent since he left, so I went up to ask him for ten dollars for some food money for the kids.

"I saw him on the porch, and I walked in the screen door and came up behind him, but afore I got there he turned around and saw me. Right away, he says to me, he says, 'I'll tell you one thing. Don't you never ask me for no money cause I don't pay for no dead horses.' I turned on my heel and I left, and I never asked him for a thing.

"We got through that winter, the Lord only knows how, and then the next thing I knowed he was up in Newport jail. We hadn't heard nothing from him for the whole three years, and then he started in writing me, asking me to bring the kids up, telling me how hard it was to be away from his family, telling me how much he missed us."

"What'd you do?" I was afraid to ask. I'd heard this story before, and I waited for the ending I was used to.

"I wrote him back," she said. "I told him, I said, 'Let me just tell you one thing. I don't pay for no dead horses.' "

I was stunned. After she left I sat there for a while. This woman had a "mind of winter," as Wallace Stevens would say. She saw the "nothing that was not there and the nothing that was." What did she have that the others didn't—all the people I had seen who would have been up to Newport jail telling the kids to "be nice, now, Daddy's sorry." Come lie to me and be my love.

What was it people needed badly enough to buy the tears in his eyes when in their heart of hearts they knew better? Company, sometimes? Money? Sex? And these were folks who hadn't run out of money and out of food in the New England winter with small kids. What did this woman have that the others didn't? What did this woman have that Ginger didn't, who couldn't be alone for two seconds without clutching at someone?

Was there anything I wanted badly enough to go up to Newport jail? I certainly hoped not. Then again, I'd never tried to dig a twenty-foot well with kids to take care of and winter on the way.

My hat was off to her. Maybe it was true, as Marge Piercy wrote, that "Nothing is won by endurance/But endurance." But sometimes that is a lot.

I was still thinking about her when Melissa, my secretary, came in. "FedEx," she said. "I signed for you." I threw it on the desk hardly glancing at it. FedEx was routine: Lawyers never seemed to use the snailmail anymore. My mind was on Katy, and it wasn't until I swung around that I noticed the return address:

> Wilbee Cingu
> Never-Never Land Enterprises
> 64 Martin Luther King Blvd.
> Cross Roads Junction, NH

I looked again. Wilbee Cingu. I didn't know any Wilbee Cingu, and there were law firms that *should* be called Never-Never Land Enterprises but weren't.

I looked more closely. Wil-bee-c-ing-u. Uh-oh. I didn't have to worry about finding Willy. He had already found me. Fear pushed its way up in my throat, and I took a deep

46

breath and tried to calm down. Willy had gotten the jump on me, and I hated it as much as I thought I would. I didn't mind walking down a dark alley to meet him—well, I did, actually, but there was nothing I could do about it—but I could not tolerate sitting in one while Willy walked toward me.

I had a friend who twenty years back had been the first female police officer in her state. She once had to climb a dark stairwell by herself in an apartment building with a man waiting at the top with an ax. Nobody knew how she did it. I did. She was the one doing the climbing.

I hesitated a second. A letter bomb was feasible. Willy could do it. On the other hand, he wouldn't be there to see the results, so it wouldn't be all that enjoyable for him. If he sent a letter bomb, my diagnosis of sexual sadist was wrong. I almost smiled. I didn't usually have to have *that* kind of faith in the diagnoses I made.

I opened the letter. "Free at last," Willy quoted. "Free at last." I'll bet Martin Luther King didn't have Willy in mind when he said that.

"By now," Willy wrote, "you must be wondering what your role in Never-Never Land will be. After all, 'reality is the product of the most august imagination.' Show me yours and I'll show you mine." It was signed,

partytime@postoffice.worldnet.att.net.

I stared at the letter for a long time. It wasn't a very long communication, but it said a lot. I knew what was in Willy's imagination—fairly horrific ways of torturing people—and if Willy was planning on bringing them to reality, then somebody was in for a bad time.

I didn't really want to see Willy's imagination brought to life, up close and personal. The only people who saw Willy's imagination brought to reality were the victims. If he was planning on personally showing me "his," then I was the one who was in for a bad time.

So he'd managed to tell me that, yes, he was up to his old tricks and, guess what, he had plans for me. Worse, he said it without anything he could be prosecuted for. It was a threat that didn't look like a threat, even if I could tie it to Willy, which I doubt very much that anyone could. Willy wouldn't be on any of the main networks with their billing records. Willy would have software that would access the Internet directly, and he could dial up from any phone in the world.

At least I didn't have to feel bad about not taking it to Adam. What could he do about it?

What could *I* do about this was a bigger problem. I tried to think. Jesus, he hadn't been out ten minutes before he got in touch. Had he been planning this?

All right then, what role did Willy have in mind for me in Never-Never Land? I had no doubts that Willy saw himself as Peter Pan and no doubts too about what his plans were for the "lost boys" he'd inevitably pick up. But what about the females—given that he was talking about my role—where did I fit? There were only two female roles in *Peter Pan*—Tinker Bell and Wendy—and nothing terrible happened to either of them.

Well, there was also the Indian Princess. As I remember, her role had something to do with being tied at the stake in a cave while the water rose. That would be a reasonably unappealing prospect.

One thing was clear: Willy was inviting me to communicate with him via e-mail, and he didn't have the address.

I didn't really want to play games with him, and if I corresponded with him, he'd have my e-mail address and one more way to worm his way into my privacy. But if I didn't, I wouldn't have any clues at all about what was coming next.

What a hand to play by myself. Didn't I know anybody I could talk to about this who wouldn't just advise me to move to Afghanistan? No, I did not. Not even Marv.

The phone rang. I jumped and then took a moment to steady myself before I picked it up. One letter from Willy and I was already spooked. "It's the ED," Melissa said. "The on-call doc wants to talk to you."

"Who is it?" I asked.

"She didn't say," Melissa answered.

"Put her on," I said. In my heart of hearts the ED was still the ER to me, but it was true that the "emergency room" had been a lot more than a room for a long time now: a small city was more like it. "Emergency Department" really was more accurate but still bothered us old-timers. An ER by any other name was still an ER.

"Michael, this is Suzanne. I'm in the ED, and we have a patient of yours down here, a woman named Camille Robbins."

Fortunately, Suzanne Stenson was one of the sharpest psychiatric residents Jefferson had ever produced. This was fortunate because dealing with a crazy patient wasn't half as bad as dealing with a crazy psychiatrist.

"What brought her in?"

"Who is more like it. You know Harvey, runs Sweet Tomatoes? He found her hiding in the shrubs this morning outside her house. Her damn dog wouldn't let him near her, and he was getting ready to call the police when she seemed to come out of it and called the dog off. It looks like she was having some kind of flashback.

"Harvey drove her in. She was disoriented and confused and in and out of flashbacks."

Oh, Lord. I just hoped Harvey knew something about dogs. I had the feeling he didn't, or he'd have called the police the first time that rottweiler looked at him.

"Michael, the problem here is the dog came with her. I hate to say this, but the staff down here are more worried about the dog than your client. Nobody here wants to get within two feet of him, which is a big problem since your client is clutching his lead like it's a lifeline. She says he's a seizure dog. Is that true?"

"It's a 'she,'" I said, "although I'm not surprised you didn't get close enough to look. Her name is Keeter. As far as I know she is a seizure dog, which means that she can go anywhere. She's also an attack dog so be careful."

"Look, if people here were being any more careful they'd shoot her."

"Why don't I come down and see Camille."

"Why don't you."

"By the way, she just told you I was her therapist or she asked to see me?"

"She asked to see you." Good. That meant we had at least some connection, however new and fragile. Suzanne went on, "One more thing, Michael. She needs to be admitted, but we can't admit that dog."

"Legally, you have to. She's a service dog."

"Legally we do, so we're not going to recommend admission for Camille because of it. Nobody thinks she would part with her, and we just can't put that dog on the ward. Risk management would go nuts, the other patients would go nuts, and I am well and truly worried the dog would go nuts. Just so you know, it's not an option."

Great. I had a woman so confused she was hiding in the shrubs having flashbacks, and hospitalization was out. But I couldn't really argue with it. I wouldn't put Keeter on the ward, either. What if Camille did lose control of her and she ate five or six patients? On the other hand, what was I supposed to tell Camille if she wanted to be admitted?

Probably the truth—which meant I'd have to take the flak

for it later. If the higher-ups wouldn't admit Camille because they had no way to manage the dog, they'd never be willing to tell Camille that. That would be admitting she *needed* hospitalization and they didn't provide it—too much liability if something happened to her later. The administration would want the resident to tell Camille hospitalization wasn't needed.

Medicine has always had an ambivalent relationship with truth. It has been frequently harder to get medicine to admit the truth than to find it—witness that whole long history of lying to dying people about what was going to happen to them—as if they weren't going to find out, anyway. The good part was the hierarchy already thought of me as a "loose cannon," so I didn't have a lot to lose, reputation-wise—if you could call that a good part.

I put Willy's letter in the drawer. Unfortunately, the damn thing might be evidence for a future crime, and besides, I wanted to be able to reread it and think about it. There must be some way to figure out more about what Willy had in mind.

I headed down to the ED. Fred Flintstone had designed the elevators, so I took the stairs like most of the rest of the staff. I walked in the ED and headed for the nurses' station. "I'm looking for Dr. Stenson," I said. I was wearing my hospital ID pin with "Dr. M. Stone" on it, so the nurse, whom I didn't know, merely glanced up before directing me to a room down the hall. The movies didn't always get it wrong. It wouldn't be hard to impersonate a doctor. Great. Willy was already turning me into a complete paranoid. Already, I was thinking about how easy it would be for him to get access to the places I hung out.

I found Suzanne in the doctors' room writing notes in the chart. The doctors' room had a counter running around the room at sitting height, and docs were scattered around the room writing or making calls. Generally physicians wrote notes every time they saw a patient. This sounded good and it was good except it resulted in charts so thick that, after a while, nobody bothered to read the whole thing. Every once in a while, of course, that caused some sort of Big Problem.

Suzanne was an exception. She read the charts from cover to cover, no matter how many times the patient had been admitted. Suzanne kept reading for a moment before she looked up.

When she did, I saw the familiar circles under her eyes that told me she had been up all night. Medicine works its residents dangerously hard, putting them on twenty-four- or even thirty-six-hour shifts routinely. There are only a few states that outlaw it, and unfortunately, Vermont isn't one of them.

Of course, this is terrible for the patients, who get lousy care, and awful for the residents, who come to hate their lives. There is, too, the minor problem that it is bad for their training since nobody can think when they are that tired.

Despite all the excuses the hierarchy makes, it is done solely for one reason: money. Hiring people to work all those shifts would cost a ton of money. Residents are cheap, and basically, they have no rights.

Suzanne was slim—who had time to eat?—with shoulder-length dark hair and bright eyes. I don't know why psychology spends so much energy trying to develop IQ tests. You can make a pretty good guess at how bright people are by their eyes. Anyone who looked at Suzanne's and didn't know she was very, very bright indeed, needed an IQ test themselves.

"So," I said to Suzanne. "Always glad to have a patient of mine brighten your day. I know how bored you get sitting around with nothing to do."

"Actually," she said, "we don't see that many of your patients down here. I thought you were losing your touch, but, shucks, I found out you had only seen her once. I guess we can't expect even you to fix people in one visit."

"I don't know why not," I replied. "Managed care does. So, what do you have?" I knew Suzanne didn't have a whole lot of time.

"Not much," she said. "What happened to this woman? She can't seem to tell us, and all we've got is she was crouched in the bushes hiding, going in and out of flashbacks."

"What's she saying during the flashbacks?"

Suzanne sighed. "Not much. She just goes into a panic state and curls up in a fetal position. Then we all start looking at the dog and hoping she doesn't think we're the problem."

"Meds?" I said.

"Enough Haldol to drop an elephant—assuming she didn't give it to the dog."

"You hope she gave it to the dog."

"A thought . . . ," she replied. "The question here," she went on, "is what do we do with her? We've done all the polypharmacy we can. We can't admit her. Does she have any relatives or friends who would look after her?"

"Not that I know of," I replied.

"So," she said, leaning back in the chair and crossing her arms, "what do you want us to do with her?"

"Fix her," I said. "What else?"

I headed out to see Camille. I would have preferred to read the chart first, but Suzanne still needed it.

On the way down the hall I fretted. Despite the fashionable view found in any pulp newspaper, good therapists don't tend to make patients worse. I had thought Camille was stabilized when she left my office, so why was she here? If she wasn't a regular visitor here, if this wasn't something she did every day, I'd have to face the fact that the therapy session had caused her to decompensate: It was a little tough believing in coincidence.

And if therapy was the problem, it meant I had a bigger one. If Camille couldn't talk *at all* about what happened without falling apart, no matter how long we spent putting things back together, or how indirectly we approached it, how were we supposed to get anywhere? She had to cross *some* open ground to get to any kind of shelter. What was I supposed to do if she couldn't do it?

Worse, I had a bad feeling Camille wasn't the only one who was facing open ground. This morning Willy had just been a vague possibility, a maybe-he'll-show-up-maybe-he-won't shadow in my mind. Now, he was setting up obstacle courses on my front lawn and sending me a written invitation.

The largest of the ED rooms looked like a miniature gymnasium broken into small areas by curtains. Groups of people were scattered through the room in the small areas; each group was separated from the other only by the curtains, partly drawn in some places, totally in others. The curtains didn't do much for the patients. True, nobody could see your mangled body as you lay there having it poked and prodded, but each patient could hear everybody else's business. It didn't help to be lying there with your broken elbow listening to a child crying on one side as they stitched up his face and an elderly woman sobbing on the other as they coded her husband for a heart attack.

But the ED, like the operating room, is one of the places where the patients' physical needs take precedence over their emotional ones. "Guest relations"—as the policies are called that try to humanize hospitals—tread lightly in the ED. You have to keep someone alive before you can worry about his or her feelings. A big room with everybody together meant staff could get back and forth from one patient to another quickly if they needed to.

I walked around the room and then realized, what a surprise, they hadn't been willing to put the dog in the common room. I headed back to the nurses' station and asked for Camille. I was directed to a small treatment room with the door shut. I knocked lightly and then poked my head in and asked, "Can I come in?"

Camille was sitting across from the door facing it with her back to the wall. At first she looked blank, and I realized she didn't recognize me right away. She looked spacey and disoriented and slowed down. I wondered how agitated she would be without the Haldol, which would likely control the flashbacks but was a major tranquilizer and antipsychotic and probably made her feel awful. Nobody who'd had it ever seemed to want to take it again no matter how crazy they felt.

I slowly opened the door and walked in. Camille's face focused and brightened. I could have been her best friend. It was the same kind of thing that happens when you run into someone you barely know a few thousand miles from home. Relationships are always relative.

I moved slowly. People with Posttraumatic Stress Disorder are edgy, and there isn't enough Haldol in the world to fix that. I sat down as far from Camille as I could get, which wasn't far enough. I knew anybody within ten feet of her would seem like an intrusion right now.

Keeter had lifted her head when I walked in. She was lying between Camille and the door. I didn't know much about the etiquette for dealing with guard dogs, but people always like it when you acknowledge them so I figured Keeter would too. I started to speak to Keeter and realized I shouldn't do anything to imply she was the dominant figure here, so I spoke to Camille first.

"Hi," I said softly. "I hear you've had a rough time." She

didn't say anything, just put her head in her hands and started crying, or maybe she just continued crying. Her face was red and puffy and streaked with tears already.

"Good afternoon, Keeter," I said evenly. "Keeping a good eye on things, I hope." Keeter did not respond at all. She looked like she was thinking, "Ha, oldest trick in the book."

"He's back," Camille said. "I knew he would be."

"He's back?" I echoed. This was going to be tricky. If I asked her too much I'd throw her into another full flashback, and she'd go away completely. But sooner or later I needed to know whatever she could tell me about whatever had happened. How much was it safe to ask?

Camille nodded and didn't say anything.

"The same guy?" I said, to prompt her.

She nodded again.

"You saw him?" I asked. It occurred to me that I needed to confirm the extent of the flashbacks. I was just assuming I knew what her flashbacks were like, but there are all kinds of flashbacks: emotional flashbacks, somatic flashbacks . . . a full-blown sight-and-sound-hallucination being the most extreme.

She shook her head sideways.

"You didn't see him?" That was a little odd. I had pegged Camille for full-blown-there-he-is flashbacks.

She shook her head again. "It was dark. He must have been there the whole time." She paused to cry some more. "I was in bed."

"Camille, you know about flashbacks, right? You know he wasn't really there, that this was a flashback?"

She looked directly at me, and for a moment her gaze was so focused and intense it surprised me. "It wasn't a flashback," she said firmly.

There was a pause. I wasn't sure what to say. Camille just kept looking at me.

"You mean you think he was really there?"

"He was there. He was really there."

There was another pause. If she believed the guy was really back, her level of panic must be incredible. Flashbacks were bad enough, but at least with flashbacks she knew the perp wasn't really there to drag her off and start the whole thing again.

"Camille," I said softly. "How could he be back? Wasn't Keeter with you? Do you think Keeter would let someone like that get close to you? Weren't you home with Keeter?"

"He was there," she said insistently. And then she looked down again. "I never thought Keeter could stop him. Nobody can stop him."

There was another pause while I tried to regroup. This woman had probably had thousands of flashbacks. What had made this one so different? What made her think he was really there? Before I could speak, Camille went on. Her voice had dropped to the point it was hard to hear her. "He said it would be worse this time, much worse."

What did this guy do to her, anyway? It must be rape, but Jesus, what kind of rape? There were some grim possibilities: rapes with objects, rapes while the person was being strangled. I had one client who was raped next to the grave the perp made her dig for herself.

"How could it be worse?" I asked. It is amazing how well you can carry on a conversation when you have no idea what the other person is talking about. Maybe it helps not to know; you lead less and listen better.

Camille didn't answer. I'm sure she didn't know. She had ceased paying any attention to the tears, and they were running freely down her face. Her nose was running too, and she was only sniffling to stop it. If she got any more panicky she wouldn't pay attention to that either. There is a level of panic where the social niceties—even hygiene—disappear.

I spied a Kleenex box on the table and reached over to give one to her. She ignored my outstretched hand as though it weren't there and started compulsively rubbing her wrists. A chill ran up my spine; I knew what that meant.

I didn't know how far I could go, but I kept on. I couldn't ask her how long it lasted, she wouldn't have any idea, so I started at the other end. "Where did they find you?" I asked.

"Nobody found me," she said. "I prayed to God over and over, but He didn't help. Nobody helped."

I tried again. "When it was over . . ."

Camille interrupted, and it was the first time I'd seen even a flash of anger. "It wasn't over," she said. "It's never been over."

I was silent for a moment trying to figure out how to ask. "Where did you go?" I asked. "When you got away?"

"I never got . . . oh . . . ," she said as she realized what I was trying to ask. "To a kennel," she said, finally. "I crawled over the fence and hid with the dogs. I was too scared to go to a house and I . . . I didn't have any clothes. I thought I'd be safe with the dogs." She paused. "No, I didn't," she said, flatly. "I didn't think I'd be safe anywhere." I was starting to put things together—but there were still about a million things I didn't know.

"Did he let you go?" I asked. It didn't sound like the kind of situation that would have been easy to get out of.

"I had a seizure," she said, flatly. "I hadn't had one for years. I don't remember much. When I came to he was saying I wasn't worth killing. I guess I wasn't, but sometimes I think it would have been better if he had. At least I wouldn't have to go through it again."

Her voice had a kind of resignation in it that gave me the creeps. This woman really thought her tormentor was back and had no belief whatsoever that she or anybody on earth could stop him from doing it again—whatever it was. Worse, the son-of-a-bitch had annihilated her self-esteem to the point she thought she wasn't even worth killing.

By now her nose was starting to drip, but she was paying no attention. Reflexively, I started to try to hand her a Kleenex again but realized the one I had was all balled up. I tossed it and picked up the Kleenex box to pull out another. I heard a sharp intake of breath from Camille. Surprised, I looked up.

Her pupils were dilated wide open, and then they contracted to pinpoints. She was sitting rigidly, grasping the arms of the chair on both sides. Her knuckles were white. Her face started to get the kind of unfocused look that said I wasn't in the room anymore.

"Camille," I said urgently. "Look at the chair; look at Keeter. What do you see?" She was losing contact with her surroundings, and sometimes you can keep people grounded in the present by getting them to focus on what's around them. If she could look at Keeter or the room or anything around her, it might help her stay in the here and now.

It didn't even slow her down. Her eyes never even flickered toward Keeter. Instead, she slowly raised her hands and touched her cheeks. "Dear God, not my nose. Just my nose, leave my nose. I won't be able to breathe." Her voice was getting sharp, and her breath was coming in panicky grasps. "Don't cover my eyes," she said. "I can't see . . . I can't see," she said, her voice rising.

"What?" I said. "What's on your face?"

She turned her face toward me as a blind person might, her eyes showing no recognition at all. "Can't you see?" she said. Then I lost her entirely. She quietly slipped off the chair and curled up in a fetal position, covered her head with her hands, and started rocking back and forth. Silence filled the room only to be broken by Camille making some sort of slight sound. If I had leaned forward, I could have caught it, maybe. I didn't. I knew what it was.

Keeter hardly reacted to any of this. She just looked dead tired, as well she might be. Her owner had been acting like this for probably the last twenty-four hours.

I looked down at the Kleenex box in my hand, trying to understand what had just happened. It just looked like an ordinary Kleenex box. I started to put it down and froze. There, on the table, sitting behind the Kleenex box until I picked it up, was the problem. I flashed back to my office. "Mummy," she had said, and I had thought she had been calling for her mother. Boy, the things people tell me that I just don't hear.

It was a simple thing sitting there on the table. You'd find it in anybody's house, in every hospital. Most people thought of it as a reassuring thing to have around. It was nothing really, just a large, ordinary roll of adhesive tape.

7

Suzanne had the big problem, of course. Once Camille showed up at the ED, she was Suzanne's responsibility, and Suzanne couldn't exactly put her on the street in the shape she was in. She could leave her in a treatment room for hours and hours—I'd seen that happen—but it was going to be more than a few hours before Camille came back to earth.

We called Harvey—neither of us thought a neighbor was likely to know much about Camille's friends or relatives—but neither of us knew anybody else to call. There wasn't anybody else we could think of who even knew Camille, and Camille was now too out of it to answer any more questions.

The call to Harvey yielded zip. Camille had hardly spoken to him or his wife, and Harvey could not remember ever seeing anybody go in or out of Camille's house except her. Dog or no, somehow Camille had to be admitted, at least temporarily.

There was a huge fight with the powers that be. I took as much of the flak as I could—Suzanne was a shoo-in for chief resident next year if she didn't alienate the entire hierarchy first, which this little episode might. In the end we came up with a compromise. Camille was going into a twenty-four-hour bed. Some psychiatric beds were reserved for short-term crisis patients, and those beds were only available for twenty-four hours at a time.

Keeter got special attention. She was not to leave Camille's room the entire time except to be walked outside. I wondered who was supposed to walk her, but decided against asking. At the end of twenty-four hours, if Camille wasn't able to leave the hospital and go home, she was to be committed to the state hospital. Let them deal with the dog, seemed to be the administrative point of view.

Suzanne and I just looked at each other. Neither of us mentioned to the "risk-management" person we were dealing with that Camille would never meet the criteria for commitment. These days to be committed you had to be actively homicidal or suicidal—and that meant have the gun in your hand and your finger on the trigger—plus be mentally ill. Camille was certainly ill enough but not planning on killing anybody, although both Suzanne and I were both considering it at this point.

Suzanne and I had a different plan. We thought the dog was more committable than Camille. Maybe if she wasn't better after twenty-four hours, we'd just commit the dog and Camille could go along.

It had taken us the entire day, and all we had bought Camille was twenty-four hours in a safe place to put herself back together. Neither of us was surprised. It was always tougher dealing with the hierarchy than the patients.

"Keeter," I said sternly when I left, "keep your cool. Do not cause any trouble. No snacking. Not one little obsessive-compulsive disorder. Not a single major depression."

As I left I passed the resident coming in to take over for Suzanne, who, mercifully, would finally get to go home and sleep. "Watch out for the antisocial in 102," I said as I passed him in the hall. "Mean as a junkyard dog."

I stepped outside in the cool spring darkness and glanced at my watch. Eight o'clock. It wouldn't be light this late until June. I particularly hate winter, where you go to work in the dark and come home in the dark. There was a reason God said, "Let there be light." If I was God, it would be the first thing I'd say too.

I went back upstairs to my office and retrieved Willy's note before I left. I put it on the seat of the car and just looked at it a moment before starting the car. Surely, I wasn't thinking of answering it tonight. I was too tired from all the fighting over Camille, too zonked from watching her deteriorate in such a painful way. I wasn't in shape for it.

I drove home with the note still sitting on the seat. When I did respond to Willy—which wouldn't be tonight—the big issue would be what to say.

Dealing with Willy wasn't exactly like dealing with anybody else I knew. The closest thing maybe was an antisocial personality disorder—a bully, in short. There were rules for dealing with bullies. You never cowered and you never blustered. And most of all, you never got into a power struggle. Antisocials would cut off their noses to spite their faces, they would go to jail, they would literally die—or worse, kill you—before they'd lose a power struggle. So, instead, you gave them choices. If you do this, this will happen. If you do that, that will happen. Up to you; not my choice.

"That's fine," I had said to one who had announced he was going to tear up my office. "Sure, if you choose to, you can tear up my office. No problem. Now, here's the deal. If you tear it up, you go to jail. If you don't tear it up, you don't go to jail. Up to you. If you want to go to jail, you can go to jail. If you don't want to go to jail, then we can sit down and talk about why you're so upset. But you need to understand this: Either way—whether you go to jail tonight or you don't, I am not going to jail." He had sat down.

It wouldn't work with Willy. I knew in my soul it wouldn't, but what would? Nothing. So you took your best shot.

This time I didn't hesitate to get out of the car in the dark. Willy wouldn't be waiting. This much I knew about him: He loved foreplay. He wanted to talk, so he'd give me time to answer. I walked from the car to the house feeling safe for the first time since before I had been attacked. I dropped my stuff in the living room and walked out onto the deck.

The outside lights lit up the small stream below. I hadn't been out on the deck much recently, and I had almost forgotten how the stream looked at night. Water always looks different at night. It comes alive like some nocturnal animal that sleeps during the day. Look at water long enough at night and you would swear the light was coming up from below, braided through the gurgling stream like phosphorous. I'd seen that too. Dipped my oars in real phosphorous, leaving arcs of light as it dripped off the circling oars.

Somewhere, a thousand miles or so straight south, most of my people were probably sitting out on the water tonight, just like I was. One way or another, most of them live on the water—on the ocean or an inlet or at the least a river. In my family, my little stream wasn't a very big deal in the water department, but I couldn't imagine living without it. I went back in, got some ice tea, came out, and sat down. I felt the day start to slip from my shoulders.

I sat quietly and let the water from the stream mesmerize me. Water is pretty much all my family has in common. I have all kinds of relatives: bright ones and dumb ones, nice ones and mean ones. I have a Mama that makes barracudas look cuddly, and once upon a time I had a Daddy who'd rather drink than fight. But every single one of us has salt water in our veins.

I'm the black sheep. Not my cousin Mary Lou, who turned into a total drunk and was picked up by the police passed out in the street outside Hardee's. Mary Lou found God and straightened herself out, and my family decided Mary Lou was a testimony to the healing powers of the Lord. Not my nephew Buddy, who spent a couple of years in a military stockade for something or other—I didn't even want to know what. That was just considered youthful hijinks.

But a good Southern girl like me going up to live in a place that froze a body to death all winter and where, everybody knew, the people were as cold as the weather? I laughed out loud, thinking if Willy did kill me, nobody in my family would be surprised. What do you expect if you're going to live up North among strangers?

How would Mama deal with Willy? Mama wouldn't see the problem. "Shoot him on sight," she'd say, as if that settled it.

"It's not that simple, Mama. It's all going to be shadow and sleight of hand. By the time I see him it'll be too late." I don't know why I carry on conversations with Mama as much as I do: I couldn't live within seven states of her.

On impulse I walked inside the tiny A-frame and started to pick up the phone. For the first time I noticed the message light flashing and hit the button to play it.

Marv's voice came on, tinged with anxiety. "Michael," he said. "Thank you for seeing my client. I gather from your notes the group was not what she was looking for.

"I'm actually calling because I read in the paper that Willy got out. I am terribly sorry. I'm wondering if this is likely to be a problem for you? I'd be happy to consult with you any time about him. And . . . well . . . I hope other matters are going better."

I hadn't told him why I'd landed on his couch, but I knew Marv was well aware the only kind of thing that could put me in that kind of shape was Jordan. "Let me know if I can help. And please come back whenever you like."

He was an amazingly benign man, and maybe I would wind up on his couch again. I picked up the phone. From the benign to the . . . , but that was the problem with Mama, I never even knew what to call her. I brought the phone back outside and sat down again. I looked at it for a moment and then sighed. Might as well. I dialed and waited. If Mama was there she'd pick it up immediately. Mama didn't dillydally around.

"Hello," the voice said. Mama never identifies herself, no matter whose phone she answers. She just expects everybody knows who she is.

"Mama, this is Michael."

"Michael, well land sakes, girl. It's been many a moon since I heard from you."

"Phone works both ways, Mama." How did I do this? I could get in a fight with Mama within *seconds* of being on the phone with her.

"Well, we been busy planting the garden. You know how much work that is. There hasn't been time to breathe." Mama wasn't one to let things go. I tried to think if I had ever in my life heard Mama take even *part* of the responsibility for anything going wrong. Probably not. This was going nowhere, as usual.

"Mama, tell me about attack dogs." Mama did know her dogs.

"Attack dogs. Girl? They don't call them 'attack dogs' any-more. Doesn't look good in court. You know how people sue over every little thing these days. Goddamn lawyers are ruining the country."

I had the feeling getting eaten by an attack dog didn't meet my definition of a little thing, but I let it go. Too, Daddy had been a lawyer, but I let that go also. "Right, protection dogs. That's not what I'm asking. I want to know how a female protection dog would likely act if she had an owner who couldn't control her. Is she going to get mean? What's she likely to do?"

"Well, that owner shouldn't have her. That's ridiculous."

"I don't run the world, Mama. There's nothing I can do about the fact that somebody has a protection dog who shouldn't. I just want to know how the dog is likely to act."

"Is she mean? Some of them are just naturally mean and some aren't."

"I don't know. She looks mean to me, but I can't tell."

There was a pause. "One thing's for sure, she'll take over."

"What do you mean? Turn on her owner?"

"Not necessarily. But she'll start making decisions on her own. A good dog won't just protect a person. They'll protect their territory. Your girl will pick out her territory, and before long you won't see any more mail. The UPS man won't come around either. Lord, there was one over on Harker's Island, he attacked the UPS *truck* when it was coming down the driveway."

"Would she let a stranger get into her owner's bedroom while the owner was there?"

"Michael, you ask the stupidest questions," Mama said with a snort. And to think I wondered where my lack of tact comes from.

I didn't say anything. It seemed clear there hadn't been anybody in Camille's room last night. I hadn't really thought so, but she had been so oddly sure. "Sounds like you got somebody with some trouble," Mama volunteered.

"The world is full of trouble," I said.

"Ain't it the truth?" she said. It was a rare moment when Mama and I agreed. I almost felt uncomfortable.

I said good-bye, hung up, and wandered back inside. I opened the fridge looking for some more ice tea and saw cartons of Chinese food. Christ, Adam. I had almost forgotten about him; last night seemed a zillion miles away. I got up and walked around. No sign he had ever been there: no note, nothing. Maybe he'd come to the end of it. No question someone could get a little tired of my stuff. I couldn't tell how I felt about that; maybe the comment about Jordan was still too raw.

I got the ice tea and, on impulse, sat down at the computer as I was walking by. I'd just compose the note tonight. I wouldn't send it. I'd just play around with it. I opened up my e-mail program and stared at the screen. What exactly was my plan? I sat there a while before I wrote.

> I'll be interested in what you choose, Mr. Willy. Sure, you can start the same old routines again, but aren't they a little "been there, done that" by now? Of course, you will eventually get caught, but a lot of people actually seem to like prison. Maybe you're one of them.
>
> I don't think you have a choice, anyway. I personally do not believe you could control your appetites if you tried. You're not really their master; you're more like their slave. Either way, I'm not involved. I don't have a role, Mr. Willy, except maybe the Greek chorus, or else Cassandra predicting doom.

If Willy had an Achilles' heel it was his narcissism. He wouldn't like the notion that he couldn't control his appetites. In Willy's mind he wasn't a slave to anything. No sense in not trying to turn that narcissistic grandiosity against him.

My hand hovered over the "Send" button. It would be

smarter to wait. Let twenty-four hours pass at least. Make Willy wait. Responding too soon might be read as a sign of anxiety. Besides, I wouldn't feel safe once I sent it.

I pressed it anyway. The story came to mind of the scorpion who bit the horse carrying him to safety across a stream. When the horse had asked why, the scorpion had said, "Because it's my nature." I had my nature as surely as Willy had his, and it was my nature to serve and volley, not to sit back at the baseline and wait for the ball.

I don't know what got me so nervous about the whole thing afterward. I just kept seeing the "Send" button in my mind, although this time it was labeled "Start," instead.

It was Saturday, but I didn't wake up feeling any better. I had that pregame edginess I'd had in high school before a big game. Winning was a big deal at the time, although even then I had had enough perspective to know Lombardi had gone off the deep end when he said winning was the only thing. Winning wasn't the *only* thing when you're playing a game. But actually, when you're dealing with a sexual sadist who wants to maim and murder you, maybe it is.

I ought to be circling the wagon trains and handing out rifles, but it was hard to circle a single wagon. I needed to be rallying the troops, but I didn't. It wasn't that people didn't want to help. It was just that I didn't exactly know how to take their help without feeling diminished somehow.

I put the coffee cup down on the table next to the bed and stood up. My whole train of thought was depressing. I hated running into my own limitations, and I seemed to do it all the time. I could do this; I couldn't do that. I had more knots in my psyche than any sailor knew.

I needed to expand my horizons — at least get back some lost territory — and today was as good a day as any. Ridiculous to think I couldn't go play ball in a gym alone. I had done it my whole life. Just because someone strangled me in a gym. It wasn't the gym's fault.

But why did he have to do it in a gym? Why contaminate my favorite place in the whole world? Why not a beauty parlor or the Miss America pageant or a meeting? Any meeting. Why not the Chairman of Psychiatry's office? I could live without any of those places easily.

Well, in all fairness to my attacker, probably because it would have been hard to find me in any of those other places. I'd never been to the Miss America meat market in my whole life, and I didn't hang around beauty parlors. In Psychiatry, my hatred of meetings was legendary. Not to mention that I went to the Chairman's office only when I had to, usually about some dumb meeting or other I'd missed.

I went to the closet to get my precious high-top basketball shoes and started to bend over to pick them up. But as I did so, I could suddenly feel a forearm pressing into my throat. I straightened up and tried to catch my breath. Jesus Christ. Was this going to plague me for the rest of my life? I had Posttraumatic Stress Disorder, and I hated it.

Having PTSD meant every time something *reminded* me of being strangled, I had the same feelings and the same physical sensations I had when I *was* being strangled. It also meant reminders would kick off intrusive memories and sometimes even nightmares. Camille had the same thing, only worse. She actually heard the perp's voice. My PTSD wasn't quite that bad. But it was miserable enough.

I bent over to get the shoes again, but the memory of my assaulter's face close to mine came up so vividly I shuddered involuntarily and stood up again. I backed away from the shoes and just stared at them.

I can do this. I can make myself do this. It crossed my mind that it might be more sensible to go to the gym with someone else the first time. But as John Belushi would have said, "Nah." I didn't want to. I could just see myself: "Adam, I'm scared to go to the gym alone. Will you come hold my hand?" Unbelievable. Impossible.

I started to reach for the shoes and then stopped. The memory of being strangled was so strong I was short of breath. I sat down on the bed and thought about it. Damn it, I could make myself take those shoes and go to the gym, and some day I'd have to. But it was clear whenever I did, I'd pay a price: I'd kick up the memory again big time.

People with PTSD avoid things that remind them of the trauma for a reason. I knew that. If I went to the gym, the price I would pay would be intrusive memories and a constant feeling of being suffocated. Not to mention nightmares. I could do it. But maybe I'd better get rid of Willy first.

Between the perp in my head and the one on the street, Willy was the bigger threat, I figured. Don't get crazy because you can't stand to be controlled. Being strangled will be sitting in your head whenever you get around to it. But how many wars can you fight at once on how many fronts? If you use up your resources tackling that, you'll have less to deal with Willy.

Hell of a thing. Every fiber in me wanted to grab the b-ball shoes and say, "Fuck you, you SOB. Do your worst." But I didn't. I was going to have to live with this for a while; that's all there was to it. If I didn't, I'd end up with two assaulters in my head, assuming I still had one.

I have a surgeon's mentality—a knife-happy surgeon. Cut it out! Get rid of it! That is my favorite thing to do with problems. I couldn't believe I was consciously, deliberately making a decision to live with something—worse, something akin to a leech on my psyche. But it was true that if I didn't live with it I might die with it. And death was the kind of problem you just didn't want to get into.

Next to my b-ball shoes were my riding boots. Why not? I was so frustrated I felt like punching something. Why not go tackle a few fixed cross-country jumps? I sighed again and reached for the boots.

I hopped in my car, which was clean and Spartan. I can't believe people spend money on cars. All cars do the same thing. They go from here to there. My idea of a car is something with four wheels and a seat. Well, okay, a motor that starts in the winter and doesn't break down. Whatever car I've had, it is always Basic Car. Small. Cheap. No frills.

Not like the Porsche a friend had when I was a student. He lived upstairs from me, and he was out two or three times a night when the alarm went off. Thieves are drawn to Porsches like mosquitoes to blood. Forget it. I never had a car I had to lock because I never had a car anybody wanted to steal.

I picked up the Interstate and headed out to the old Braxton Farm. There was a trendy riding academy closer in, where all the students and the professors' children rode, but it never crossed my mind to go there. The academy barn always looked freshly painted. Once, I went by there and they had flower boxes on the barn windows. Too precious for me. I had found an old farm in the country that trained serious event horses and that was often looking for riders to exercise them.

The sign on the gate simply said "Braxton's Farm." Braxton had been gone a century. Joe Higgins had the place now, but Braxton's Farm it was and Braxton's Farm it would stay. I pulled up next to the weathered barn and surveyed the scene. The exterior of the barn looked like it always did: gray and battered. The fences all needed a new coat of paint. Joe never got around to details like that. But the place was neat and clean and looked like it was designed to be more comfortable for horses than for humans.

Mud season was beginning to relent. The outdoor ring looked ridable, if barely. That was disappointing. I was planning on using that as an argument for going cross-country since the cross-country course was on a hill and dried out sooner in the spring. Joe thought me a little too gung-ho for the cross-country course and often restricted me to the ring. Worse, since he'd built the indoor ring, I didn't even get outside half the time.

I found him saddling up a young chestnut mare I didn't recognize. Joe was a trim, good-looking man in his sixties with graying hair wearing a flannel workshirt with riding pants and boots. I'd never seen him in anything else. He looked a lot like the barn: weathered but solid with no frills.

"Good," he said, looking up. "I was just thinking about you. I'm taking this new mare on the cross-country course for the first time, and I was wishing somebody was here to take Freight Train with us."

Had I died and gone to heaven or what? I didn't even have to argue with him. "Delighted," I said. "What's going on with Freight Train?" Freight Train was a very capable, reliable jumper, and I didn't usually get to ride problem-free horses.

"His new rider is what's wrong with Freight Train. I wish to God parents would quit buying horses their kids can't handle. Freight Train's going to hell in a handbasket. He's jumping all strung out, and he's going to kill that kid if I don't get him under control."

It seemed odd to be taking a horse on the cross-country course to get him under control. Usually, that kind of work was done in the ring, where horses were much less pumped up than in the open air galloping free. But I didn't say a thing. I sure as hell wasn't going to talk Joe out of it.

"Control, Michael. I want this horse under control. I should work him in the ring, but I don't have time. The kid's parents are insisting on a novice event next weekend, and right now, in the mood he's in, Freight Train will eat that kid alive on a cross-country course." Joe stopped saddling and looked over the horse's back at me. "We are taking these jumps slow and easy, Michael, or we are coming back to the barn. Half the time you're worse than Freight Train."

"Hey, I just got here. Don't take it out on me." I was miffed. Joe and I had a running argument about whether I jumped too fast or not. It was a bum rap. Just because I couldn't see lolly-gagging around in front of a jump. I always jumped in control, or at least I tried to.

I went in the tack room to get Freight Train's gear. The tack was shiny with leather oil, and the smell of leather oil was sweet in the air. Each horse's halter and bridle were hung neatly on a hook and labeled. The saddles were on racks across the room.

I got Freight Train's halter and bridle and picked out a jumping saddle—a big jumping saddle—that would likely fit him. I dropped his tack off near the cross-ties where I would saddle him and went off to fetch him with his halter and a lead line. All the stalls had wooden signs with the horses' names on them, and I wandered around until I found him. I could have asked Joe, but I didn't feel like it. He was too crabby today, and I was still miffed.

The top half of Freight Train's stable door was open, and I looked in to make sure it was really him in his stall. The horse inside was too big to be anybody else, and I opened the bottom half of the stable door and stood for a moment just admiring him as the sun slanted in across his stall.

He was a big bay thoroughbred at seventeen hands. He had thick, tough legs unlike most thoroughbreds, whose spindly legs are their downfall. The sunlight made stripes across his shiny, brown coat and it looked almost red where the light hit it. Freight Train turned to look at me with his big, curious eyes. Even munching his hay, his eyes had that deep thoroughbred light in them.

Ah, thoroughbreds. They have heart like no other horse. Who else will literally run themselves to death for you if you aren't careful? Who else will look at a cross-country jump and start salivating? They go when they shouldn't go, couldn't go, would damage themselves by going. You might have to put on the brakes a lot, but you never have to pedal.

All right, they have their flaws—high-strung natures, spindly legs—and more than a few have lousy personalities, just plain cranky. A lot of thoroughbreds would as soon bite you as look at you, and if you haven't been kicked by a thoroughbred or dumped by one, it means you don't ride them. But in the end there are thoroughbreds and then there are a lot of other animals.

"Freight Train, dear heart," I said, slipping on his halter, "care to go for a spin? Perhaps a turn around the cross-country course." Freight Train's ears perked up. Of course he didn't recognize the words, but he could hear the excitement in my voice.

I led him out of the stall to the cross-ties. Freight Train allowed himself to be led quietly. I hooked him up and went to get the cleaning supplies.

By the time I got back from the tack room, Joe had his mare saddled and was in the indoor ring warming her up, so I had the aisle between the stalls all to myself. The barn was silent except for horses munching hay and the occasional snort or wall-kick.

Something started to ease inside of me. There are only a few holy places in the world. High on my list are an empty gym with no one there but me, and a clean barn with well-cared-for, contented horses munching their hay.

I brushed Freight Train's dusty coat in short, easy strokes

working backward from his neck to his haunches: Horses are always dusty and need to be groomed daily. Freight Train's coat was shiny, a tribute to his diet and the frequent brushing. He seemed to like the stroking and stood quietly. I probably brushed him longer than I needed to—Joe would be yelling at me soon to get going—but the rhythm of the quiet brushing in the nearly silent, sunlit barn was balm to my agitated soul. What was it Will Rogers said? Something about the outside of a horse being good for the inside of a man? Make that "person," and he got it right.

I picked up the hoof pick out of the box of cleaning supplies and lifted each of the big guy's feet in turn. I cleaned out all the muck on the bottom of each hoof and carefully traced the grooves with the hoof pick. I inspected his feet carefully and then felt all four legs from the knee down. I couldn't feel any heat or swelling in any of them. On a cross-country course, a lame horse who couldn't jump properly could kill you, so it wasn't just altruism that made me check carefully to see if Freight Train was fit.

But he was. He felt like a million bucks, and he looked like a million bucks, so I put the saddle on and was just finishing putting on the bridle when Joe brought his horse in from the indoor ring.

"Going to take all day?" he said. Whatever had gone on in the inner ring hadn't lightened his mood any.

"Oh, you know me," I said, "just trying to avoid the cross-country course. One more sec."

Joe snorted, and I ran to get my helmet and riding gloves. When I came back he and his mare had already started off. I scrambled onto Freight Train's back and headed after him. It was a bit of a feat getting up there, given how big Freight Train was and the fact that no one was around to give me a leg up, but I never had the patience to go find the mounting stand.

Freight Train perked up a bit as we left the barn, but didn't get antsy until we passed the outdoor ring and the cutoff for the trail rides. When there wasn't any other place we could be going except the cross-country course, his whole mood changed. He was like a kid who couldn't contain himself. He wanted to go, and I wouldn't let him, so he started dancing in place. He got so many steps out of every yard he looked like a parade horse. Freight Train pulled his head in and arched his neck so my pulling on the bit didn't do any good: His neck was as far back as it would go.

I laughed out loud and reached down to pat his neck. "Easy, big guy," I said. "We'll get there." I continued to hold the reins in one hand and pat his neck to calm him down as we made our way down the road. I don't know why I love this so much. Maybe because around people I always seem to be the one with the throttle wide open. Thoroughbreds are so antsy, around them I feel like mellowness itself. Or maybe I love being around them simply because I know so well how they feel.

We rounded a curve, and the hill with the cross-country jumps on it came into view. Freight Train got serious about moving along and gave up his dancing in place for some serious pulling on the bit. I took the reins in each hand and squeezed and released, squeezed and released. It wouldn't do any good to pull steadily. Freight Train would just brace against the pressure or get the bit in his teeth, which meant real trouble.

As the first jump came in sight I let Freight Train canter, and we started circling in slow circles a long way from it. Without saying anything, it was clear between Joe and me that he would wait for me to do whatever I needed to do to get Freight Train under control. The new mare would follow Freight Train over the jumps.

Freight Train wasn't happy about circling, but he tolerated it until he reached the part of the circle where he was facing the first jump. Then he tried to leap forward and take off, but I was relentless. I made him circle again by holding tight the rein away from the jump and loosening the other. Freight Train's head was pointing toward the circle, but for the whole first quarter of it his body tried to gallop sideways to get to the jump.

We circled this way a few times, then the next time around I switched circles so he was heading into a circle on the other side and making a figure eight. Poor Freight Train was so intent on getting to the jump he didn't see the new circle coming up and didn't switch leads when I pulled him to the other side.

That put him galloping with his outside foot leading on the new circle, and he damn near fell on his nose. He stumbled, corrected himself, and switched leads. The message I'd sent was clear: Pay attention to me, Freight Train, or you're going to fall on your head.

We did a few more figure eights, and then I headed for the first jump.

It was a particularly tough one: a platform only two feet or so high but a good five feet deep. It had no wings, and it was only ten feet wide, which meant it was very easy and tempting for a horse to run out on either side. The jump looked like a simple upright until you were right up on it, which just increased the chances a horse would try to go around.

The issue for Freight Train wasn't that it was a platform—he knew this course—it was whether his strides would be right coming into it. No matter how good a horse is at jumping, he still has to take off the right distance from a jump. It has to be far enough away that he won't hit it going up and close enough that he can clear the whole thing coming down. Ideally he would gallop with even strides to the jump and magically find himself exactly the right distance from the jump to take off.

That wouldn't happen by accident, not even with an experienced jumper like Freight Train. It was my job to lengthen or shorten his strides from farther away so that by three strides out he would be coming in perfectly.

If he came in wrong, he'd either have to leave out a stride and jump long—not easy when the jump is five feet deep—or he'd have to take an itsy-bitsy stride and "chip" it—also not easy when you're moving at thoroughbred speed. A couple of thousand pounds has a lot of momentum when it's moving right along.

Either way, the price of screwing up was that he could land on top of the jump or fail to clear it in the first place. This would be a really big problem with a cross-country jump because they are rigid and fixed. The jump we were facing was made out of logs nailed together, and they were just about thick enough, say, to hold up the World Trade Center. Come to think of it: It is strange that I love this so.

Freight Train didn't want to listen to me. The sun was shining, and the jump was just sitting there, and by God, he was a thoroughbred, which meant he was born and bred to move at intoxicating speeds. But the whole point of the stupid circling was to establish who was the boss of this operation, and he reluctantly slowed in response to my constant hassling.

I measured the distance from the jump to where I thought the third stride out would be. I decided Freight Train wasn't coming in right so I shortened his stride even more. He responded reluctantly, but he responded.

As we got closer to the jump my own adrenaline started to soar, and I could taste the bitter edge of fear in my mouth. Putting your life on the line will always get your attention. Unless you're a loony, it'll scare the bejesus out of you. "Take your best shot, fate," I thought as I always did, "and then leave me alone till the next time"—a strange mantra but one that always comes to mind.

By three strides from the jump Freight Train was coming in right. I eased up slightly on the reins and got ready to jump. By this point Freight Train could figure out for himself what he needed to do, and he kept his stride even as we approached.

He took his last stride and soared into the air. He jumped big as horses usually do when faced with rigid, wide jumps. I stood up in the stirrups and threw myself forward so I could release the reins up his neck. He needed to be able to stretch out in the air as much as he liked without hitting the bit. Novice riders always hold on to the reins to balance themselves, and it's a wonder some horses don't just stomp them to death once they finally get off.

Freight Train had a hang time that Michael Jordan would envy, and it seemed like I was flying forever. The exhilaration hit me like, well, a freight train, and by the time I landed I had enough endorphins for major heart surgery without anesthetics. I was in the zone. I could hear birds chirping with a singular clarity and see every leaf on the nearby trees stand out distinctly. Everything had a color and vividness that nothing but jumping or drugs can produce.

I looked back as we cantered up the hill, and Joe had gotten his mare over the jump, although barely. She looked spooked and shaken, and Joe looked determined. To a new horse a cross-country jump is a formidable thing.

I laughed out loud as we cantered. All those snide male comments about women and horses miss the mark. All that junk about that "big thing between their legs." We don't confuse horses with men; we aren't making love to horses when we ride—we are the horse. It is like becoming a centaur and suddenly acquiring four powerful legs. Freight Train and I for this moment in time were a unit, a finely oiled machine, and we were leaping like gazelles over every obstacle in our path. Jesus, life was sweet.

The second jump was a far simpler one: an upright made of

logs with wings that went out at an angle and almost guided the horse to the jump. We were doing fine on the approach, when Freight Train suddenly veered to the left. Surprised— the jump ahead was nothing compared to the last one—I tried to recover my balance and press with my left leg to straighten him out. But Freight Train kept moving at an angle and looking at the trees. I glanced over—what was spooking him— and caught a glimpse of something yellow.

Yellow. What's yellow? Deer aren't yellow. But I didn't have time to think about it. Freight Train was still coming in at an angle, and we were almost on top of the jump. He chipped it. Lucky it was a small one.

I looked back. There was no way to warn Joe about whatever it was that was in the trees. But his mare was so nervous about the jumps she didn't seem to be paying attention to anything else, anyway.

I made a long, slow curve to the right toward a stand of trees. To get to the third jump we had to canter down a lane through the trees, and it was close to my favorite part of the course.

Freight Train and I were alone in the tunnel of trees—Joe and his mare were still pretty far behind—and I could hear birds on both sides. The trees were so close and so vivid I felt like I could reach out and touch them. It gave me time to think about the yellow something I saw—thought I saw—in the trees. I came up blank. It certainly wasn't hunting season, and the course wasn't close to any hiking trails.

Whatever it was, it was gone. Freight Train seemed fine. My head was thoroughly in the zone by now so everything seemed in slow motion. The sound of Freight Train's hoofs drumming on the hard-packed dirt sounded like some kind of old, lost sound vaguely remembered, almost like a heartbeat.

As we approached the end of the trees, fear broke through my endorphin-soaked brain. The next jump was a killer, loosely speaking. It started with a sharp turn to the right so that we'd be going downhill. It was fairly scary to canter downhill without jumping, but the jump itself made it worse. It was a drop jump. This meant you leaped over something on one side expecting to land at the same level you took off, only to find the ground was several feet lower on the other side. The jump hid the drop so an unsuspecting horse wouldn't see—until it was too late—that the small two-foot solid jump in front of him hid a three-foot drop straight down on the other side.

There was also the problem that we had done a U-turn and were coming back to the same bunch of trees that had spooked Freight Train—although this time from the other side.

I could feel Freight Train tense as we got closer to the end of the tunnel, and I took the time to put the reins in one hand and pat his neck. This time I was standing in the saddle and leaning forward. He wasn't going too fast now, and the point was just to keep him moving over the jump.

I saw the jump ahead and squeezed my legs slightly. Freight Train's strides weren't coming in right, and this time I thought I'd lengthen to pick up a little speed; going downhill make horses cautious, and they tend to slow. This jump was such a horse-stopper that I just wanted to get Freight Train over it. I didn't much care about the form.

The jump was close after the tunnel of trees, and the three-stride-from-the-jump mark came up quickly. Freight Train still seemed a little off to me, so I squeezed even more to lengthen his last three strides. We weren't going over this pretty, but I'd be damned if we weren't going over it.

Suddenly, from the stand of trees on our right, something white broke from cover and ran right in front of Freight Train. I saw the blur in my peripheral vision and thought "uh-oh," but the whole thing happened too fast to do anything.

Freight Train immediately shied to the left, away from the intruder and, unfortunately, the jump: horses instinctively protect their legs by not stepping on strange things. I was already standing up in the stirrups and leaning forward, and there was no time to get back. Freight Train went left, but I went straight. I flew through the air toward the jump. The world seemed to flip, and I hit the jump hard with my back and bounced over it, landing the three feet down on the other side.

If I'd had any presence of mind, I'd have been worried that Joe wouldn't see Freight Train was loose and would take the jump and land right on top of me. But I was too stunned to worry about anything: I tried to remember what happened, but couldn't. I just lay there. It didn't even cross my mind to get up.

I heard the sound of feet running—Freight Train had gone back down the tunnel of trees, and Joe had seen him and pulled up. Then Joe was next to me saying, "Are you all right?"

I didn't answer for a minute. For some reason I hate that question. People always ask it when you get hurt before you even know if you are all right or not. You're supposed to say, "Yes, I'm fine," even if you aren't, so they can quit worrying. I couldn't seem to find enough breath to say anything, and Joe said again, "Are you all right?"

When I didn't answer he said, "Michael, can you move your legs?" That freaked me, and I said, "Of course I can move my legs," and then tried to move them. They did move, which was very reassuring. I sat up, and then it came to me.

"It wasn't Freight Train's fault," I said to Joe. "Something ran across the course right in front of him." Which was very weird, come to think of it. I had never heard of an animal running toward danger. I got a little more oriented and sat up,

ANNA SALTER

asking, "Is Freight Train all right?" The world started whirling when I sat up, and I leaned back on my hands and closed my eyes to stop the spinning.

"He's fine," Joe said.

"Well, go and check him," I said testily with my eyes still shut.

"To hell with Freight Train," Joe said.

"He's a forty-thousand-dollar horse, Joe. Go and check him. I'm all right."

Joe grumbled, but he went off, and I was glad for the moment alone to collect myself. I got up slowly and tried to brush the dirt off my back. I found I had to move very slowly to keep the world from spinning, and I walked over to the jump and leaned against it with my eyes shut again. Joe came back with both horses in tow, and I straightened up. "He's fine," he said.

I looked at the horses. Both had grass coming out from their bits where they had used their freedom to graze on the new grass just starting. Both looked totally unperturbed at my predicament. Horses are not big in the empathy department.

I tried moving again. The world had gotten reasonably stable. I walked over to Freight Train and started to get on.

"Are you all right?" Joe said.

"Of course I'm all right," I responded tersely. "You asked me that already."

"Well, you're getting on the wrong horse," Joe said. "It's the only reason I ask."

I looked at the horse I was getting on, and it was Joe's mare. I stepped back with whatever dignity I could summon—which wasn't much—and moved over to the other horse. Maybe I was in worse shape than I thought.

"We're going home, Michael," Joe said.

"You know Freight Train has to go over the jump," I

responded. Joe knew you should never let a horse get away with not taking a jump for any reason. No matter what the reason for balking—except maybe sudden death—the horse went over the jump it refused before you went home. Joe knew that.

"Fine," Joe said. "I'll take him over."

"Joe," I said slowly, "I need to go over the jump too."

I could hear him sigh, but he didn't say anything. "Give me your crop," I said. He gave me the crop and a leg up on Freight Train. I held the crop down my leg where Freight Train couldn't see it. Ordinarily, it would be the last thing I'd need with Freight Train, but this time might be different.

We turned and trotted up the hill. I was not going to try to make the sharp turn from the tunnel in the trees again—no point in making this harder than it already was. I wiggled various parts of my body as I went, trying to figure out if everything worked. Everything seemed to, but I did not feel well and this was going to be a major deal getting over this jump. What the hell was it? A Goddamn psycho rabbit? What would cause a rabbit to run in front of a galloping thorough-bred?

Joe got on his mare and positioned himself to the left of the jump to discourage Freight Train from shying the same way he had before. Ordinarily I would have told him I didn't need the help, but this time I kept my mouth shut.

We trotted to begin with, the trees on our right and the jump straight ahead. One thing was for sure: I could throw away the left rein. Freight Train wouldn't shy toward the trees where the intruder had come from. Why had I thought that? It wasn't an intruder; it was just a stupid rabbit. If Freight Train went anywhere it would be to the left, like he had before.

We started cantering halfway down the hill, and I could feel Freight Train's body tense as we got closer. This time I was sitting as far back in the saddle as I could get in case he did balk. I saw him cut his eye toward the trees, looking, no doubt, for another rabbit. I was holding the right rein so tightly he couldn't possibly move his head to the left, but his hindquarters started drifting. Freight Train wasn't even thinking about the jump ahead. He was expecting trouble from the trees.

I had the crop in my left hand, but Freight Train didn't know it. I took the reins in my right hand and cracked him sharply on his left hindquarters. Surprised, he shot forward—the trees forgotten for the moment.

The jump was right in front of him, and he wasn't ready. I hit him again, more sharply this time, and he took off, awkwardly and late, but he did take off.

He wasn't exactly balanced, and I didn't feel like I was flying—more like falling. He stumbled when he landed on the other side and almost went down on his nose. I fell forward on his neck when he stumbled.

Freight Train caught himself, and so did I, and neither of us went down, although it was close. We were over. I pulled him up, more relieved than I wanted to admit, and Joe came trotting up, probably more relieved than he wanted to admit.

I considered whether I could get through the rest of the course. I just hated to call it quits, but I felt like shit. Freight Train would do fine, but could I get through it? Luckily I didn't have to make the decision. "We're going home," Joe said, and started off on his mare before I had a chance to argue. To be truthful, I didn't really want to.

I followed behind, and we walked back to the barn. Neither of us said anything. When somebody got hurt, Joe always got angry—from worry, I think, but it wasn't pleasant to deal with. I'd given him enough flak about it over the years that he'd learned—at least around me—to keep it to himself. For my part, the vertigo kept coming and going, and I was working at just staying on the horse.

I started to unsaddle Freight Train at the barn, but Joe took the saddle out of my hands. "Go home, Michael," he said tersely. "You look like shit."

I didn't even think of arguing. I just headed for the car. I looked back and saw Joe watching. He was probably wondering if I'd get in the wrong car. For Christ's sakes, I was moving under my own steam. How bad could it be?

I got in the car and headed for the highway, but once out of sight of Joe I turned onto a logging road that went up by the cross-country jumps. There was something I had to do, and tomorrow would be too late. I drove as far as I could, then got out and walked up the hill. I headed for the thicket of trees that had spooked Freight Train. It seemed to take a long time to get up the hill. You don't realize how much ground you cover on a horse.

I pulled aside some bushes and headed into the bramble, looking at the ground the whole time. It took me a few minutes, but I found what I was looking for—sort of. Surprised, I knelt down and touched the ground with my fingers.

There in the soft, wet dirt was a footprint. But it wasn't a large male who had stood in the thicket. There was the imprint of the ball of somebody's foot—small, about the size of mine—but where the heel should be there was only a small, deep hole. A woman had stood in the thicket, a woman who hadn't expected to be there and who was no doubt cursing her shoes as she stood. It just couldn't be Willy, not unless he had crammed his feet into a small woman's spike heels, which, come to think of it, I wouldn't put past him.

I stood up, completely mystified, and thought about it. Willy was famous for attracting female admirers. I had even run into one leaving once when I went in to see him. Had he conned someone into keeping an eye on me? It couldn't be a casual hiker. Nobody wore spike heels on a hike.

I put my hand on my back while I thought. It was beginning

to hurt like a son-of-a-bitch, and when I put my hand on it, I felt a knot right in the middle of my spine. I put my fist next to it and compared them. The knot stood out roughly as far as my fist.

I swallowed hard. I'd played b-ball too long to be upset by the average sprain or broken nose, but the memory of Christopher Reeves could send me into near hysteria. With a knot like that, the ED was calling my name.

9

I was relieved to see it was Jack who finally walked into my cubicle in the ED. Ordinarily I avoided him. Jack and I had spent some time together, back before I got religion, or my version of it, anyway, and quit going out with married men.

Right now I didn't feel like avoiding him. He was a very good doc, and he'd take good care of me, and at this moment that seemed like a big deal. Jack wouldn't miss a cracked vertebrae, say, the kind where you go to sleep feeling fine and wake up after it severs your spinal cord.

My head felt like someone was hitting it with a hammer, and I smiled bleakly when he walked in. "So," he said. "Up to your usual quiet life, I see."

"There was this rabbit with a pocket watch," I replied. "Kept saying he was late. Fool ran right in front of my horse."

Jack took my face in his hands and lifted it. I closed my eyes for a second against the pain. Any movement was starting to make my head feel like an anvil had been dropped on it. "Headache?" Jack said.

"More or less," I replied.

He looked back and forth from one eye to the other. "Are they all right?" I said, trying to sound casual. I knew pupils of different sizes were not a good sign.

"More or less," he said. "Any nausea or sleepiness?"

"None," I said. "Just good old-fashioned pain."

"So what else is wrong with you?" he asked.

"This." I got up off the examining table and turned around. I lifted my shirt up to show Jack my back.

"Impressive," he said. "We'll need to get a look at that." He put his hand on my back and ran it over the bump. Even in the pain I was aware of how gentle his fingers felt. That man did have nice hands. I sighed inwardly. The estrogen vote was coming in again. If I ever became a multiple personality, it would be a running battle between the quasi-reasonable part of me and my estrogen-steeped, who-gives-a-shit brain stem.

"Have you seen this?" he asked.

"No," I replied. "I just felt it."

"Take a look." He turned and got a mirror and held it over my shoulder where I could turn my head and get a look at it. My entire back was discoloring from one side to the other. The knot in the center looked as bad as it felt.

"Oh, boy," I said.

"Lady," he said, "whatever you're trying to prove, you've already proved it." I laughed. Jack was quoting something a guy who played in the pick-up basketball games had said to me one time.

"Could be I should stick with the less dangerous sports." It just slipped out, and immediately I wanted to hit the "undo" button and take it back.

Jack didn't respond. Things between us had gone beyond that kind of flippancy. Worse, it was a kind of painful reminder of the difference in how he saw the affair and how I did.

He sat down and filled out the paperwork for the X-ray. It seemed to take him a long time. Finally, he handed it to me. "If you ever want to put something on the line beside your tush," he said, "call me. Otherwise, I've got a rowing machine."

It hurt, but I deserved it. I took it without reply.

I got through the wait for the X-ray and the wait for the radiologist to interpret it and the wait for Jack to come back and tell me it was fine. I'd banged myself to hell and back, but I hadn't actually broken anything. I had a concussion—even I had figured that out—but it looked like I hadn't fractured my skull or done anything permanent to my precious little brain cells. This was good—I was very attached to those little cells.

By the time I got home, my head hurt so badly, I had to put it on the steering wheel and wait for a lull before I could get out of the car. By then I was nauseated, but I was pretty sure it was from the pain.

I locked the door behind me and more or less glided up to the loft. It hurt less if I walked very smoothly. I lay down carefully on the bed and didn't move. I had only taken Advil at the hospital, but I found that I was drifting off in some spacey, exhausted way.

The phone rang, and I didn't even think about answering it. The machine was turned up, and I could hear Marv's voice. "Michael," he said, "I need to check in with you. Something came up in a session that you should know about." His voice sounded somewhat urgent, but I didn't care—not in the slightest. I didn't care what anybody said in any session. I didn't much care about anything. I was too damn tired and in too much pain.

Time passed. A whole day and night of it, and I only got off the bed when I had to. I tried to brush my teeth, but it jarred my head too much. I woke up every time I turned over in the night because turning my head would start it throbbing again.

Marv had called again, and it sounded like whatever it was, was important to him, but it still wasn't to me. My whole world had been reduced to a focus on keeping my head as still as possible.

Besides, if I spoke to Marv, he'd know immediately how hurt I was: There was zero chance I could fool him. Then he'd tell people, and they'd come out and scurry around. I'd have to deal with them, and I just didn't have the energy. The only call I answered was from Jack; I was afraid he'd come out to check on me if I didn't.

There was a little voice inside that said, "Call Marv. His voice doesn't sound right," but I ignored it. Chicken Little could have come to my door, and I would have said, "So, the sky is falling? I know that already. It fell on my head."

10

I just didn't do well with the head thing. I called in sick to work Monday and Tuesday—a flu bug, I said—and it wasn't until late Tuesday that I could even walk around without gritting my teeth. Finally, I got well enough to remember there was an outside world and noticed the machines that kept me in touch with it.

I might as well tackle the phone. I was halfway through listening to the messages when it rang. Impulsively, I picked it up and said "hello."

I felt a jolt when I heard Adam's voice. "Michael," he said. I was supposed to say something back, but I couldn't remember what—besides I realized I was holding my breath. When I didn't speak, Adam went on, "Look, I don't want to bug you; I only have a couple of things I want to say."

It didn't sound like Adam. He didn't sound all that warm—worried maybe, but not warm—and his speech sounded rehearsed. "First, I am sorry I brought up Jordan."

"Now isn't the time to talk about it," I responded. Oh, Jesus, if he triggered Jordan again I would surely lose it.

"I know that. I figured that out," he added dryly. The second thing is—the only thing I want—is for you to promise me you'll call me if Willy contacts you."

I didn't say anything. I was not, I was absolutely not ready to discuss Willy with Adam. I didn't want Adam anywhere near me right now. He stirred up too much stuff, and I needed a clear head to deal with Willy.

I sighed but didn't say anything. I hated to lie to Adam, and his request sounded so sincere and so . . . reasonable.

"Michael, has he contacted you already?" Adam said sharply.

"I'm thinking, Adam. Don't read too much into it. I have to think about whether I can make a promise like that." I hadn't lied yet.

"If I have a problem," I said, "you'll be the first to know."

There was a pause.

"That isn't good enough," Adam said.

He was taking away all my wiggle room. "All right," I said, giving up. "I promise." Why do some people force you to lie?

"Okay," he said, sounding relieved, and I got a full body flush of guilt; the man trusted me. "We can talk about other things later," he added, and he was gone.

After he hung up I just sat there. If it was possible to make my relationship with Adam worse, I had just done it. But what are you supposed to do when somebody has a gun to your head? This wasn't my fault. People should not pressure their friends into lying to them.

But when I thought about it I realized there were all kinds of things I could have said. Like "no," for starters. Why didn't I just say, "No, I'm not promising anything, Adam, but I'll keep your request in mind." The more I thought about it, the stranger it seemed that I had agreed. Adam always had an unsettling effect on me. I couldn't think straight when he was around. Not to mention that I could hardly think at all with this hammer banging on my head.

But it was bigger than that. There was a reason I lived alone. Relationships are like magnets for me: They pull me off course. Expectations, demands—I have that female thing that hates disappointing people. After a while, in every relationship, I start feeling less "me." Pretty soon, I'm so watered down I can't stand myself, and then I get out.

I decided to put it aside—after all, Adam had *invited* me to lie to him; he had practically *insisted* I lie to him—and I walked over to the computer. Willy was still out there, and I needed to quit obsessing over Adam and figure out what he was up to. I had thrown down a gauntlet to Willy, sort of, and it was going to be interesting to see how he responded.

I checked on my e-mail, and yes, there was a message from "partytime." I stared at it for a moment before I opened it. Just seeing mail from Willy gave me a bad case of the dreads. I finally double-clicked on "partytime," and Willy's letter popped up on my screen.

> Well, well, my good doctor. I should prove to you I can control my appetites—a little reverse psychology, perhaps? Next you'll be proscribing the symptom! But no, I can't see you in the Milan school. My dear, you must think I am an oppositional adolescent to be bought off so easily. Oh, Michael, you do amuse me.

So he knew a little something about psychology. Big deal. A lot of people know about the Milan group and their focus on proscribing the symptom. If someone was truly oppositional they'd quit having the symptom just to win the power struggle.

But interestingly, I hadn't been proscribing the symptom. I had just been playing to his narcissism, which, for all his smarts, he still didn't see.

> Still, all in all it was a disappointing communication. Perhaps you are simply less clever than I thought. Or then again, stress has a way of eating into your soul like acid, doesn't it? You start wondering when and how and . . . what.

> You need solace! Distraction from the inevitable. There's still time—some anyway. Get yourself a dog, a rottweiler, maybe, and keep her. Perhaps some flowers—Camellias say. Have a little Kiwi fruit or quiche Lorraine.

I froze. For a moment I couldn't breathe. I read it again and again. I got up and walked around the room and sat down and read the last paragraph again. I got up and walked again, still reading it and telling myself it couldn't mean what I thought it meant. I could be wrong; I had to be wrong.

But what were the probabilities? I had a client named Camille, one named Kiwi, and one named Lorraine. He'd even capitalized the names, for God's sake. Get a rottweiler and "keep her." Keep her. Keeter.

I needed an outside person to read this and tell me I was crazy. I got as far as the phone and stopped. Anybody I knew who looked at this would tell me to spend the next two years in New Zealand.

But how could Willy know who my clients were? How could he possibly know? Had he broken into my files? Had he followed people who went in and out of my office? How could he know? Was he tapping my phone? Had I spoken to them on the phone? He couldn't have gotten into my computer files. I didn't keep my clients' names on my computer.

I read the message again. It had to be what I thought it was. It made no sense otherwise. Quiche Lorraine and Kiwi fruit? He just couldn't pull those out of a hat.

So he was here. Close enough to watch my office. But how would he know their names? Was he following them and then checking out who lived at that address? But even if he did? He might somehow find out their names from where they lived, but how did he get Keeter's name? I kept going over and over it like a broken record. Had he broken into my office? Had he read my files? But if he was following people, he knew where I lived, too.

I was going in circles. I got up and got a glass of ice tea to settle my nerves and sat down to think. Ice tea is mother's milk to Southerners, and somehow, under stress, I always like to touch something from the South. I looked at the ice and twirled it in the glass while I tried to clear my mind. "In ghostlier demarcations," Wallace Stevens had written, "keener sounds." Well, things were pretty ghostly, and I was hearing something all right, but what? "In ghostlier demarcations, muddy but insistent noises." Stevens had never written that.

I remembered something from long ago. I had gone sailing with some friends in college. We'd been on a twenty-four-foot Erickson, a little Clorox bottle of a boat, when the motor went out and, worse, the fog rolled in. I had been assigned the job of navigating, and I had gone below with the charts while others steered and kept a lookout—as best they could—for other boats. The fog had been so thick you couldn't see three feet ahead, and the little boat didn't have radar.

Nobody had really gotten freaked out until the ferries started coming. We'd hear the sound of their motors grow louder and louder, but nobody could see a thing. Then when the motors were so loud that we were all just waiting to be run over, the sound would slowly start fading. The damn things were passing us so close we could practically touch them, and we still couldn't see them.

"In ghostlier demarcations, the sound of ferries." That was closer to the truth. I could hear Willy in the fog, but I couldn't see anything. It was a lot like the ferries, with one difference: Willy wasn't in the fog. You might say he had radar of a sort, but the ferries used it to avoid us, and Willy would use it to circle me and circle me, getting closer all the time. More like a hammerhead shark than a ferry.

That wasn't really news. No matter what I told anybody, I knew Willy would be on my doorstep—or more likely outside my window—from the moment I heard he was getting out of jail. But I never thought he'd drag my clients into it.

I thought of Lucas, the mass murderer. When he was five years old, his mother asked him if he loved the family mule. He said he did, and she shot it in front of him. She knew she could hurt him most by hurting things he loved.

I had no children. I lived alone. I wasn't somebody you could easily threaten with things like that. But the sanctity of my therapy office was important to me, and the people I took care of were important to me. What made me think Willy wouldn't figure that out?

There were a couple of things I had to do. I got dressed and pulled the fanny pack I kept my magnum in from a drawer. I put on the fanny pack and then checked the gun to be sure it was loaded. Without children in the house, I could keep my gun loaded, and I did.

I threw a couple of speed loaders in the pack, grabbed my car keys, and headed for the car. I was moving too fast, and my head started hurting again. I slowed down—Jesus, I hated slowing down when I was trying to get somewhere—and slowly glided my head to the car.

I never noticed the ride in. It was one of those deals where my mind was so preoccupied, my brain stem took over the wheel. I got to my private practice office in Carlotta's house and sat outside. The lights were on in her part of the house, and I had no choice whatsoever. Carlotta had been my best friend since college—which I hoped to God Willy did not know—and I had to go talk to her about this.

I thought of about eighteen ways I could approach this without telling her the truth, and none of them worked. I gave up and got out of the car. Between my prickly sense of privacy and Carlotta's safety, my privacy was going to have to take it on the ear.

I went around to the back door, which opened on the kitchen. I knocked as I opened it with my key. Carlotta was standing in the kitchen in her favorite white satin pj's, mixing her nightly protein drink. Carlotta's way of living is a little different from mine. My favorite night wear is a T-shirt. She turned around as I came in and said, "Greetings, Dr. Michael. Want a milk shake?"

"No, thanks," I said and sat down at the kitchen table. I ran my fingers absentmindedly over the top of the table. It was an extraordinary object: a thick piece of solid redwood in a free-form style supported by a handmade pottery base. At the sound of my voice, Carlotta turned around again to look at me briefly, then went back to making her drink. "What the hell happened to you?"

"Fell off a horse," I said. Carlotta turned around again and looked at me. "Nothing serious," I said. "Jack was at the ED."

I didn't say anything more, and shortly Carlotta finished futzing with the blender and sat down. She didn't say anything either, just drank her drink and waited. I suppose it was obvious I wasn't there just to visit. Finally, I got going.

"How are things with Hank?" I asked. Hank Holden was a judge Carlotta had been seeing.

"Fine," she said.

I took a deep breath. There was no way I could fool Carlotta, so I might as well cut to the chase. "Why don't you go stay with him for a while?"

"Michael . . ."

"I'm not going to get into it, Carlotta. I'm just not. But I'm telling you, go stay with Hank."

"So he's here."

I shrugged.

"You're wearing your fanny pack."

I shrugged again. I got up and poured myself some milk shake just to be doing something.

"You haven't told Adam about this."

I sat back down.

Carlotta's face—which was ordinarily composed—looked like a kaleidoscope of emotions. Anger had passed through it and fear and some other things that went by too quick to identify.

"Michael, you are a goddamn fool."

"True," I said. Hard to argue with that.

"Why me?" she said.

"There's nothing specific about you," I said.

"Then I'll stay. It's you he's after."

"I wouldn't do that," I replied.

"Why not?"

"He knows some things he shouldn't know," I said carefully looking down at the table. "It may be he got into the office."

I heard Carlotta's sharp intake of breath but didn't look up. It really wasn't a comfortable thought. Carlotta quit arguing.

"Hank's out of town until tomorrow."

"I'll stay tonight."

"Is that going to help or hurt?"

"Good question, but I have a gun and you don't. You need to think about a gun course," I said firmly. This was on old argument; Carlotta hated guns.

"If I quit hanging around you," she replied, "I wouldn't need one."

Which was probably true.

"Adam doesn't know," Carlotta said flatly.

I didn't reply. It wasn't a question.

"You know I'll call him," she said.

"It'll just cause an argument," I replied. "I, uh . . . I promised him I'd tell him if Willy showed up."

I knew I didn't have a prayer.

"That was dumb," was all she said.

Carlotta stormed off to bed. She hadn't said a whole lot, but she was as pissed as I could remember her being. Who could blame her? I had brought a maniac into her life who might even have gotten into her house, no doubt while she was sleeping. Now she had to move out without knowing when she could come back, and on top of that she had to worry about me.

Plus, when she thought about it, she would figure out I had more or less lied to her at lunch when I reassured her that Willy would take off for the hinterland and not come after me. Then she'd get doubly pissed.

And worse, what could I say? I don't know why I hate for people to worry about me so much. I just do.

So, as close as I could figure it, I was now in trouble with just about everybody I knew. I hadn't returned Marv's phone call when he told me it was urgent. I'd lied to Carlotta and Adam; one of them knew it and the other was about to.

It could be I wasn't easy to be friends with. It could be I was pretty exasperating to be friends with.

On the other hand, it could be people didn't know how to be friends with me without trying to control me. And that was on top of my not knowing how to be friends with them without feeling controlled.

It could be all of it was true.

103

A fault line. Willy couldn't know it, but he had hit a fault line. He had just applied a little stress, and the earth was splitting right where the fault line was. So maybe I should get a little proactive and try to keep it from splitting all the way through. Maybe I should call Marv and try to keep at least one relationship intact.

But I knew I wouldn't pick up the phone. I just didn't want to call Marv—who knew why? I didn't even know if it was because of this fault line, or a different one altogether. How many fault lines are there in my crazy psyche? How many high school football players are there in the state of Texas?

11

I woke up in the middle of a bad dream. I was driving through New York City, and halfway across I realized I had lost something. Something had just slipped away, and whatever it was, it changed everything. There was no longer any point to getting to wherever I was going, and, for some reason, it was clear there was no point to going back and looking for it. Something was gone that mattered enormously, and I woke up hungover with the loss.

I was so preoccupied with the dream, it took me a moment to realize something was different. Then it hit me: My head didn't hurt. For the first time since I hit the jump, my head wasn't the center of my universe. I slipped out of bed, testing my new pain-free state, and almost jumped with glee when nothing dreadful happened.

I didn't jump, however. Instead, I walked gingerly to the kitchen, moving only slightly more confidently as I went along. The memory of the headache was still with me, and I didn't want to start it up again. Carlotta had made coffee for me, so I guessed she wasn't terminally pissed. I poured the coffee and climbed back into bed.

Whew. What was that dream all about? I couldn't believe it was about my friendships and the pressure this thing with Willy was putting on them. Everything looked better without a headache, and I began to think that maybe I had overreacted.

Carlotta and I had hung out together through marriages and divorces. I tolerated her obsession with all things feminine. She had tolerated my bitching about it for two decades.

Women take their friendships seriously, and someday Carlotta and I were going to end up in an old-age commune sitting on a green porch with white rockers, talking about our old lovers. Women live with the fact that we will likely outlive any partners for a decade or more, so you can't make long, long-range plans with a partner.

No, it would be the friendships that lasted in the end. Carlotta and I would be rocking back and forth, trading outrageous stories—some of which would be true—smoking something and drinking brandy until we were giddy. Might as well develop a few bad habits when it was too late to matter. The problem was, if I didn't get Willy off my case and get busy, I was going to be weak in the story department.

So what was that dream all about? Jordan? How many months till the anniversary of her death? Five. Early for the anniversary reaction to start kicking in. I hoped the anniversary reaction wasn't kicking in. It was a pretty miserable business.

If not Jordan, Adam? I couldn't be getting that attached. I hoped I wasn't getting that attached. What was I losing? What was slipping away?

I gave up on it and got dressed. Carlotta was gone, and I was running late. I didn't have a meeting at psychiatry until ten, but I had something I had to do first. I went into my private practice office and unlocked the filing cabinet. There sure weren't any signs that Willy had gotten in. How the hell could he have gotten into a locked cabinet in a locked house with dead bolts? Who knew?

I pulled out all my files on clients and put them on the couch. Even though I was only there part-time, I'd been doing therapy for a while, and there were still a lot of files. I went off to the basement and came back with some book boxes and put all the files in boxes and took them out to the car. I wasn't sure this would work, but it needed to.

I drove over to my bank and walked in. There were several women sitting at desks in the lobby. I picked the one with the least set hairdo as the best bet. Set hairdos are always a bad sign. She was free, so I went over and sat down. "I'd like a safety deposit box," I said. "Actually, I'd like a bunch of them."

"Fine," she said pleasantly. "How many would you like?"

"Uh, quite a few," I said.

"Quite a few?"

"Well, how big are they?" I hadn't brought the file boxes in yet. I didn't want to freak her. "I mean, what is your largest size?"

"Well," she said, sitting back and looking at me with a puzzled expression. "They're all twenty-four inches deep. The largest size is, ten inches high by fifteen inches wide."

I made a quick calculation. This would take a lot of boxes. "Just a minute," I said. "Why don't I bring in the stuff."

It took me several trips to bring in the files, and by then I had her full attention. "The large-size boxes cost $100 a year," she said tentatively. "Usually people use these just for . . . are you sure . . . ?"

She'd been trained not to ask so she didn't, but I answered her anyway. "Securities," I said folding my hands on the desk and looking straight at her. "My great-aunt died."

She looked at me for a long moment. Either I was one of the richer folk she had ever met, or I was a lying drug-runner storing my dope—I'd actually heard from dope dealers in my practice that they stored their dope in safety deposit boxes. I could almost see her thinking, "Could be either."

"Let me see how many we have available," she said and went off, glancing over her shoulder at my file boxes as she disappeared.

Why is nothing ever easy? I had to go to three branches to find enough safety deposit boxes, and by then I was considerably poorer and had missed another meeting in Psychiatry. Still I felt so relieved I almost felt light-headed. If this would shut down the flow of information to Willy, it was well and truly worth it. Besides, it was diagnostic. Any new info that Willy got after this point couldn't come from the files—well, any new information after I did one more thing—but first I had to go to Psychiatry.

I practically sneaked into the Psychiatry Department. I didn't want to run into anybody who was at the meeting I'd missed. How was I to explain where I'd been? "Well, actually, I think a sadist may have broken into my office and read my files, so I put them all in safety deposit boxes." Pa . . . ra . . . noia, they'd be chirping.

I could have put my private practice files in my Psychiatry office, but if Willy could break into my other office, surely he could break into Psychiatry. The department was housed in a building right across the street from the hospital, connected by tunnels, and the hospital was open twenty-four hours a day. In any event, my Psychiatry files were not going to be a problem. They were all housed in Records in the main hospital, and nobody could find them over there. Hell, I couldn't even get them half the time.

I thought I had successfully slipped in unnoticed—my secretary, Melissa, had not been at her desk when I went by— but I hadn't been in my office ten minutes when I heard a knock on the door. I turned around to see Toby, the Chair of

Psychiatry, standing in the doorway. Whoa, the meeting hadn't been that important.

"Got a minute?" he said.

"Sure," I said with an attempt—a poor attempt—at enthusiasm.

Toby walked in and sat down on the couch. We had never gotten along. Toby had told me once I wasn't a team player, and I had thought it was a compliment. That miscommunication was the first of many. Toby thought I was a loose cannon who went her own way and did whatever she did without considering how it impacted the department. He told me once that I didn't care at all about the *financial* goals of the department, and his voice couldn't have been more outraged if I had mugged a little old lady on the street. I knew he thought I cared even less about *his* opinion than I did the financial goals of the department. How could he believe such things?

But Toby didn't know everything. He told me once I saw him as just a bureaucrat. I didn't see him as just a bureaucrat. I saw him as a complete pompous asshole who ought to be shot first when the revolution came. It comforted me to know I had *some* social skills after all.

I braced myself for a diatribe, but Toby was unusually subdued. I couldn't stand waiting. "I missed the curriculum meeting because I had an emergency with a client," I said. It was the only excuse Psychiatry wouldn't challenge. This lying business just got easier as you went along, and I was beginning to really get into the swing of it.

"That's not important," Toby said. "We'll send you the minutes."

Excuse me? What did he say? I was stunned into silence. It was a reasonable response. What was wrong with Toby? Was he sick?

"I wondered . . . you see people in your private practice?" I only did consults, teaching, and stupid committee-sitting in my role at Jefferson.

"Sure," I said, wary now. Oh, Jesus, don't let it be any relative of his.

He sighed. "My neighbor called. Their daughter goes to Jefferson U. It seems there was an . . . incident. Lucy was at a fraternity party, and she'd been drinking—quite a bit. She had sex with this boy at the party—willingly, she says. But she woke up, and she was being raped by several young men— three, I think, including her date." Toby looked away. Both of us knew if it hadn't been his neighbor, he would have likely said it was her own fault for getting drunk. He was not the most sensitive person I knew when it came to victims; unless it was a client of his. Toby did better by his own clients than he did by just about anybody else.

He went on. "She kept passing out and was too sick to do much to stop them, but she did keep saying 'no.' She's quite distressed." Toby looked acutely uncomfortable. I realized it couldn't have been easy for him to come to me, and I wasn't sure why he had. There were lots of good therapists in the department who saw victims in therapy.

"You want me to see her?" I asked.

"No, no," he said. "She already has a therapist. It's just that . . . the young man . . . well, he doesn't deny those men had sex with her. He says she consented."

"Not terribly likely," I said, "unless Lucy acts out a whole lot."

"Not at all," he replied firmly. "I've known Lucy all her life. She's very levelheaded. The thing is—her parents are distraught. Lucy wants the university to do something, and the young man is claiming that Lucy egged them on and invited it. Her parents are afraid what it will do to her reputation—and, I suppose, theirs. And Lucy is adamant that something has to be done."

"The police?" I said.

"Nobody's called them," he said. "Even Lucy doesn't want that kind of publicity."

I sighed. The police are much better at handling rape cases than universities are. But I knew, too, how few victims are willing to involve them.

"Toby, exactly what does Lucy want out of this? She isn't involving the police. Has she actually filed a formal complaint with the university?"

"She has," Toby said. "But, as you can imagine, the discipline committee has two conflicting tales in front of them. Lucy simply doesn't have any proof. I doubt they'll do much."

"What about the other guys?"

"Thus far, the young man won't name them, and Lucy doesn't know who they are."

"Even if the discipline committee agrees with her, what does she think they can do? The university isn't going to send anybody to jail. What does she think can happen?"

"She wants to know who they are, and she wants them gone—all of them—expelled. She says she doesn't want to walk around campus wondering if this guy or that one raped her. And"—he raised his eyebrows wryly—"she wants them to say they're sorry."

Pleeeease. People can be so naive about offenders. Did Lucy really think it would mean a damn thing if they could be coerced into apologizing? It is like asking a mugger to say "sorry."

"How can I help?" I had to admit my war with Toby seemed pretty minor compared to this. This whole thing could go very badly if it wasn't handled well, and Lucy, if she had already been traumatized, could get retraumatized pretty easily. Not to mention that if her family disagreed with what she wanted to do, there was the potential for a split that might never heal.

"The young man has agreed to go to a counselor for an

evaluation, but I'm afraid—well—according to your last Grand Rounds, anyway—since most therapists are not trained in detecting deception, they often end up colluding with offenders—at least that was the implication." Implication, my foot. That was what I said, and I was merely stating the obvious.

Toby went on. "I'm referring to the research you presented on mental health practitioners and the fact that they are no better than the average citizen in detecting deception—which I gathered from your stats was not exceptional." Exceptional? The average person is no better than chance at detecting deception, and mental health is right in there with them.

"I thought . . . I just thought . . . you deal with offenders—I thought you might . . ." He took a deep breath and finally got to the point. "Would you take a look at this and maybe interview this young man and see what you think? See if there's anything you can do to prevent this from blowing up and hurting Lucy?"

Good grief. First of all it was a shock that Toby had actually listened to my last Grand Rounds. That alone was unbelievable. And he had learned something? I was incredulous, and then I realized how much it must have cost him to admit it. This pompous asshole was genuinely fond of Lucy and her family, and he wanted help for them badly enough to come with his hat in his hand to the one person in the department he personally disliked the most.

My opinion of Toby rose a notch. I had always taken him to be a hard-core narcissist, but narcissists never put anybody's needs above their own. Maybe Toby wasn't a total, died-in-the-wool, card-carrying narcissist like I had thought. Maybe he was only 99 percent narcissist, but he had a functioning 1 percent he could pull out of a hat when he needed to. It was something, anyway.

"I will," I said. "But you have to understand this. I will interview him, and I will use some of the new stuff I was talking about that detects deception. But—and it's a big 'but'—you have to know, Toby, I'll call it the way I see it. If I conclude he's telling the truth, I'll back him. And, even if I don't think he's telling the truth, the best I may be able to do is recommend a polygraph. Offenders don't usually confess without one."

"I have no doubt," he said dryly, standing up, "that you will call it the way you see it. I have a lot of faith in Lucy, or I wouldn't be here."

I was still worried about Toby's expectations. "I don't work wonders, Toby," I said. "Just so you know, if he's lying, I may be able to figure it out, but he's not likely to change his story. And in the end my knowing he's lying isn't going to help a whole lot."

"Oh, just give it your best shot," he said with a wry smile, and I would have sworn there was a twinkle in his eye.

12

There was one more thing that had to be done, and the easiest way to do it was to call Adam. Not a chance. It might be the easiest way to deal with it, but I wasn't calling him. I had to know somebody else who could help.

I couldn't just open the yellow pages and look for a private eye. Some investigators are very skilled and others are a rip-off, but there wasn't any way to tell the difference from an ad. I wasn't even sure there were any in the Upper Valley who were any good. Rural New England just doesn't have a big need for private eyes. Everybody already knows who is having an affair and with whom. Finding out that kind of thing is what keeps most private eyes in business.

My problem wasn't whether my spouse was having an affair. My problem was whether Willy was bugging my office, and the grapevine couldn't help me very much with that. Damn it, if I were in the city, there were probably places that specialized in sweeping your office for bugs.

But of course. Danny. I didn't know him well, but I had been involved in a situation where the FBI was brought in. Danny was a senior special agent in the local branch, and he had been called in. When I worked with him he said he was retiring in a few months, and he thought he'd do a little private work after that. I opened the yellow pages and found him. He had a small ad that said nothing about the incredible credentials he had for that kind of work.

Danny was tall and lean and wore wire-rimmed glasses. He looked like an accountant — which actually he was, by training at least — but he was also somebody who had twice rescued U.S. hostages in South America. He was good on a negotiation team — he could talk to anybody and you couldn't help but like him — but he was always thinking a whole lot more than he seemed to be.

Both times in South America, Danny had got information on the phone with the kidnappers that was used to track them down and storm their hideouts. And he was also one of the people kicking down the door. All this I knew from Adam, who had a buddy in the FBI. It wasn't like Danny told you a whole lot about his work.

I had liked him, and we'd had lunch a few times, but it was a little weird. He could be funny and likable, but he always managed to sit with his back to the door, and if you looked carefully, you'd see that he was always scanning the crowd — even when he laughed.

I'd thought about what it would be like to be in bed with him — my fantasy life is, shall we say, a rich and varied one — but I concluded he'd have to have the side of the bed farthest from the door, and he'd be constantly scanning the room even when he . . . laughed.

But a case was another matter. I dialed his number and waited. I smiled thinking he knew who I was before he answered the phone. What were the chances that Danny had the kind of Caller ID that gave you the person's name as well as their number? Oh, about 100 percent. I was gratified that his voice was warm when he answered.

"Hello, this is Danny Barns," he said.

"Danny," I began, "this is Michael Stone." He would never admit he had known who it was, and I wouldn't put him on guard by mentioning it.

"Doc," he said. "How are you?"

Private eye work was pretty boring, he said, but he did a little consulting on the side, and that was interesting. He didn't say to whom, and I didn't ask, but I had a feeling he was still tied up with the old agency in one way or the other, and it was probably very interesting. We went on like that for a few minutes, and then I got on with it.

"I want to hire you," I said. I was prepared to tell him the truth. I didn't think there was any other way to get him to take it seriously. "Somebody may be bugging my therapy sessions. It's somebody I know, and he's sent me a teasing message that sounds like he knows who my clients are. I don't know how he'd know, and I want to be sure he isn't bugging me."

"What phone are you calling from?"

I laughed. Adam had told me once how many people who thought they were being bugged called about it on the same phone they thought was bugged. "I'm calling from a different office."

"How do you know he bugged you? Could he have gotten into your records?" Danny asked.

"Maybe," I answered. "They're in the same office—this is all in my private practice—but I've got dead bolts, and there's no indication of a break-in. Anyway, I've put all the records in safety deposit boxes, just to be sure."

I was struck by how focused and intent he was. His voice was all business with none of the warm, fuzzy overtones I'd seen him use when he wanted to. This was a whole different side of Danny than the public one I'd seen before, closer to the bone, I thought.

"How much does he know?"

"Beats me," I said. "All he's done thus far is drop their names."

"That doesn't sound too bad," Danny responded, sounding less interested. "Could be he's just watching your office and following people."

"Maybe," I said. "But he's not someone who'd be satisfied with a cheap thrill. He's a planner. Likes long, drawn-out, meticulously scripted stuff. If names were all he had, he wouldn't have dropped them just like that. Whatever he's up to, this is only the opening volley."

There was a pause on the phone.

"What kind of 'scripted stuff'?" Danny asked finally.

"Uh, well, he's a sadist. Card-carrying. Not a nice man. And he's more or less told me some things he wishes he hadn't." And right now, I thought, I wished he hadn't either.

"Well, is it 'more' or 'less'?"

"Actually it's 'more.' A whole lot more than he'd like me to know now that he's been suddenly released from a lengthy and just incarceration by a group of judicial assholes I hope he moves next door to."

"How does today sound?" Danny offered. It looked like I had gotten his attention back, which was probably not a good sign. It was like being a "great case" in medicine. Anything that interests the doctors is bad news for the patients.

"Sounds good," I replied. "If you've got the time." He said

he'd make the time, and we agreed to meet at my office first thing after lunch.

It turned out it was a big deal sweeping for bugs. Microphones are about the size of the tip of a pencil these days, and they can be anywhere. If someone gets access, he can put them in a wall socket, in the receiver of the phone, almost anywhere. Those two places are most common, Danny said, because bugs need power, and the only way not to have to keep coming back to change the batteries is to hook them directly into a power source.

Bugs can also be on any frequency. Great, so we had something that was practically microscopic in size and it could be on any frequency. But technology works both ways. Danny went all over the room with his bug detector, a small device that went up and down the frequencies. Nothing, nothing, and more nothing. Danny did it thoroughly. But nothing.

"It could be turned off," he said. "You can turn them on and off remotely. He could be just turning them on for the therapy sessions. How cautious is he?"

"I wouldn't say cautious," I said. "He's pretty egotistical, and he likes to brag. On the other hand, he's not exactly a fool, and he's telling me he's bugging me so he has to expect I'll look for it. This could be a problem if he's just turning it on for therapy sessions. I can't exactly ask a client to have a seat while I sweep for bugs."

"Sure you can," Danny said, "if you ask the right client. You're about to have a new client. What kind of problem would he have that would interest your perp so he'd stay tuned?"

"Pedophilia," I replied without hesitating. "If he heard a pedophile in here, he'd stay tuned."

We made a plan. Danny would call and leave a message on my private practice phone asking for an emergency appointment. He'd identify himself as John, no last name, and ask if he could come in as soon as possible. He was having some thoughts, again, about children, and . . . well, he needed to talk to someone quick. I'd call back and set up an appointment at nine A.M. on Friday. My usual nine A.M. was Kiwi, someone Willy had mentioned. If he was bugging, he was bugging her. I'd cancel Kiwi and put in "John" instead, who'd show up right on time with a small device in his briefcase.

13

Alexander Hammil, Lucy's alleged tormentor, wasted no time in calling me. He sounded unbearably preppy over the phone, but I reminded myself preppies are obnoxious by nature, but that doesn't mean they are all rapists. I told him my terms, and he still wanted to see me, which meant he was either an arrogant little twerp or he was telling the truth.

I told him I would send him a letter outlining what we had talked about. Never, I knew, *never* trust what someone says on the phone in a situation like this. He'd have to sign my letter and bring it to the appointment with him before I'd see him. He seemed impatient with all of this and wanted to know if he could pick up the letter to speed things up. Sure, I said. I'd have it ready tomorrow and I'd see him in my private practice office on Friday.

I hung up the phone and sat down at my computer to write. I knew I could screw up myself and the situation royally if I didn't set things up properly:

Dear Mr. Hammil:

I am responding to your phone call requesting an appointment regarding the matter before the university's discipline committee. I am writing the conditions under which
I will see you in order that there be no possibility that we
might misunderstand each other. As you know, Lucy
MacDonald has filed a complaint with the university
saying that you and several other men had intercourse
with her without her consent. She claims she was incapacitated from alcohol ingestion and passed out repeatedly.
She states that she did tell you and the other men "no" and
that you ignored her protests. You have asked me to
evaluate you in terms of the charges against you.

I have explained that standard psychological tests will not
determine whether or not a specific event happened and
that there is no psychological profile of a rapist. I have
agreed only to interview you but have been clear with all
parties in this case that the greatest probability from this
assessment is that I will be able to make no firm determination of any sort.

Ordinarily, a psychological assessment is confidential.
However, in this case I have explained that I will only
evaluate you if the results are available to both sides of the
dispute. This is so whether I conclude that there is a
possibility you committed the offense as alleged or whether I agree with your description of events or whether I can
make no determination. You have agreed to sign a release
of information prior to my evaluating you consenting to
these terms.

I have explained to you that you should consult a lawyer
prior to agreeing to this, and you have informed me that

you have already consulted a lawyer and he has indicated his willingness for you to pursue this evaluation. Please be sure that your lawyer sees this letter and is fully informed of all conditions attached to this evaluation.

If this is agreeable to you, please sign this letter and the attached release of information and return both at or before your appointment time.

I gave the letter to Melissa for Mr. Hammil to pick up and called up Lucy. There wasn't anything I could really tell her until Hammil signed the letter—not even that he had an appointment—but I told her I had agreed to look into the matter. She sounded so relieved that I wondered what Toby had said about me. I asked her for a written statement of exactly what happened to her from the time she left her dorm until the time she got home. I told her I needed it by Friday with a signed release to share it with Mr. Hammil.

Lucy agreed readily. Probably doing something felt a whole lot better than doing nothing.

By Friday, my ducks were in a row. At nine A.M., "John" arrived right on schedule. At his request I pulled down the shades and only then did he take his bug detector out. "John" started wandering around the room scanning it with his bug detector, all the time talking about his preference for children, how long he'd been out of jail, and how much he didn't want to go back.

I was amazed. Danny couldn't have been any more convincing if he was sitting down and concentrating on what he was doing. I was the one who was having trouble concentrating. I was hearing one thing while at the same time Danny was wandering all over the room, climbing on chairs to check the ceiling, crawling on his hands and knees to check the floor, without ever missing a beat.

"Nothing," he finally said, after a full hour of crawling and climbing and checking and rechecking. "At least nothing that's turned on now."

"Good," I said, relieved. "So, it's wait-and-see time. Maybe it was just the records."

He turned to go and then stopped with his hand on the doorknob and turned back to me. Clients do that all the time. "Doorknob comments," we call them. They are invariably the most important part of the session. "You're in over your head," he said flatly. It didn't sound like he meant to be hurtful. It just sounded like a factual assessment of the situation.

I just shrugged. What could I say?

"There are other ways to play it," he said.

I shrugged again.

He paused a moment longer as though waiting for me to say something, but I didn't. I just didn't feel like trying to explain myself. Besides, I wasn't sure I could.

"All right," he said, "you want some advice?"

"Sure," I said. For some reason, advice from Danny didn't seem as threatening as Carlotta or Adam.

"Don't stay on the defensive. Don't sit around waiting for him to find you. He'll have everything on his side: the time, the place, the circumstances. If you're going to play this by yourself, at least find out where he is and go after him."

"Right. And what do I do when I find him?"

"Don't hesitate."

I didn't respond. I knew what he meant. Adam had once told me that a surprising number of women who have guns and know how to use them still get raped or murdered. They don't pull the trigger, he said. They hesitate too long. It sounded like Danny thought I might be one of them.

He handed me a card with a number on it. "You can always reach me with that," he said. It didn't look like the number in the phone book. Probably a mobile phone, I thought. Maybe a number not everybody has.

Then he handed me the bug-sweeping device. "Sweep before every session," he said. "Maybe he had a cold today. Maybe he took the day off. It doesn't mean he won't be back."

He left, and I sat thinking for a moment. I felt better but wasn't sure why. I hardly knew Danny. He had so many layers of onion skin, I wasn't sure if there was a real Danny under all of them. If there was, you'd never know it if you'd found it.

But that meant I could listen to his advice without feeling bad if I didn't take it, and he could give it without being that upset if I didn't take it. If I got myself killed, Danny would work that crime scene just like any other. Probably it was not a sign of major mental health that Danny was the only person I could even imagine talking to about this. To hell with it. Alexander Hammil was waiting.

I pulled up the shades—the room looked serious with the shades drawn, and I did not want Mr. Hammil on guard—and walked out to greet him. He had arrived right on schedule, and I went out to the waiting room to find a tastefully dressed, good-looking young man sitting confidently on the couch.

He stood up when I walked in. Oh dear, this was going to be one of those "yes, ma'am, no, ma'am" things. "Hello," I said reaching out my hand. He shook it with exactly the right degree of firmness. "I'm Dr. Stone. I'm glad you came in, and hopefully we can clear this whole thing up today.

"I am running a little late, and I thought to expedite matters I would have you fill in a brief questionnaire for me. It just gives your version of what happened. I'm afraid it looks a bit long, but there's only one question on most of the pages, and it really would help, if you don't mind." I handed him a questionnaire and a pen and said quickly, before he had a chance to protest, "Would you like some coffee? Tea?"

He said "no," and I turned to go before he had a chance to

think things over. I glanced back and saw him shrug and sit down. Well and good. The interview had begun.

The questionnaire was a simple one. It asked him to explain what he did on the day of the alleged rape from the time he got up until the time he went to bed. It asked him his opinion of how these charges came about. It asked him why I should believe him, and it asked him if he was lying. I left the door of my office partly open so that I could walk by and see how he was doing.

He wrote furiously for twenty minutes, and then he put his pen down. I came out a couple of minutes later and collected the questionnaire. I offered him coffee again, and this time he accepted. I told him I needed a few minutes to look over the questionnaire.

I read through the questionnaire. All I wanted to know was whether he said he didn't do it. Over 90 percent of people lie by omission rather than commission. Unless you ask them a direct question, like "Did you do it?"—unless you force them to lie—the vast majority of people evade the question. For some reason it turns out to be hard to say, "I" (first person) "didn't" (past tense) "do that" (thing he was charged with).

I went to the last page first. It asked why I should believe him and whether he had been truthful in his statement. "Why should I lie?" he had written. "I was raised to tell the truth. It's not the sort of thing I would do." Uh-oh. There wasn't any-place where he said he didn't do it.

I started from the first page of the questionnaire and read forward. There wasn't a single place where he denied it, if you read carefully. I read his description of the day. There were indications of missing time, changes in verb tenses, out of sequence information, and changes in pronouns—all of the sort that were consistent with deception. We had a problem. He was a lying little twerp after all. But knowing it was different from proving it. For that I needed his help.

I walked out again and smiled. "Your questionnaire is very helpful," I said, "and it clears up a lot of things. I wonder if there is one more thing I could ask you to do. Here is Ms. MacDonald's story of what happened. Could you just take this red pen and cross through everything that she says that you don't agree with. Then on every line that you cross through, I want you to write a number and initial it. Then I want you to put that number on this clean sheet of paper and write what really happened."

I went through it a couple of times to make sure he had it. He was plenty bright, but he wasn't expecting this, and his mind was on other things—mainly impressing me—so it took him a couple of rounds to get it.

"If you'll just do this, I'm fairly confident we can clear this whole thing up today." He agreed. It sounded good to him, and he sat down to work with relish. When he had finished, I came back and asked him if he was sure he had crossed out everything that wasn't true.

"I think so," he said.

"Oh, no," I replied. "I don't want you to *think* so. I want you to be sure. Absolutely sure. I want to give you all the time you need to be *sure* you have crossed out everything you don't agree with. So take a few more minutes and go over it."

I turned to go, and he looked perplexed and sat back down. In a few minutes he knocked gently on the partly opened door. "I'm done," he said.

"Great," I said, standing up from my desk and walking over. "You're sure you've crossed everything out you don't agree with?"

"As far as I can tell," he said.

"Well," I said. "I don't want you to have any doubts. Sit back down and go over it again. Don't come back until you are really *sure* you have crossed everything out that isn't true and have written in *exactly* what really happened."

He was pissed off, but he sat back down. For this to work he had to be *committed* to what he had written, and I was prepared to go on indefinitely until he made that commitment.

This time when he came back he was ready for me. "I'm finished," he said. "I've gone over everything," he added quickly.

"You're sure," I said. "You've crossed out everything?"

"I'm sure," he replied. He did not want to sit down and go over this again.

"Come on in," I said and opened the door. I looked over the statement as he sat down. He had followed instructions carefully, and there were red lines on a number of places on Lucy's statement. Each one had his initials next to it and a number. I took the extra sheets of paper he had given me and went back and forth going from the numbers he had put on Lucy's statement to what he said really happened on the other pages. Finally, I shook my head.

"I'm not sure you and Ms. MacDonald mean the same things by some of your terms," I said. "Just so I'm sure. What do you mean by 'assault'?"

"Assault?" he said, surprised.

"Assault. I don't mean that you need to come up with a dictionary definition, but just roughly, say, what do you mean by the term."

"Well, I'd say assault involves inflicting some sort of violence on someone."

"Against their will?"

"Well, sure. Most people wouldn't agree to violence being inflicted on them," he said sarcastically and then caught himself.

"And what about 'passed out'?"

"Unconscious," he said.

"Would you write those down?" I said sweetly, handing him

back the piece of paper where he'd written what really happened.

He paused for a minute to think it over, but couldn't see what the problem would be, so he wrote them down. "Would you sign them?" I asked.

"Why should I sign it?" he replied.

I rolled my eyes heavenward for him to see. "I've got material from you and Ms. MacDonald, and I want to be clear what's what, plus this whole thing is very emotional, and I don't want Ms. MacDonald, or even you later, to claim I made anything up. It's standard procedure. Is there something wrong with the definitions that you don't want to sign them? If there is, just change them."

He looked at them again and then signed them.

I picked up the statements again—Lucy's version and his rewrites—and looked back and forth from one to the other. I shook my head, perplexed, but kept reading. Silence filled the room. He started shifting in his seat. I just kept reading and let the anxiety build.

Finally, he couldn't stand it. "Is anything wrong?" he asked.

"I think so," I answered, but didn't elaborate. I went back to comparing the statements point by point.

He waited a few more minutes and then said, "What's wrong?"

I waited another long moment before I answered.

"Well, you and Ms. MacDonald agree on what happened. I wasn't expecting that."

"We agree? We don't agree. She says we raped her. I never said that."

"But," I said, holding the statements for him to see, "in Ms. MacDonald's statement she used the word 'assault' three times and 'passed out' five, and you didn't put a red line through any of them. You crossed out other things, but you never once crossed out those words." He looked quickly at Lucy's state-ment, and then he blanched. "I . . . I . . ."

"Well," I said while he sputtered, "here's what I think. I know there's a whole lot of truth in what you said. A whole lot. Well, let me put it this way." I took a piece of paper and drew a horizontal line with 0 on one end and 100 on the other. "I know you're not down here," I said, pointing at the zero. "I'd be willing to bet that you aren't anywhere close to here," I said still pointing at the zero.

"But I know, too, you haven't told me everything," I said, pointing at the 100. "Where would you say you are?" I asked, holding out the pen for him. "Just put a line at what percent-age of the real story you've shared."

It was hard, at that point, to put the line at 100 percent because, for one thing, if he did he was admitting that Lucy had been correct in her use of the words "assault" and "passed out." He put a line at 95 or so, but that, too, was actually a confession of sorts.

"You know," I said looking at the mark, "I think I know what the problem is. I can understand your objecting to being called a 'rapist' just because you got drunk and things got a little out of hand. After all, a sex offender is somebody who jumps out of bushes.

"But the thing I don't understand is why you don't really tell your side of the story. If I don't miss my guess, you were almost as drunk as she was. I'd be willing to bet that, if she was incapacitated by alcohol, so were you. She can't really use alcohol as an excuse for her behavior and not yours—if you were really as drunk as I think you were.

"Maybe I'm wrong, but I don't think you really thought she meant it when she said 'no.' Hell, it was probably so weak, you might have thought she was just playing. Not to mention that you couldn't really control those other guys anyway."

He looked shell-shocked, and he was sitting completely still. The breeze from the window was ruffling his hair. Without that he'd have looked like a statue. "Is that true?" I asked. "Were you drunk too?" Then I realized my rhythm was off. I should have had him saying "yes" all along and getting used to answering the questions. Shit, a little thing like that could make the difference in his fessing up and not.

"So you were drunk?"

"Everybody was drunk," he said. "Roger just kept pouring vodka in the punch, and by the end it was about 100 proof. And you're right," he said rallying. "I was as drunk as she was." I had given him only one way out of the blind alley, and he had decided to take it.

"Had you just met her or did you know her?"

"I had just met her."

"So she was a pretty easy lady, because you had just met her and she had already hopped into bed with you," I said shaking my head. "I can see why you didn't take her 'no' seriously. You must have thought she was just fooling around. Was that it, or did you think she really wanted you to stop?"

"No, no," he said quickly. "I assumed . . . I just thought . . . well, I mean she was coming on to everybody downstairs, I was just the one who took her up on it." He was getting bolder now and moving into the new version I had offered him. "She was fucking my brains out, and I just thought, hell, she'd probably take on anybody. Besides, it's not like I invited them in."

"They came in on their own?"

"Sure," he said, "we were getting it on, and they just walked in and . . . and . . ." He lapsed into silence.

"At that point, what could you do?" I said helpfully. "There were three of them, and you were drunk to the max. If she couldn't do anything to stop them because of the alcohol, you probably couldn't either."

"I couldn't. Heck, I didn't really know what was going on, I was so drunk."

"What I don't get," I said, "is why you're taking all the heat by yourself. If all of this is true, why is it your word alone? Why don't you have these guys backing you up? Then it would be four to one instead of just your word against hers.

"You can do what you want to, but I'll tell you what I think. I think you'd better not walk out of here leaving a lie. Because once the committee knows you are lying about part of it, they're going to think you're lying about all of it.

"I think the real story is important. I think you need to tell them how drunk you were and why you didn't believe her 'no' was any more than playing games. I think you need to tell them that this wasn't any kind of plan and you didn't invite those guys in, they just walked in.

"Now, it's up to you; but if I were you, I'd tell the committee who the other guys were and get them to back up your story. Because if you don't, the committee is going to wonder why not. The only reason to hide them is to protect them if they're guilty. Otherwise, you'd want them backing you up.

"But you do what you want. I'm going to give you the pen and paper and the chance to set it straight. To be honest, with her that drunk, I don't really want to write a report that says you are lying. It makes it seem like it was all your fault.

"But read my lips on this one, Alexander—this is a one-shot deal. When you walk out of here, the evaluation is over and I write up whatever I have. Don't come back later and tell me you didn't get a chance to give your side of the story, because this is your chance right now. Here's the pen. Here's the paper. Take it or leave it. I'll write up a report that says you're lying if that's what you want me to do."

I handed him the pen and stood up quickly. "Let me get you some more coffee," I said and walked out before he had a chance to reply.

14

The moment Alexander Hammil left, I xeroxed his confession and left the office with it. If he had the sense God gave a mosquito, he would rethink his visit with me and head straight for his lawyer's office. His lawyer would pick up the phone to rescind Hammil's release before Hammil finished his first sentence.

I drove straight to my tiny A-frame—the one with the unlisted phone number—and sat down at the computer. It didn't take long to do the evaluation, given that he had confessed. He had rationalized and minimized to the max, of course, but he had admitted that the other men had walked in uninvited and Lucy had repeatedly said "no." He admitted, too, that he knew she was in and out of consciousness and too incapacitated to do anything except say "no." And, miracles of miracles, he had named his fellow rapists.

That didn't leave a whole lot for me to add. I gave him points for fessing up, but added that rationalization and minimization were typical of sex offenders and were strong predictors for relapse. If Hammil thought there was nothing wrong with doing it this time, he wouldn't think there was anything wrong with doing it the next time.

I called up Tom Gaines, Lucy's lawyer. The only thing I had told him before the eval was to be available on Friday morning. Tom hadn't asked any questions, but I was pretty sure he'd be there. His secretary answered on the first ring and put me through.

"Miss Michael," Tom said when he got on the phone. "How is my sweet little Southern flower doing this morning?"

"I can't believe you get away with that stuff up here," I replied, but I said it jokingly. I'm a sucker for a man with a Southern accent. I had accused Tom before of taking lessons to keep his accent pure. He played his Southernness to the hilt, and it lulled a lot of people into not taking him seriously, which was a big mistake.

"Actually, I'm quite well. And I think you will be too. It appears your client has been telling the truth."

"Now, Miss Michael, you know all my clients tell the truth," Tom said sardonically. "But this one for sure," he added.

"Well, it seems Mr. Hammil has had a change of heart and fessed up. I'm faxing you my eval, which includes a full written and signed confession."

"Wonders never cease," Tom said. "And you had nothing to do with this, I'm sure," he added.

"Nothing to speak of," I replied. "He just walked into my office and decided to tell the truth. But in case there is any charge of arm-twisting, I'm also faxing you the release he signed in advance, which suggests he consult a lawyer, etc. This release ought to be good for about another fifteen minutes, so I'll send this report just as soon as we hang up."

"Just so you know," Tom said. "I am never going to let any

accused client of mine get within two hundred yards of you, so don't even ask."

"Why not?" I replied. "If they're all telling the truth."

I hung up the phone and faxed the report. When it went through I breathed a sign of relief. I hated getting stuck with info I couldn't use. It made me completely crazy to see a case go down the tubes when I had information that would turn it around but couldn't use it because someone had rescinded a release. Without a valid release, nothing left my office no matter what. Idly I checked my e-mail. I wasn't expecting anything, but since I was sitting in front of the computer, why not?

There was a message from "partytime." So Willy had something to say. What was it this time?

I double-clicked on his message.

> Bravo! I am pleased to see my faith in you was justified. Exceedingly deft handling of that poor schlemiel. My Lord, these amateurs are so naive it's almost refreshing. Putty in your hands: truly an impressive display of your skills—and your own capacity for deception, which was surprisingly impressive.

What was he talking about? It could not possibly be Hammil. He hadn't left my office more than an hour ago, and I had just finished sweeping for bugs when he came in. For a moment I was confused.

> It does make me wonder, though. You are quite a manipulative little bitch, aren't you? And, perhaps, not as naive as you pretend? "Tell me, Mr. Willy. Teach me, Mr. Willy." A little bit of a Colombo routine, perhaps? What is it they say? "Payback's a bitch."

Shock was running through me. There wasn't anybody else Willy could be talking about except Hammil. But how could he have heard that conversation with Hammil? We had swept for bugs minutes before he came in. How could he possibly have known to turn the bug off for "John" and not for Hammil? Could he have some kind of device that Danny's bug sweeper couldn't pick up? Was that possible? I couldn't believe that. Danny would have the latest, most up-to-date gizmo.

I looked at the second paragraph. The tone of Willy's communications was changing. He was calling me names, devaluing me, making excuses for going after me. He was working himself up. Which meant, of course, that he was moving in. Willy was tired of foreplay and heading for the main event, whatever that was.

I read and reread the message. It felt like a locomotive was picking up speed and heading straight for me, and I was like some kind of small animal mesmerized by the light and standing stock-still on the track. Worse, I was a *confused* small animal, obsessing over how Willy was getting his information instead of getting off the track. But there wasn't any way off the track. And how *was* Willy getting the information?

It wasn't the records. So much for the safety deposit boxes. If it was a bug it was one an FBI agent couldn't find — which, knowing Danny, didn't seem possible. But it had to be a bug. He had to be turning it off and on, but how would he get the info to tell him when? Nothing made any sense. And he was escalating too fast for me to catch up.

The phone rang, and I jumped. I stared at it for a moment before I answered it. I picked it up, and for a panicky moment I held my breath, expecting it to be Willy on the other end. It was Marv, instead, and I let out my breath in relief. Jesus, I was spooked. "Michael," he said with annoyance in his normally warm voice. "I've been trying to reach you."

"I know, Marv," I said trying to pull myself back into the present. "I'm sorry. I've just been tied up with some weird stuff."

There were lots of people I would have bit my tongue off rather than say "sorry" to, but Marv somehow wasn't one of them. He was so benign I never felt defensive around him. Not that I'd tell him I had fallen off a horse, of course. That was going too far.

His tone changed instantly. "Weird stuff?" was all he said. Marv could get people to say more by saying less than anyone I knew, but I wasn't in the mood to fall for it.

"It doesn't matter," I said, still staring at the computer screen. "What's up?"

"I need to consult you on Ginger." Guilt flooded me immediately. The albatross I had handed over to Marv to get her off my neck was pulling on his. Maybe that's why I hadn't wanted to call him. Somehow I just knew from the few minutes I spent talking with her in Marv's waiting room that Ginger was doing her millstone routine.

"I'm happy to talk about her," I said with forced enthusiasm, "but, Marv, tell me right up front: Are you going to ask me to take her back?" That, of course, was the real reason I hadn't called. I transferred her to Marv in hopes that the dynamics would be different with a male. They obviously hadn't been, so Marv would be justified in saying he couldn't be of any further help.

"Your taking her back isn't the answer," Marv said gently. "But I have to come up with some kind of plan, and worse, I made a serious mistake with her, and I need to discuss it with you."

I sat up straight. Marv made a *serious* mistake. I was so surprised I didn't speak for a moment. All therapists make minor mistakes all the time, but Marv was handling Ginger as cautiously as he knew how, and he was the best therapist I knew. What kind of *serious* mistake could he have possibly made? Oh, Lord, don't tell me he crossed some kind of boundary with her or let her cross some kind of boundary with him.

Shit, if I hadn't been so self-absorbed and focused on my headache and on Willy, I'd have called him back immediately. Great, he needed help from me within days of my camping on his couch, and I hadn't even returned the phone call.

"Are you free now?" I said evenly. No sense in beating my breast on the phone with Marv. Why didn't I just go and give him the help he was asking for?

"Yes," he said, relieved. "Right now would be fine."

He said it quietly, but somehow the way he said "right now" made me think it was all the more urgent. "I'll be right there," I said and hung up the phone. I grabbed my fanny pack and strapped it on. Willy's latest communication had left me no doubt that I'd be carrying it for a while. I picked up my car keys and started for the door. But fate just wasn't cooperating. As badly as I wanted to go see Marv, I never made it.

15

I almost did. I was almost out the door when the phone rang. I started to keep going, but then I thought it might be Marv. Maybe he wanted me to bring something with me. Maybe he was calling to tell me Ginger was camped outside his office door again and we should meet somewhere else. That turned me around. I picked up the phone, but it was Melissa, my secretary.

"Michael, I called the other office, but you weren't there. I'm sorry to bother you at home."

"No problem. What's up?"

"You had a very strange call from someone named Harvey, and I thought you might want to know about it. He said his neighbor was acting very peculiarly, and he needed to talk to you right away. I said I'd try to reach you. Do you want his number?"

I took it. Harvey was Camille's neighbor, and I thought guiltily that I hadn't yet called Camille to reschedule our appointment. She had gotten out of the hospital over the weekend, but I had been trying to keep my head from falling apart on Monday and had canceled our appointment. I should have called by now to reschedule, but I had gotten caught up dealing with Lucy's rapist. The biggest problem with being a therapist is all the balls you have to keep up in the air.

I called Harvey. "Michael," he said, sounding very relieved, "I don't know what to do about Camille." Harvey knew she was my client, since we had gotten permission from Camille to call him when she was in the hospital.

"What do you mean?" I said. "What's going on?"

"I haven't seen her very much since she got out of the hospital. I've been trying to keep an eye on her, but she hasn't been out all that much, not even to walk the dog." Harvey was the kind of neighbor everybody should have. He had been aghast when we called him from the hospital and he realized Camille was that ill and had no friends or relatives around.

But Camille hadn't grown up in the Upper Valley. She had only moved here a few years ago, after the attack, and she had been a recluse ever since. How do you make friends when you never leave the house and never talk to anyone? The only people she had talked to had been a couple of therapists whom she had seen before me—neither of whom had lasted very long. Both therapists had wanted Camille to talk about the assault, and Camille had left therapy because she couldn't do that without falling apart.

As for relatives—Camille didn't have any to speak of. She had told me her mother died a few years ago, and she hadn't seen her father since her parents' divorce when she was twelve. There weren't any siblings, and if there were extended family, she didn't know about them.

She survived on disability—which in her case, was well deserved. She truly couldn't work, and through no fault of her own. But if someone didn't work and didn't go out socially, they could live a hell of a long time in a place without knowing anybody.

I thought briefly of Camille's former life. There had been plenty of friends in Boston, but she had left all of them behind. She was fearful that if anybody knew where she had gone, somehow the perp would find out. It didn't make sense, but then trauma makes the fear center in your head the size of a watermelon, and that doesn't leave a whole lot of room for logic.

Harvey went on. "Then a little while ago, she started screaming, just screaming. Michael, it was chilling. I started to call the police, but then it stopped, and I wasn't sure I should. I didn't want to freak her. So I went over.

"The whole place was quiet. I knocked, but nobody came to the door. It was so silent it gave me the creeps. I thought all dogs barked when they heard something. I just got back, and I wasn't sure what to do, so I decided to call you first. Should I call the police . . . or the hospital . . . or somebody?"

I considered it. What could the police do? There would likely be a confrontation with Keeter. If Camille was in a major flashback and couldn't call her off, Keeter wouldn't be likely to let strange men anywhere near Camille.

This would not be a good thing. The police would have to do something to Keeter to get to Camille, hopefully temporary but maybe permanent. Keeter was Camille's only sense of safety. If anything happened to Keeter, Camille would be in even worse shape than she was now. And, even if the police only did something temporary to Keeter, it would confirm Camille's greatest fears that Keeter could be gotten around.

Calling the hospital wasn't even an option. They had zippo for outreach. Harvey could call the community mental center. They had outreach, but they didn't know Camille. And they didn't know Keeter. Actually, the problem was more that Keeter didn't know them, any more than she knew the police.

"No," I said. "I'll check on her. Give me the address, and I'll swing by." I put the words out there and then immediately wanted to swallow them. I hate going to clients' houses. It seems like a kind of boundary crossing to me. It always has an impact on the relationship. It makes it more social and less professional.

But what could the police or mental health guys do if they came? Even if they didn't shoot Keeter, no doubt they'd haul Camille off to an inpatient unit, which would lead to her sitting around an emergency room for seven hours or so while people fought about what to do with her. If Camille could stay at home, she should. But I had no doubt she was exhibiting a level of craziness that would keep the police, particularly, from seeing it that way. If they came, they'd surely take her in.

"Michael," Harvey said. "Why isn't there somebody looking after her? Did the hospital just release her with nobody?"

"Oh, Harvey," I said. "You've missed about fifteen years of so-called progress. You know all those people eating out of trash cans and sleeping in dumpsters in every city? A whole lot of them are mentally ill. This society has taken the "enlightened" position that the mentally ill can look after themselves. Hospitals literally put people on the streets who have no money, no place to sleep, and who are hearing voices.

"It's supposed to be about 'least restrictive environments,' but it's about money and what it costs to feed and house them." I had hated community care for the mentally ill since it first came in. Mostly, it meant no care at all.

"But this is the Upper Valley!" Harvey's voice had outrage in it. I knew from the waitresses at Sweet Tomatoes that Harvey was a gentle soul who paid staff fairly and treated them well.

"Makes no difference," I said. "We don't have as many mentally ill as cities do, but hospital mental health units are pretty much revolving doors everywhere. Managed care won't pay for extended stays, and anyway, these guys rarely have any kind of insurance. People go through those revolving doors here like everywhere else."

Harvey was silent, probably speechless. If he thought this was bad, I should tell him about all the abused children I'd seen returned to violent, even sadistic parents under the rubric of "family preservation." "Child annihilation" was more like it.

I hung up and thought about what I had just agreed to. I just hated to go to clients' houses, but what could it hurt? I'd just assess the situation on my way to see Marv. I couldn't do a lot for Camille but see that she was safe and not suicidal. But then again, that wasn't small potatoes. I called Marv to tell him I had to make a stop on the way and walked out.

Camille's house was a small two-story colonial with a fenced-in yard a few blocks from the main street of town. All the towns in the Upper Valley are small enough that there is no such thing as a town house, but Camille had gotten as close to Main Street as she could. I had expected to find something like that. The remoteness and isolation of the country wouldn't appeal to her right now.

Thank God for the fenced-in yard. It wouldn't necessarily keep Keeter in—the fence wasn't that tall—but it would keep kids from wandering into her territory.

I walked around to the back of the house before I knocked just to see the whole setup. There was a park behind the houses on that block, a good place to take Keeter to play. No doubt that had made the house more appealing, since that tiny yard wouldn't do much for a dog that big. Not that Camille would have been letting her run much lately. She probably had poor Keeter's collar glued to her wrist.

Harvey had been leaving for work, so I didn't stop by. Restaurant owners, or Harvey anyway, didn't seem to fly into work at eight o'clock like the rest of us. He was always wandering in just in time to get ready for the lunch crowd. His wife taught school, so I knew she wouldn't be there either. I walked up to Camille's house and knocked on the door.

No answer. No bark.

I tried the bell.

No answer. Where was Keeter?

I couldn't just leave Camille like that, knowing she was inside. What if she had hanged herself, it suddenly occurred to me. Jesus, I should have thought of that earlier. I was going to beat myself up forever for not letting Harvey call the police if something terrible had happened to Camille.

But then again, maybe she was just afraid of who might be at the door.

"Camille," I called out. "It's Michael. I need to talk to you."

There was silence.

"Camille, answer the door. I really have to know you're all right."

Still silence.

I started to threaten calling the police—I didn't really have a choice if she wouldn't let me in—when I heard, "Michael?" The voice was faint, but it was there. At least she hadn't hanged herself. It was something. "Is it really you?"

"It's really me, Camille. Please open the door."

I heard the sound of footsteps. Camille hadn't been far, and the door opened up just the length of the chain inside. Camille peered out. "Are you alone?"

I wanted to say, "No, I brought a serial killer with me," but thought better of it. I have that weird sense of humor that kicks in at tense times, but I try to keep a leash on it. Not everybody appreciates it, and I was pretty sure Camille wouldn't.

"Of course," I said. "I'm alone." She still seemed to hesitate, but then she closed the door and took off the chain. She opened it slowly, and I stepped in.

The first thing I noticed was Keeter in a crouch about ten feet from the door. She was so tense her muscles were bunching. She looked like an ad for a weight-lifting magazine for dogs. "Meet Ms. Canine Olympia. Tell us, Ms. Keeter, how do you maintain that rippled look?"

"People," she'd say. "Breakfast of champions."

I had to admit the crouch looked like the kind dogs spring from, and the only thing that looked remotely like a target was me.

But Keeter knew me, I reminded myself. She should, anyway. I took a deep breath and started to approach her to say "hello," thinking once Keeter recognized me she'd go off red alert.

"Michael," Camille said sharply. "I wouldn't do that."

I stopped. "Why not?" I asked.

"She's a guard dog. I mean really. She used to protect a service station at night after it was closed. She's trained to let someone get *in* the door and then attack. She's really bad about her territory. Just don't move toward her. When she's in that frame of mind she feels trapped if you move toward her."

I backed up. On second thought maybe I wouldn't say hello. "Why doesn't she bark?" I asked.

"Training," Camille answered. "She was trained to stay quiet and ambush an intruder." I halfway turned back to Camille. I couldn't bring myself to fully turn my back on that coiled spring on the floor, but the more important thing was Camille and the fact that she was making sense.

I noticed for the first time that she was clutching a bottle of pills. "What are the pills?" I asked tensely. Maybe my suicidal fantasies weren't so off after all.

"Haldol," she said. "I thought he was here, and I just lost it. I heard him. I finally got it together enough to take Haldol. I took double," she said sheepishly.

No wonder she was making sense. "Do you remember screaming?" I asked.

"No," she said and paused. "I heard some screaming, but I didn't realize it was me. Was it me?"

"It was you," I said. "Your neighbor Harvey called me. He was afraid you needed help, and nobody came to the door when he knocked."

I kept checking in on Keeter out of the corner of my eye as I talked. She looked like she was relaxing somewhat. Her muscles didn't have that tightly clenched, one-more-inch-and-you're-mine look.

"Oh," she said. "I heard someone at the door, but I just thought it was him coming back." I knew who "him" was by now: the sweet soul who had kidnapped her, taped her face and head, no doubt raped her, but also probably tortured her. I didn't know the details, but I knew they were bad enough to have almost destroyed the woman in front of me.

"No," I said, "It was just Harvey. What happened?"

"He was back again," she said. "The only way I can cope with it is by eating these," she said holding up the Haldol. "Sometimes I just wish he'd kill me and get it over with."

"Let's sit down," I said, "and talk for a minute." Camille sighed and then let me into the living room. Keeter looked better, but I took a wide berth around her just in case. Some friend she was. Enter the wrong door and you're morning snack.

"Camille," I said after we were seated, "do you really believe it was him and not a flashback?"

"I don't know," she said. "It didn't seem like a flashback. The flashbacks have always been to things that really happened. I mean, I'd wake up and see him duct-taping my face—I could feel it—or that he was . . . he was . . ."

"Stop," I said. "Better not to think about it. It's been a bad morning, and you could trigger another whatever-you-want-to-call-it. But what do you mean? How is this different from the other ones?"

"These are never about what he's *done,*" she said thoughtfully. "He just keeps threatening what he's *going* to do."

"It isn't a replay of things that happened before?"

"No," she said. Keeter had come in and lain down at her feet. I guess she had finally decided I wasn't there to rob the gas station or mug Camille. Camille scratched her head. Keeter laid her head on Camille's feet and turned her belly up. It was a side of Keeter I hadn't seen. It was a side of Camille I hadn't seen either. She was thinking a whole lot more clearly than she usually was after a flashback. Maybe she needed to double her meds.

She was also a better psychologist than me. She was right. A flashback was *always* a repeat of the past. Always. That was the point of a flashback. The brain regurgitated images of the trauma. It didn't make up new possibilities. And Camille had told me about this before. The voice had said it would be worse next time, but I hadn't thought about how *unlike* a flashback that statement was.

"And there's another thing," Camille went on. "He's just *talking.* I can't see him."

"What do you mean you can't see him?"

"In all the other flashbacks I saw him. I saw it happening all over again, over and over. This is just a voice out of the dark. He gets in. I don't know how, but he gets in." She sighed hopelessly. "I don't expect you to believe me."

But I was starting to wonder. Flashbacks aren't auditory. They may have voices in them, but they are mostly visual. Unless she was having a psychotic break. Psychotic hallucinations are usually auditory. There is no reason you can't have a psychotic break on top of PTSD. Except she was too old. Most psychotic breaks occur when people are younger than Camille. Not to mention that if this trauma was going to trigger psychosis, why hadn't the attack itself triggered it? Why now?

It occurred to me for the first time that her attacker might really be back. What if the same kind of thing was happening to her that was happening to me? What if she was being stalked by a sadist? I hadn't even thought about it because Camille had terrible PTSD and a long history of flashbacks. I just thought it was more of the same.

But a good percentage of sadists do come back. They call their victims or watch them. The only good data on this came from FBI studies of interviews with caught sadistic rapists and even serial killers—serial killers don't kill everybody they attack, particularly before they get into a killing pattern.

In the interviews they described frequently coming back after the rape. They'd stand outside their victims' houses and watch them or call them on the phone just to hear their voices. It's kind of a reverse form of PTSD. The perps get emotional flashbacks too, but they *want* to relive the memories. The reliving brings an aftertaste of the violent high all over again.

Too, some of them actually attack the same woman twice. The number of women who have been attacked more than once by the same stranger is larger than most people know.

I hadn't considered it partly because I was dealing with Willy, and it seemed too bizarre to have both of us stalked by a sadist at the same time. Yet two rare cancers might be unlikely for an internist to run across in the same week, but how unlikely is it for a specialist? And what was my specialty? Trauma.

But even if the perp really was back, how was he getting into her house? Why wasn't Keeter going bananas?

"Tell me about Keeter," I said. "How did you get her?"

"I met a guy who owned this string of protection dogs," she said. "He had a route. He dropped them off at service stations and department stores and stuff at night and then picked them up in the morning. I tried to get a dog through a regular trainer, but they wouldn't sell me one because they didn't think I could handle him."

Good thinking, I thought, but I didn't comment. Reputable dealers try not to sell dogs to people who are going to let them eat small children. And Camille had surely been in the kind of shape that would have told any vaguely responsible person she couldn't handle an attack dog. "So how did you meet this guy?"

"By accident," she said. "I told a guy I knew at a local service station that I was looking for a protection dog. I used to take my car there, and we were just talking one day while I had some work done on the car. I was getting ready to leave. I just couldn't stay in Boston anymore after the . . . Well, I kept thinking he knew where I lived and he'd come back. I hardly told anybody I was going. I was afraid he'd find out somehow."

"He," I knew, was always the perp. She never called him anything else. He was on her mind so much she always thought I knew whom she was talking about when she said "he."

"I had to have the car fixed. I didn't tell Chris what happened, but he probably figured something. I always took my car there so I knew him before, and afterward, I was a lot . . . different." Her eyes started filling up. There was always the ongoing grief for who she had been.

"You know," she said as the tears started, "I've lived alone since I was sixteen. I never had a problem. My mother was depressed all the time, and she drank. I could never get her to stop even though I tried all the time. I couldn't bring anybody home because Mom would be staggering around in her nightgown, and finally I just left. I put myself through school, and I did everything by myself. I told the other nurses it was ridiculous to need an escort to the parking lot. I just didn't know . . . I never . . ."

Camille cried for a few minutes, and we were both silent. I had never met the woman she was describing, although something about Camille had always shone through the jumble of fear and anxiety that surrounded her. There was some core of all that she used to be still there, but it was very far away.

"Chris introduced you to the trainer?" I said softly. A part of me wanted to keep talking about her life before the cyclone, and today she could. But my anxiety about the perp being back was growing, and if he really was back, she might not have a life to talk about if I didn't find out more about how he was getting into her house.

"Chris called him and called me back to say I should talk to him. He thought he'd sell me a dog if I really wanted one. He said he wasn't a regular dealer, just a guy who had some dogs he rented out to service stations and places like that."

It didn't surprise me that it had been that easy to get a dog. While dealers are attuned to ethical issues around guard dogs, there is a whole netherworld out there of macho types who own guard dogs or breed a few and who think everybody should have one. Some are survivalists or military wannabees or whatever.

"Did Chris use the guy's dogs in his service station at night?"

"Sure," she said. "That's how he knew him."

"Did Chris know Keeter?"

"I don't know," she said. "Why?"

I ignored the question. "Why was the trainer willing to give up a dog?" I asked. "He didn't usually sell them, did he? I mean, you said he wasn't a regular dealer?"

"No, I don't think so, but, well, Keeter wasn't behaving too well. Wait a minute. Chris did know her, because I remember him telling me I should think twice about getting her. He said she wasn't too stable. I forgot all about that. But the other guy said she just needed somebody with her. He said there was a difference in being alone all night in an empty building and being with an owner all the time."

"What was she doing that was so bad?"

"I don't know for sure," she said. "I think she was maybe a little too aggressive or something. I think Chris said she gave the clerk a hard time when he tried to open the store in the morning. Chris said he didn't have any trouble with her, but he couldn't be there every day. I don't care what she did," she said defiantly. "I had to have a dog, and nobody else would sell me one."

"Was she already trained as a seizure dog?" I said doubtfully.

"No, I took her in for training right after I got her. There was a training center in Manchester. Actually," she said sheepishly, "she didn't do that well. She didn't really graduate, but I needed a guard dog more than a seizure dog, so I kept her. I just tell people she's a seizure dog," she said looking down, "so they'll let her come with me. Otherwise, there're a lot of places that won't let her in, but she didn't really get her papers.

"She might do the right thing, I mean if I had a seizure, but she might not. The guy said she was unreliable."

I looked at Keeter again. Great. She was an unreliable guard dog who'd had a little training in seizures and was unreliable there too. What the hell would she do in an emergency? Who knew?

So where did all that leave us? The guy who sold her the dog was out as the perp. She hadn't met him before the attack, and it would be too much of a coincidence for her to meet him afterward. But Chris wasn't out. Chris was somebody whom Keeter knew and who could walk into a building that Keeter was guarding without her taking his throat out. That had been their relationship. Keeter guarded the gas station until Chris got there.

And the fact that Chris knew Camille before the attack fit. A lot of attackers know their victims casually. That's how they target them. Camille wouldn't have recognized him. She had told me the perp had been wearing a ski mask, and somebody wouldn't recognize their grandmother if she were wearing one of those things.

But wouldn't Camille have recognized Chris's voice if she knew him? Maybe, maybe not. People who are abducted are so frightened they hardly recognize their own voices, and Camille had only known him slightly.

If Chris were the perp, what a stroke of luck he had. Camille comes in, and he gets to gloat over how horrible she looks. Then she tells him she wants a guard dog, and he puts her on to one who knows him and who won't react if he walks in on her turf.

But I didn't know Chris was the one. For one thing, he had warned her against Keeter. Still, whoever it was, one thing was for sure: Keeter wasn't perp-proof. There were people who could get into the house without her raising a fuss—her trainer and Chris, for starters. Not to mention that everybody who knew Keeter had rated her as unreliable.

"Did Chris know where you were going?" I asked.

She thought a minute. "I don't think he knew exactly. I told him I was going to New England. No, wait, I remember him saying he used to live in Vermont, and we started talking about it, so I think I did tell him the general area. Why do you ask?"

Uh-oh. I needed to talk to Adam right away. This might not be a job for a therapist after all. If there was a perp outside her head and not inside it, it was strictly a job for the police. I had zero expertise in catching perps.

But that, of course, was what Adam had been telling me all along about Willy. Willy was surely outside my head as well as inside it. But this was different, I reasoned. It made sense for me to turn Camille's case over to Adam and not mine. Unfortunately, the voice in my head failed me when I tried to think why.

Well, shit, just face it. This was different because it wasn't me. This was about Camille. And she didn't sleep with Adam, and she didn't have a crazy, prickly, porcupine thing about her boundaries, and most of all, maybe, she wasn't Mama's child.

There was that other thing too. I knew I couldn't tolerate Adam's rescuing me twice. I'd resent hell out of him for it. Mama's child. Unfortunately, I was truly Mama's child.

I got some paper from Camille and wrote out a couple of permission forms. Camille had had a so-so experience with the Boston police after the attack. One officer had been pretty sensitive to her confused state, and the other had pushed her to give all the details. When she couldn't—she dissociated when she tried to talk about it—he had been impatient with her and finally left.

Some progress has been made in twenty years of feminists harping about the way rape victims are treated. Cops no longer routinely hook victims up to lie detector tests, and some places even have women cops do much of the interviewing. But the truth is, there are far more rapes than women cops available to interview victims, and old attitudes still die hard. Camille's experience with the police had been better than that of most rape victims in a big city environment.

And, in all fairness, Camille would have been impossible to interview. She was found nude, in a dog kennel. She was dissociative and couldn't talk about what happened without losing it and becoming completely incoherent. Cops are oriented toward catching perps, and Camille wouldn't have been any help at all. They would have had a nasty crime on their hands with an eyewitness who was useless to them. I could see a cop getting frustrated with that.

I told Camille what I had in mind and she agreed. She still

saw the police as a help, and she didn't mind my bringing Adam in or contacting the two police who had investigated the attack before. But she never would have called them on her own. The perp loomed too large in her mind. She didn't think anybody could stop him.

I left uneasily. If Camille was in danger, I didn't like to leave her there, not even with Keeter, since Keeter wasn't proving to be too helpful on this one. But even if Keeter did know Chris, I reminded myself, and Chris was the perp, that didn't mean she would let him *attack* Camille. Camille was her owner now, and Chris had never been. She had been trained to let Chris into a building she was guarding, but she had never been trained to let him attack her handler.

And all training aside, there was the business of Keeter's genes. A rottweiler had protect-your-owner written into its DNA.

For once I used the car phone. I have a prejudice against car phones, but I had finally bought one when Adam threatened to give me one if I didn't. I had explained my prejudice to him—buy a car phone, and the next step is a phone in the shower, and soon there is *no* time you aren't connected to the world. I didn't like being connected to it as much as I was, and I surely wasn't looking for more—but he hadn't been impressed.

He just said he had a prejudice too, a thing about friends of his who routinely confronted sex offenders riding around alone without car phones, not thinking for one second about whom they were dealing with. What was I going to do, he had asked, if I were followed and run off the road—look for a pay phone?

I didn't like using it, but I wanted to be able to say enough alarming stuff to the dispatcher that she would track Adam down if he wasn't there, and I didn't want to do that in front of Camille. But I was in luck. He was there and free, and she put me through to him. I told him I had a client with a problem that might be outside her head rather than inside, and I needed to talk to him about it. He said to come on in.

He was writing something when I walked through the open door of his office. "Hi," I said softly.

He looked up and smiled. "Come on in," he said and pulled up a chair for me. The smile didn't go away when he sat back down, and for a moment I remembered how I loved to touch the smile creases in the corners of his eyes with my fingertips. I knew all the planes and creases of his face by touch.

For a moment there was silence, and the atmosphere started to pick up a charge. I remembered Hawaii and the feel of the sand on my bare back. I remembered my loft and the moon shining through the skylight across his bare chest. I remembered his fingers sliding between . . . I looked at him. I saw the look in his eye and knew he was remembering something too, whatever it was.

"Don't start," I said.

Adam didn't speak.

"I'm here on business," I said.

Adam still didn't speak.

"Look, if you're going to —" But Adam interrupted.

"Michael," he said, "I haven't said anything."

"Oh," I said. "That's right. . . . Never mind."

How could this man discombobulate me like that? I shouldn't let myself get in the same room with him.

"Just projection," I said, sighing. "I'm talking to myself."

"Keep talking," he said.

"Never mind," I replied.

I started to tell him about Camille. Adam didn't seem to be paying that much attention — whether he admitted it or not, he had a look in his eyes I knew pretty well — until I started talking about why I was no longer sure she was having flashbacks. A lot of cops would have dismissed what I said—I had zero for hard evidence—but Adam wasn't a lot of cops.

He got very focused, and wherever he had been, he wasn't anymore. I told him about Chris, and he got even more interested. He knew as well as I did that sadists could and did return. If there was a way to get around Keeter, then what Camille was saying wasn't all that improbable.

"How sure are you?" he said, finally.

"That they're not flashbacks? I don't know. They just don't sound like flashbacks. How do you have a flashback to something that never happened? I guess I'd have to say pretty sure."

"How do you know she isn't making it up?"

"The whole thing? From the beginning? As in Munescheusen? Oh, I'd stake a lot on that. You can't fake the way she was in the hospital. Pupils dilated, shallow, rapid breathing, skin color changes. She was in a full-blown panic attack."

"Crazy?"

"Crazy? As in paranoid? And has panic attacks because she believes what she says?" Actually, I hadn't even thought about it, but it didn't sound right.

"I don't know. The content of her delusions isn't right. I don't know why, but paranoids all have the same kinds of delusions: People are broadcasting through their teeth; aliens have planted a transmitter in their skulls. This isn't anything like any paranoid delusion I've ever seen."

"Yeah, but they do have a thing about people going after them."

"True," I had to admit. "I guess I can't rule it out completely, but I don't buy it. I'd have to think about why." I paused while I tried to figure out why I was so sure it wasn't paranoia.

"Paranoids have this suspicious way about them," I said finally. "They check your office. They decide you're one of *them.* They keep looking for hidden recorders. I don't get any of that from Camille.

"But it's all the more reason to check with the original cops on the case. I can't say it's impossible. But I'd say if the original incident happened like she said, there's not a lot of reason to think she's making this one up." I knew that was where Adam would start anyway. He'd want to get the original crime reports and find out how far the Boston cops had gotten on solving the case.

"Now, Michael, don't get upset. False Memory Syndrome?"

I rolled my eyes. "Adam, we've gone through this. The false memory zealots have zero—and I do mean zero—evidence there is any such thing. And there is a whole lot of evidence— as in tons—that there isn't. But even if you were a died-in-the-wool false memory crazy, you wouldn't apply it to this case. This is out-of-family-stranger attack. Not exactly the kind of case that's a candidate for the false memory bullshit.

"Besides, I really don't think the issue is going to be the original attack. I have a feeling Boston will confirm that she was found just like she said. I think the issue is going to be whether that attack did something to her so profound that this guy is back only in her head. Even by the backlash's reckoning, that wouldn't be a false memory issue."

"I'll check it out," he said, "and call you."

I gave him what I had. Bit by bit, I had gotten little pieces of what happened from Camille. She knew the exact date that she had been abducted, and, of course, she knew the name of the hospital where she had worked. She wasn't as sure where she had been found. Everything immediately after the attack was hazy, but she remembered one of the detective's names very clearly. She had dissociated by focusing on his name badge when he was hassling her.

I left reluctantly; I just felt like hanging around. A part of me wanted to say, "So your lover is a porcupine. So?" Maybe I wanted to say, "All right, so you *could* find a less prickly lover. But could they hit the jumper from the corner?" Maybe most of all I wanted to just say, "Dinner?" But I didn't say any of it. I just said, "See ya." I figured he knew what I meant. No sense in belaboring things.

On the way out I thought about it. Once in a while I used to pick up those books that said things like "Men are from Mars; Women are from Venus." They always made me feel like I was from Pluto. I didn't seem to fit.

Things were fine up until fifth grade. Then all the other girls started sitting on the rocks at recess and combing their hair. Boring, boring, and more boring. I couldn't cope with the rocks, so I played tight end on the football team. Needless to say, there weren't a lot of other girls playing.

I knew what I was doing. I was rationalizing the fact that it would kill me to sit down and talk to Adam about our relationship. Some part of me knew I should, but I just didn't want to. And Adam was only slightly better than I was at that sort of thing. Although, come to think of it, when a hard-nosed police chief was better than I was at talking about feelings, it could be I was pretty far out there. Well, somebody had to hold down one end of a continuum. Otherwise the normal curve wouldn't work.

I glanced at my watch. I was running a little late for Marv. As in hours late. It was getting on in the afternoon, and late afternoon is prime time for therapists to see clients. Adults work and kids go to school, so the late afternoon hours are usually the busiest.

Marvin was booked, his secretary told me when I arrived. That didn't surprise me, but the note on my desk did. "I'm seeing clients till eight. Please don't come over to the house afterward or any time during the weekend. I don't really want to talk on the phone about this either. I think it best to wait until Monday and talk to you at work. Could we meet early

Monday? Name a time and I'll reschedule whatever I have to. Give the message to Rochelle."

Don't come over to the house? Name a time and he will reschedule? Reschedule a client for the sake of a meeting? That just didn't happen. Don't call. Something pretty serious was going on, but I couldn't think of any scenario that would have Marv telling me not to come by the house to talk about it. Did he have a lover I didn't know about who didn't want company? Domestic problems?

But Marv didn't have a lover except for his paintings—I was pretty sure of that—and try as I might, I couldn't think of a single painting that would object to my dropping by.

And Lord, it could not be, no, it could not be somehow that Ginger was staying at his house. Even if Marv had a psychotic break, he wouldn't permit such a thing . . . I hoped. I reminded myself of the numerous times I'd been in cases where people were astonished at some of the things their friends or family members had done. Nobel prizewinners and rock stars molested kids. Presidents of universities made obscene phone calls. And every one of those people had other people who loved them and absolutely could not believe they would do such a thing.

Almost 10 percent of male therapists get sexually involved with clients. It isn't like it is even that uncommon. But not Marv. If Marv had made a mistake anywhere near that serious, I was going to set records for astonishment.

But if it wasn't that, then what? Why didn't Marv want me over to his house? The world was making less and less sense every goddamn day.

16

As long as I was at Psychiatry I might as well tie up some loose ends. I called Toby and caught him between power lunches. His secretary put me through right away. Amazing how accessible he was when you were doing him a favor. "Toby," I said. "This is Michael. I can't tell you any of the details because I don't have permission, but things worked out pretty well in that case you referred me. You might want to give Lucy a call."

"I'm very glad to hear that," he said, and his voice sounded genuinely relieved. "I'm very appreciative of your help."

"Happy to," I said, and I meant it. Toby was rarely on the side of the angels, but when he was, I didn't mind hanging out with him.

And I wasn't sorry to have Toby owing me. In the world of faculty politics, people pay their debts. In fact, Toby did almost nothing but. He generally paid more attention to whom he owed and who owed him than whatever issue was under consideration.

No doubt I'd be in trouble again, and no doubt there would be a time I needed support from Toby, and almost always when that happened, I was on the low end of the power continuum and not somebody Toby would get a lot of points out of supporting. I didn't mind at all having a chit from Toby in my pocket.

I stayed and worked for a while, and it was dusk when I finally strapped on my fanny pack and walked out to the car. My head was full of lying fraternity rapists and eavesdropping sadistic ministers, and most of all my head was full of worry about Marv and Camille.

What was it Stevens wrote, "We must endure our thoughts all night until the bright obvious . . ." Stevens, master of the midway zap. In the beginning, he was talking about a snow-storm, and by the end you realized the snowstorm was inside his head and not outside. Maybe someday all of this was going to turn into the "bright obvious," but right now a snowstorm was an understatement. It was more like swimming in mud.

Dusk settled in all around me as I drove home. I hate dusk—for the same reason I hate snowstorms—inside or out. I can't see. I can see more at night once my eyes acclimate than I can when everything is betwixt and between.

There is, I admit, the occasional splashy sunset at dusk. But it is only occasionally that dusk has a little glory to it. Nine-tenths of the time it is just a messy transition. Now, if day just went whap, like a light shutting off, and there you were, in the sparkling night sky, that would be a transition. But every single goddamn day, you have to put up with this lingering, slow, death-of-the-light business. Thank goodness, by the time I got home the day had finished falling apart and night was blooming.

I walked out onto the deck with my solace glass of ice tea just as the full moon slipped from behind some clouds. Looking up I remembered being five years old and riding home in a car with the moon following us all the way. I remember how amazed I was: Everywhere we went, there it was—no matter how fast we went the moon always seemed to keep up.

I used to talk to the moon, sitting at the window of my bedroom. I didn't understand that the half moon and the full moon were the same thing, and I waited and waited until the full moon came back.

When it did, I wouldn't throw my usual fit about going to bed: I couldn't wait till Mama closed the door and I could drag a chair over to the window. I talked, and the moon listened. Mama wasn't exactly the listening type, and if she did listen, she was likely to say something warm like, "Don't talk foolishness, girl," or she would just snort. Mama had a snort that said "bullshit" better than "bullshit" said it. The moon never said anything like that.

I remembered sneaking out and swimming under that moon when I was older. I always have liked being outside at night—most of all when the moon was shining like it was tonight. I looked at the stream below the deck: In the moonlight it had a vibrancy that hurt your eyes it was so intense, nothing like the ordinary stream it became during the day.

But then the moon gives everything a kind of grace. What doesn't look good under a full moon? Old cars look good. Junkyards look good. Shopping malls look good.

I had the feeling, suddenly, of being watched, and at first I thought it was the moon. I shook my head and smiled, thinking how easy it was to slip back into that five-year-old person—but I stopped my head in mid shake.

The feeling of being watched wasn't benign. It wasn't a feeling of being looked after or watched over: It was something different. I looked up at the moon one last time, and then I looked at the trees across the stream.

I'd chalk it up to paranoia if, oddly enough, I hadn't seen the research. The research said people could tell when somebody was staring at them although nobody knew how. Besides, if it was paranoia, I reasoned, it wouldn't have happened in the middle of my basking in the full moon, which was one time I hadn't been worrying about Willy at all. Likely, the opposite was true. If I was being watched, it probably had taken a while for it to get through my moon-soaked brain.

I sipped my ice tea and thought about it. I didn't have my fanny pack on the deck, and it was probably not a very good idea to be out here like some kind of sitting duck. What was going on? Was this the night Willy was making his move, or was he here just to scout the terrain?

Thinking about it, I felt the bitter taste of fear in my mouth, and then I got mad. Seriously mad. I just couldn't live my life sitting around waiting for someone to torture and murder me. Willy hadn't laid a finger on me, and already he had stolen just about everything I cared about. I couldn't even sit on my goddamn deck in the moonlight without worrying about him.

I got up abruptly and walked back into the house and picked up my fanny pack where I had dropped it. Goddamn it. This was totally and completely ridiculous. Who knew these woods better than me? Willy? I don't think so. Who was used to being in the woods at night? Willy or me? Ten to one Willy wasn't sneaking out of the house at fifteen to swim under the full moon, although, come to think of it, he probably was sneaking out of the house to play Peeping Tom at that age.

What the hell. You place your bets. If Willy and I were going to duke it out, I probably had more advantage in my own woods at night than I'd get anywhere else.

I ran up to the loft and stared at my clothes hanging in my closet. I didn't exactly have a lot. A limit of 250 things in my life total somewhat limited my wardrobe. Surprise, surprise, I didn't have an official night-creeping outfit. Everything had to be black—I knew that from all the rapists I had interviewed— so what could I put together?

I didn't have any black sweatpants. My two pairs of blue jeans were blue. But I did have one pair of black dress pants. I grabbed them, pulled off my clothes, and put them on. I looked for shoes. I could wear the one pair of flat black pumps I used for work, but they would be awful in the woods. I sighed as I saw my black, high-top basketball shoes. I'd never worn them off the court before, but I guessed I could make an exception. At least, I wouldn't be on concrete.

I found a black turtleneck in the drawer and pulled it on and then a black sweater over it. I rummaged around until I found a navy blue knit cap. It wasn't black, but it was close. I strapped on my fanny pack. I looked pretty funny with my basketball shoes and my dress pants. As if I cared. This goddamn thing was going to be over tonight one way or the other.

I strapped the fanny pack on my hip and ran down the stairs from the loft and headed for the back door. Just before I reached it, I screeched to a halt. Nobody who had ever seen *Silence of the Lambs* could even think about a perp at night without wondering if he had night goggles.

What if he did? Did he know what I was thinking when I looked up at the woods, got up abruptly, and went back inside? Which door was he watching, the deck door or the back door? Even without night goggles, he could see me come out of the door in the moonlight if he was watching it. How smart was

Willy? Smart. But he couldn't watch both at once, so which door would he watch?

I paced around the room thinking and saw I hadn't locked the deck door in my haste. Absentmindedly, I locked it. I was going to have to place my bets. Which door would he be watching? There just wasn't any way to know, and I could be in big trouble if Willy saw me coming out of the house and ambushed me.

I turned from the deck door—goddamn it, I didn't want to make a random choice, but I wasn't staying inside—and my eyes fell on the wood box. The wood box. I had one of those wood boxes that's cut right through the wall of the house. To load it with firewood, you had to go outside, remove a two-foot insulated plug from the side of the house, and load the wood. It was set up so you never had to drag wood inside the house.

I threw the top of the wood box open and started pulling firewood out, throwing it in all directions on my precious hardwood floor. The plug was only two feet or so wide. Good thing I was skinny. I could fit through two feet, at least on the diagonal. I got the last of the wood out and stood up. I looked around. What had I forgotten? The lights. I walked over and turned off the living room lights. I should have done it before, but the wood box was off to the side, hidden by a sofa from the huge A-frame window that fronted the deck. Nobody could have seen me unload the wood box, but now I was about to open it. I didn't want the light to shine through the open wood box door and give me away.

The wood box wasn't big enough for me to get in completely, so I leaned in as far as I could and brushed off the wood dust from the plug. This was the tricky part. The plug couldn't be pulled inside; it would only go out. The only way to get it out was to push it out on the ground, and I didn't want to make a lot of noise. If I didn't alert Willy by making noise, he really couldn't see me slipping out of the side of the house no matter which door he was watching.

I pushed on the plug gently, and nothing happened. I pushed again and got nowhere. Finally, I started hitting it with my fist with short jabs until it started moving outward. The plug was insulated, and my fist didn't make any real noise on the insulation.

I got lucky. One side of the plug opened up first, and I was able to reach my hand around it and grab the edge before the whole thing fell. I eased the plug out the rest of the way and at least broke its fall to the ground.

I stuck my head out and just waited. It would take two or three minutes for my eyes to acclimate, and there was no point in going anywhere until they did. Soon the darkness in front of me turned into trees and a woodpile, and I put my arms over my head and started to wiggle out. I wiggled out as quickly as I could and quietly replaced the plug. It wouldn't be good if Willy found it and went in while I was out.

I crouched down for a moment to get oriented. The opening was near the woodpile, and the woodpile was high enough to provide cover, so I was okay where I was for a few minutes. I was beginning to regret the full moon. The night was too bright. Anybody could see anybody in this light, and I had several feet of clear moonlit ground to cross before I could get to the shadow of the trees.

I could hear my heart beating while I waited, but it wasn't exactly fear, it was more like exhilaration. I have always felt invisible in the woods at night, although God knows that is a myth. Every woods animal within forty miles knew there was a human about, but *people* didn't expect anybody to be in the woods at night, certainly not without a flashlight. If you wanted to hide, the woods at night were the place.

Something was bothering me, nagging at me, but I was

getting a taste of the exhilaration I had on the cross-country course, and I ignored it. I'd think about it later. First, I had to get to the cover of the trees. I crouched and duck-walked along the edge of the house, looking for the place where the distance to the trees was the shortest. I found the closest place and got ready. I knew I'd be faster standing up but a lot more visible, so I took a deep breath and wiggled across the moonlit ground on my belly.

I made it to the edge of the trees, then stood up and ran some distance through the trees before I crouched down and listened. Nobody shot me; nobody even shot at me. In fact, I didn't hear anything unnatural. Nothing big and awkward was moving in the woods. The crickets were still holding forth. I was surprised they hadn't piped down. I could hear an owl in the distance screeching — nature was having its nightly orgy of death and destruction.

A whole lot of me didn't want to go looking for Willy, gun or not. A whole lot of me just wanted to melt into the shadows and feel that nobody and nothing could find me. I was tired of being alert, of waiting for trouble, of having the rhythm of my life dictated by a goddamn predator. I did not like feeling like a goldfish in a fishbowl with a cat's face pressed up against the side. I could climb a tree right now, right up to the top like I did when I was fifteen, and the moon would blaze down on me like grace. Nobody would find me there.

But if I did, Willy would still be there when I got down — if not tonight, then tomorrow night or the next or the next. I started to move through the trees. I just couldn't live like that. I'd parallel the road and go down far enough that when I turned back, I'd come up behind him, no matter where he was watching the house from. There was a small hill across the stream from the house. Willy would be somewhere on that hill, looking down, if he hadn't left by now.

Then I stopped. I knew what was bothering me. Funny

thing to think about at this late stage, but exactly what was I going to do when I got there? Was I actually planning on shooting him? In cold blood? In the back? Or was I planning on letting him shoot at me first? In which case what I would do might be a moot point.

But what if he didn't have a gun or didn't pull one? Was I going to march him down to my house and call the police? The very thought of Willy inside my house made me completely crazy. Also, what would they have him on? Trespassing. Big deal. He'd be out in two days and more clever the next time.

I started moving again and thought of all the things Willy had done to children and would do to children in the future, and the thought of him dead had a lot of appeal. I didn't mind him dead. I didn't have a problem with his being dead. But the truth was I didn't even like to shoot silhouettes of people. So I was not going to be happy shooting at a real person. Much less if he didn't try to shoot at me.

There was also the small matter that I would go to jail for it. The law does frown on shooting people who are not armed. But that wasn't the main thing. The main thing was that I couldn't even imagine shooting anybody in cold blood, not even Willy.

This was the problem with me and Willy since he got out. He knew exactly what he wanted to do with me—whatever it was, and I truly didn't want to find out—but I didn't have a clue what to do with him.

But something had to happen tonight because I could not and would not keep living like this. I was going onto that hill with Willy, and I'd figure out what to do then.

I went straight out from the side of the house until I was far enough away that I knew I had to be behind Willy. At least he couldn't see the house if he was this far out, so unless he was leaving, I was going to come up behind him. It was also a good place to cross the stream. There were enough rocks that I didn't have to get wet and a lot of overhanging trees providing shade.

I crossed the stream on the rocks, feeling a little exposed. Shadow or not, I was still more visible crossing the stream than I was in the forest. But again nobody shot me and nobody grabbed me on the other side, and that was now my definition of success.

But once I got over, the questions came back: How smart was Willy? Smart. How smart? Smart enough to lure me into the woods? Smart enough to know I'd come after him if he stood there night after night staring at me until I figured it out? What would he have done if I hadn't? Lit a cigarette to get my attention? Turned on a flashlight?

The thought of Camille came back, blind with tape wrapped all around her head, while some aberrant asshole did God knows what to the rest of her. I shuddered, and my stomach started to turn. Was I really sneaking up on Willy? Or was he sneaking up on me? I looked down. Any step could be onto a trap.

I took a deep breath and tried to push the fear out of my mind. I wasn't sure anymore I should be out here, but I was still committed. I couldn't go back and huddle in the house waiting for him. I went forward more slowly than before, looking carefully at every step.

Thank God for New England forests. They are sparse enough that you can walk off the path and not have to bushwhack, at least at this time of year. The buds were just starting, and mostly the forest was filled with bare bushes. They were widely enough spaced that the lack of a trail wasn't a big problem. Things fill out some in the summer, and I would have made a whole lot more noise than I did now. Thank God it wasn't a Southern forest. I'd have sounded like a bear crashing through the woods if I ventured off a trail.

I took a deep breath. The whole thing of Willy having the nerve to hang around my woods just seemed so incredible. The forest had been my haven, and I was incensed that it was being used by a predator. But tell that to a mouse or a rabbit or just about any other creature in the forest. Life is a lottery in the forest. The damn screech owl in the distance had a taste for brains. You'd find rabbits in the forest where he had chewed off the heads so he could take the brains back and enjoy them at his leisure.

Oh, I knew what the politically correct thing was. The owl was killing to live and Willy was killing for the fun of it, and that was supposed to be some huge difference, but I don't really know how much difference it made to the rabbit. This moonlight-soaked haven of mine was more violent than any inner city.

And now I was part of it, more so than at any time in my life. I'd always been a visitor before. Tonight I was locked into that predator/prey thing like everybody else around me. Except for one thing—the rabbit didn't usually try to sneak up on the owl. Probably that was because she wouldn't know what to do once she got there, which was exactly my problem.

I wondered if animals romanticize the city as much as people romanticize the forest. I almost laughed as I thought of the rabbits lecturing their children on the moral superiority of the city: "At least humans don't usually *eat* somebody when they kill them, not like here."

I was getting giddy. Fear of a trap and the exhilaration of being invisible were mixing in my brain, and there were enough chemicals up there to make a junkie happy. Ahead of me was the ridge, and as I saw it, my heart started to beat double-time.

I stepped behind a tree for cover, crouched down, and stuck my head out to survey the scene. From where I was I didn't see anybody on the ridge, but I was still pretty far down the hill. I'd have to zigzag back and forth going up to the top of the ridge to make sure I covered the width of it. If Willy was waiting for me, he still had to spot me, goggles or not. I got ready to move and thought, "All right, fate, take your best shot, and then leave me alone till the next time." That crazy mantra always came back.

I had a fleeting thought of how stupid what I'd done would seem to most people. I had voluntarily chosen to be alone, at night, in the woods with a sadistic sex offender who was stalking me and most likely planning on killing me. Worse, a very bright sex offender who might well be counting the steps between me and the next snare.

Thinking about it, a wave of gut-wrenching, throw-up-time, blind panic started swelling in me. I grabbed the tree and held on. "Don't be stupid," I told myself. "This is still your arena more than his. You're only guessing that he's expecting you."

But what if Willy wasn't expecting me. Even then would he be likely just to stand there with no cover? Wasn't Willy the kind who'd set a few snares just in case? I remembered belatedly that Willy had been a scout leader among his many covers for child molestation. Had he been one of those woodsy-type scoutmasters?

I waited, and the panic started easing like the tide going out. My thinking didn't have a whole lot to do with it. It was just the way panic worked. It came in waves and, just like waves, receded.

"Goddamn it," I thought. I never had those until I was attacked. I sincerely hoped I didn't get one at some point when I needed to function in some important way, like, say, when I had a gun in my hand and Willy in front of it.

I hadn't pulled my gun yet. I don't believe a gun is some kind of magic talisman that protects you just by buying one, so I had gotten some serious training. The training said never pull a gun until you're ready to use it. I hadn't even located Willy yet. I started moving up the hill zigzag, running in a half-crouch from one tree to the next. The forest had grown quiet: By now the entire population was aware of a collision about to happen. Was Willy smart enough to listen?

I saw nothing till I got right on top of the ridge. I was moving in a crouching duck walk across the ridge when I spotted him. Even in the moonlight, there were so many shapes in the forest that I don't know if I would have spotted him if he hadn't moved. It was a slight movement, maybe shifting from one foot to the other, but it was enough.

I hit the ground. Willy was halfway down the hill and still pretty far away from me. All I could really see was a shape. He was standing in the shadow of a large tree, and I couldn't be sure which way he was looking. Had he heard me and turned around? Was he looking my way or at the house? I waited, but Willy didn't move again. I pulled open the Velcro opening to my fanny pack. It made a noise that in my mind sounded about as loud as thunder, but Willy still didn't move.

I got the gun out and started wiggling closer. If this was a trap, the only place he could be sure I would be was right here. The closer I got to him, the more likely it was I'd hit a snare of some kind.

Alarm bells were starting to go off in my head, but I put it down to the weirdness of the situation and my fear. I had to face the fact that I couldn't just shoot him, and any other scenario was pretty scary.

It was too hard to plan. I didn't have a plan. When people take their guns out, anything can happen; I just had to trust my instincts. It didn't even seem that important if he shot me—at least the goddamn thing would be over. It wasn't being shot that scared me anyway; it was being caught. My mind was racing. It seemed like I had fifty thoughts for every wiggle forward.

Willy moved again, another slight movement, and I stopped and held my breath. I was getting closer, and I was going to have to do something when I got there. I couldn't just watch him all night. I wondered suddenly what Adam would think of this. Not much. Well, fuck Adam. Adam didn't have an answer to this except to hide under his bed. I don't think so.

I realized Adam would be the only one who could figure this out. Both doors locked. Me, no doubt, dead in the woods in some very unpleasant way. Firewood on the floor. Adam would look at it, start futzing with the plug. I could see him shaking his head as he searched for footprints by the side of the house. No one else would even think somebody might do something this stupid. Adam would.

Willy crouched down, and I dropped my head to the ground. Had he heard something? Seen something? I was still fifty feet away. Too far. I waited. Several light-years passed. Willy didn't move again, and I started wiggling forward slowly: bush to bush, tree to tree, zigzagging toward Willy.

I made myself keep going. I knew the temptation would be to stop too soon, and I needed to get closer to have a clean shot if I needed one, but it was hard to keep going—a little like asking myself to crawl within striking range of a rattlesnake. And each foot forward made it more likely I'd hit a trap. Finally I was maybe twenty feet from Willy, and nothing bad had happened. I was close enough to call out and close enough I hoped to nail him if I needed to. I stayed prone on the ground, pulled the gun, and slowly extended both arms in front of me.

I fixed my gunsight on Willy, but I put my trigger finger on the trigger guard instead of the trigger. Training. Gun courses. Don't put your finger on the trigger until you're ready to shoot. I hesitated. It would take too long to move my finger if I needed to shoot. Basic rule. Don't put your finger on the trigger. Don't do it. I didn't.

My breathing was short and rapid. Goddamn it. It's hard to aim if you can't get your breathing under control. You were supposed to squeeze the trigger between breaths. What was I thinking about? I wasn't going to squeeze the trigger. Or maybe I was.

Suddenly Willy stood up, and my finger convulsed on the trigger guard. Had it been the trigger, I'd have shot. I started to move my finger to the trigger, then stopped. Something was wrong. Time stopped. It took my brain a moment or two to process the scene in front of me, but slowly it began to sink in. What was wrong with this picture?

It wasn't Willy. The silhouette was wrong. It just wasn't Willy. It couldn't be Willy. Even with a coat, even from the back, it wasn't Willy. Worse, the figure was small.

Jesus Christ. I put the gun on the ground and closed my eyes for a moment. The only thing I really feared about guns was that I'd shoot a fourteen-year-old some night who was breaking into my house to steal a stereo. Jesus Christ. I picked up the gun again and put it in the fanny pack. My hands were shaking. Tears were starting down my face. Jesus Christ. I didn't even know who was there, but it sure as hell wasn't Willy. And I didn't have a reason in the world to want anyone else dead.

I could have called out to the figure, but whoever it was might have a gun and might shoot in panic. I didn't want to start anything when I didn't know what was going on. I'd think about this later. I'd figure it out later. Right now I just wanted out of this.

I started crawling backward, away from the unaware figure now shifting restlessly, from one foot to the other, still watching the house. My God. I'd almost killed somebody, and I didn't even know who it was. I'd damn near shot somebody, and it would have been totally the wrong person. Willy would have loved that. Maybe that was the trap all along.

I was far enough away now. I got up and headed back the way I came. Who the hell was that? The tears kept falling.

But there was something else. Something about the way that figure moved was familiar. Had Willy enlisted someone I knew to help him? What revenge that would be — to con me into shooting some poor innocent kid, some kid I knew. How smart was Willy? Smart? How smart was I? Maybe the answer was "not very."

17

The figure on the ridge haunted me all weekend. I had dreams in which I pulled the trigger and then walked up afterward to find I'd shot a kid. As I got closer, the child always turned into Jordan. I woke up cold and disoriented with the metallic taste of grief in my mouth that I always got when Jordan was back.

The dreams didn't exactly surprise me. Probably I *had* damn near shot a kid—your basic horrifying possibility. And, too, anything that had to do with a hurt or dying child always brought up Jordan.

Besides, I knew some part of me thought I killed Jordan by going back to work. She died of SIDS at the day care, the first day I went back, and even though I knew infants died of SIDS with medical people standing over them, I had some crazy belief that it wouldn't have happened if I'd been there.

All this was on top of the bizarre business with Marv. It was miserable not being able to call him or stop by his house—I would have loved a little distraction—but his request was so odd I didn't even think about ignoring it.

Something very weird was going on. Surely there were reasonable explanations. Surely there were, like . . . like . . . well, who knows, maybe Willy was living there.

Right.

By eight o'clock Monday morning I was in my office. Actually, I was in my office quite a bit earlier, and by eight I was pacing. Whatever it was with Marv, I'd rather know than hang around wondering.

Ordinarily, he was late for everything except clients. But he wasn't late today. He was exactly on time, which I thought a very bad sign. I looked him over. His clothes were the same rumpled odd assortment of discordant colors as always. This was good. If he'd come in color-coordinated, I'd have panicked.

But his face was different. His face looked like a basset hound. Marv always had a bit of basset hound about him, but today he'd have won best of show.

I wanted to scream at him, "SO WHAT IS IT? CUT TO THE CHASE. WHY CAN'T I GO TO YOUR HOUSE? WHO'S THERE?" But I didn't. Marv's face told me he was miserable, and I started thinking about what he'd done for me when I came over the night I was so freaked out.

"What's up?" I said as casually as possible. There was enough anxiety in my voice to make any psychiatrist reach for his prescription pad, but Marv didn't seem to notice.

He sat down heavily in the chair facing my desk. "Michael," he said slowly. "I need to talk to you about something."

NO SHIT, SHERLOCK. COME ON. COME ON. GET IT OUT. I didn't say it. I just said, "Okay."

He ran his hand over his balding head and said, "I made a mistake, a therapeutic mistake, and I'm afraid it was a serious one."

I KNOW. YOU SAID THAT ALREADY. IT'S NOT GOING TO MATTER, MARV, BECAUSE WE'LL BOTH BE DEAD OF OLD AGE BY THE TIME YOU GET IT OUT. WE'LL BE FOSSIL-IZED. I didn't say that either. I just said, "So tell me."

"It's about Ginger." Oh, Jesus Christ. Maybe I didn't want Marv to tell me after all. I started to open my mouth, then shut it again. Marv had called me. I hadn't called him. He wanted something from me—maybe I should find out what it was before I chickened out.

"Okay," I finally got out.

Marv sighed and shifted in his seat. "She developed a very intense transference. I'm sure you're well aware of what that is like." He glanced up at me, and I immediately felt guilty for sending her to him. What a thing to do to a friend. "But at first it seemed quite stable, and nothing beyond what you had described.

"She would drive by my house frequently at night and on the weekends, just for reassurance I still existed, that sort of thing. She'd drive by in the middle of the night, too, when she couldn't sleep.

"I didn't know any of this at the time. I didn't find it out until . . . well, let me get to the point."

The shouting in my head had stopped once Marv finally got going, but for the life of me I couldn't see where this was headed.

"Unfortunately, she drove by early on the night you came to see me, and she saw your car. Of course, she knew your car because she used to do the same thing to you."

"She did what to me? She drove by my house?" Marv nodded. I automatically put my hand to my mouth. I didn't know that. I knew she drove by the office, and I knew she called my answering machine for reassurance, but I never thought about her going to my house.

"But how did she know where it was?" Surely, he was wrong.

"She followed you. She really is quite clever. The first night she followed you part of the way, then turned off. The next night she was waiting where she turned off previously, and she followed you for another section and turned off. Eventually, she got all the way to your house, and I doubt *anyone* would have realized they were being followed.

"I didn't know any of this, Michael," he said, anticipating my reaction. "Not until right before I called. I pressed immediately until she told me the whole story. I would have told you—the information release she signed when you transferred her is still valid—but I didn't know. In any case, when she saw your car at my house, she immediately got jealous—I'm not sure of whom, since she's attached to both of us—and she came back in the middle of the night to reassure herself that your car wasn't still there. But of course, it was."

"Oh . . ." It was pretty obvious what conclusion Ginger would have drawn.

"Then the next day she saw you in my office. If you remember, you were seeing a client for me. Of course, no one told Ginger anything about why I wasn't there—her appointment was much later that day, and I was back by then."

"Predictably, Ginger decided that we were having an affair. She took the office business as proof. You could go into my office when I wasn't there, and she couldn't. You saw a client in my office, but you wouldn't see her. She saw both of us as leaving her out. I'm afraid what happened fits quite well with the analytic model of the Oedipal complex: She felt totally abandoned."

For once I didn't roll my eyes. Whatever you called it, I

could well believe that Ginger felt abandoned if she thought Marv and I were having an affair.

"So what happened?"

"She decompensated."

"How bad?"

"Quite badly, I'm afraid. She became self-mutilating. She cut her vagina to punish herself for being so worthless and unlovable."

And to punish Marv, I thought, and me.

"She was really in a very difficult state. And that's where I made the mistake."

"Like what?" I said softly. I still didn't get it. What had Marv done that was so bad?

"She was decompensating on the basis of something that didn't exist. That was the irony. We weren't having an affair, so I broke my rule on nondisclosure. I told her we weren't."

He fell silent. What he'd done wasn't wise. It was never wise to share personal information with a client. It changed the relationship, and it turned things into more of a social exchange. But I could see why Marv did it. And on the surface, it didn't seem so terrible.

But then I got it. I knew how things had gone wrong.

"What *did* you tell her?" I said evenly. He would never have been able to stop at just telling her we weren't having an affair. Ginger would have insisted on knowing why I was at his house all night if we weren't.

"I didn't tell her anything about your personal life," he said quickly. This was good, because if he had put the knowledge of Jordan and what she meant to me in Ginger's hands, it would have driven a stake into the heart of my friendship with Marv.

"So what then?" I said. "What did you tell her?"

Marv took a deep breath. "I couldn't lie to a client. I really couldn't. It would have totally destroyed the relationship. And I couldn't tell her the whole truth. Worse, once I had told her something, I felt as though I couldn't leave it dangling. So I told her about Willy."

"Say again?"

"I told her you had a dangerous client who had just been released from prison and that you were quite concerned about it. I told her you had some concern for your safety and that's why you were staying at my house that night."

"Oh, my God, Marv. I can't believe you did that. What'd she say?"

"It's not what she said," Marv replied. "It's what she *did* that's the issue. With hindsight," he said miserably, "it was quite predictable. I'm afraid I gave her a perfect excuse for stalking you. She's been 'taking care' of you ever since."

"Jesus Christ," I said. "Jesus Christ." Ginger was small—no more than five-two and small-boned.

"It was a grievous error, Michael. I am truly sorry. "

"Boy, was it." We both fell silent while I tried to put the pieces together. The world was starting to make sense again, but I didn't like the picture I was seeing.

"Have you seen anything of her?" Marv asked. "Have you noticed anything?"

"Yes and no," I said. "I noticed something, but I had no clue it was Ginger. I almost killed her. She was on the ridge behind my house in the middle of the night—at least I'm betting it was her—and I was lying no more than fifty feet away with a gun in my hands. I thought she was Willy." Marv blinked rapidly and swallowed.

"And a few days before that she almost killed me," I said. She spooked a rabbit—again, I'm assuming it was her. Is she still wearing those spike heels even when she's got on jeans?" Marv nodded. "Then she was the one. She spooked a rabbit,

who spooked my horse, and I ended up wearing the jump."
Marv's face started losing color.

"We have to get her out of this, Marv. And I mean instantly.
Willy's closing in, and I have to know what's him and what's
not. I can't hesitate worrying about whether it's Ginger.
Besides, if Willy's hanging around, he knows she's there too,
and he could easily leave her as a present on my front
doorstep."

Marv looked like he would faint. "He'd do it," I said firmly.
"He'd make a joke about it. That's his style. He'd say something about doing me a favor or too many cooks spoiling the
broth. But she's right between the two of us, and that is
definitely the wrong place to be."

"Willy's 'closing in,'" he said weakly.

"Forget it," I said. "I'm getting good help on it."

Marv looked relieved. Bob Dylan was a genius: "All I suggest
is a man hears what he wants to hear." Willy's way was
amazingly easy. Just tell people what they want to hear, and
they buy it every time.

"So," I went on, "what do we do about Ginger? If we tell her
she's in danger, she'll never leave. She'll stay to 'protect' me.
You can't tell her you lied to her. It'll ruin her faith in therapists, and I doubt she would live right now without one. You
can't even keep her as a client. You've screwed up the
relationship by giving her info she shouldn't have. Besides,
she's crossing boundaries big time."

I was trying to be gentle, but it wasn't coming out that way. I
was getting more pissed the more I thought about it. If he
wanted to self-disclose, why did he disclose about me? Why
not tell her something about himself?

The analytic people would have a field day with this. So
Marv wasn't pissed at me for transferring Ginger? Ha! He'd
given her right back. Or maybe he was so pissed at her, he was

unconsciously trying to get her killed. Or maybe both. When people didn't know they were angry, they did terrible things.

That was the one advantage of being angry all the time and knowing it. I kept an eye on my anger like some sort of boa constrictor in the garden. I tried to keep it focused where it mattered—on people like Willy. But poor Marv had thought he was a gentle soul. And he was—as much as anybody is.

Whatever his motivation for nearly getting both Ginger and me killed, I didn't want to touch it. Marv was a very smart man, and he'd probably go back into analysis over this. He'd be obsessing over his navel for decades, which, God knows, was punishment enough.

We talked till noon. We tried this out and that out and the other out. We canceled a series of clients and appointments, and we refused to take phone calls. The secretaries began to worry about what horrendous crisis was in the air now.

I told him nothing more about Willy. I felt sorry for Marv for what he'd done, but I couldn't change the fact that I no longer trusted him. Under pressure, he'd betrayed me, and that fact stuck in my mind—and I'd bet in his, too. Sure, it could have been worse—he could have told her about Jordan. But somehow that seemed like poor consolation. How close *had* he come to telling Ginger about her? Would he leave her out the next time? I knew the answer rationally, but I no longer knew it in my heart.

Finally, we realized the answer to Ginger was in front of us all the time. It only took four hours for us to see it. At least, maybe it was the answer. It was a good shot, the only one we could think of. But it relied on putting unbelievable pressure on Ginger, and Marv didn't like it. He wanted to cry "mea culpa" and apologize to her on his knees. I told him he could wallow on his own time. Taking responsibility for his stupidity would be the worst thing he could do to Ginger right now.

In the end, he agreed. He couldn't think of another option.

He called Ginger to set up a meeting, and I went off to find Toby and cash in my chit. Great. The only time Toby had owed me in a decade, and it was going to last less than a week. I had no doubts Toby would go for it. He'd love not to owe me, and besides, Toby's blind spot was his narcissism just as Marv's was his anger. If I fed that enough, he'd buy just about anything.

As for my motivation . . . Sure, this one fed the boa a little bit, but at least I knew it.

18

I had to go past Melissa's desk on my way to Toby's office, and she flagged me down. "Michael," Melissa said with relief in her voice, "you're back. Chief Bowman has called twice. He wants you to call him back right away." My life was back to Zeno's paradox. I could only get halfway to wherever I was trying to go.

I almost decided to ignore the call. Getting halfway was costing me. After all, if I hadn't gotten sidetracked on Friday when I was heading in to see Marv, I wouldn't have nearly shot Ginger.

On the other hand, maybe my mistake was in not returning urgent phone calls. This was an urgent phone call, and I was about not to return it.

I sighed. I didn't mind paying my dues and learning my lessons in life. It was just that it wasn't always easy to figure out which lesson you were supposed to learn.

I looked at the relief on Melissa's face and decided to call Adam back. She took it personally when someone was upset because they couldn't reach one of us. Easy for me to say I'll call him later, but she'd be the one on the phone when Adam called back annoyed. Melissa's sole failing was that she was a sponge for stress.

I went to my office and called Adam. He was all business when he came on the line, and I knew from the tone of his voice he had something. "I called Boston and got lucky," he said. "I reached the detective who handled Camille Robbin's case. He's a supervisor now, but he remembers that case clearly.

"There's no question the original incident was genuine. She was a nurse who worked at Mass General. She was abducted from the parking lot and found the next day in a dog kennel in Concord. She had scaled a fence to get in. The owner found her when he came out to see why all the dogs were barking.

"She was nude and had cigarette burns on her breasts and labia. She'd been tortured extensively. She still had duct tape on most of her face. She had torn off just enough to see.

"Not surprisingly, she wasn't in very good shape to talk about it. In fact, she curled up in a fetal position when they tried. The only thing they ever really got out of her was that she had gotten in her car to go home. Her car was found a few days later at a rest area on I-93.

"They never got any more out of her. She was hospitalized at MacClean's, and they went out a couple of times to talk to her, but she went into flashbacks whenever she tried. They tried to follow up after she was released, but she disappeared, and nobody knew where she'd gone. They called the hospital, the neighbors . . . nobody knew where she was."

Nobody, I thought, except Chris.

"The detective was pretty happy to hear from me. They still want to talk to her."

"Why?" I said, surprised. "Are they still working the case?"

It was an awful case, but it was five years ago, and Boston cops are pretty busy.

"It's not so much her case they worried about," Adam said slowly. "It's the two murders they had within a year and a half after that with the same MO."

I tried to get my breathing restarted. Clearly, Camille's attacker had been sadistic, but my worst fear was that he was more than that: a full-blown serial killer. "The first was about eight months later," Adam went on. "A woman was found handcuffed spread-eagled to trees in the woods near Bolton. She had duct tape all over her head and cigarette burns all over her body. Death was by suffocation."

"From the duct tape?" I asked. "Can duct tape do that?"

"Sure," Adam said. "He just finally sealed the nose off after he'd had his fun. Raped, of course. Objects forced up the anus."

"There was another?" I said weakly. Jesus, if this guy was back, Camille was in some serious trouble.

"Same MO," Adam said. "Same cause of death. And then nothing. That's been maybe three and a half years. Nothing's happened since then. They thought either he'd moved on or he was incarcerated for something else, but they sure would like to find him. If he's back, they're thinking he'll start up again."

And maybe Camille was scheduled to be the first this time just like she was last time. "Did they talk to Chris?" I asked.

"Nope. They didn't know anything about him. Camille wasn't coherent, and I doubt she would have mentioned a guy she knew slightly who worked at a local gas station. She wouldn't have had any reason to.

"There's another thing, Michael. They brought Quantico in on this." Which was smart. The FBI profilers at the Behavioral Sciences Unit were very good at profiling offenders. "They pegged the guy as a white male between twenty-five and thirty-one, a local who knew her. He would have finished high school but probably not gone beyond it. He'd have a late model car and work in a trade."

How did they do that? How? I understood where they got the white male from. Ninety-nine percent of serial killers are white males, and killers tend to attack their own race, so since Camille was Caucasian the odds were overwhelming he was a white male. I even knew where they got the age from. Killers tend to attack people within a few years of their age. Camille was probably twenty-eight or so at the time, so they added three on each side. But where did the car come from?

When you asked Quantico questions like that, they just said they did the profiles based on info from interviews with caught killers. But their chief honcho had once looked at a murder scene and said that the killer had a stutter—which it turned out he had. How did he get that out of his interviews with previous killers? I'd be willing to bet he had never interviewed a serial killer in his life who stuttered.

"This is looking very grim," I said.

"I'd say so," Adam said. "As far as they know, she's the only person who's survived an attack. It may be the killer is thinking what they are—if she gets better she may remember something. Or it may be he just has a compulsion to finish the job. They were pretty excited to hear about Chris. He fits their profile, and he knew where she went."

"So what now?"

"Well," he said, "on this end I have an officer watching the house from the park behind it, but I'd like to talk to Camille. I need you with me," he went on. "I don't expect she'd take well to a strange man knocking on her door."

No, I thought, she wouldn't, and neither would Keeter.

"Can we meet at your office?" Adam asked. "I don't want to go to her house in case our perp is watching it somehow."

"No," I said quickly. Too quickly. Adam was silent, and I

tried to think of a reason fast. I couldn't. "Uh, that'll be fine," I said. It killed me to put Adam in a situation where there was even a remote chance Willy might be listening in. But the truth was, if Willy was listening in, what did it matter if it were Adam or a client? It wasn't any better to have Willy listening in on clients.

"I have an appointment with her later today. I'll talk to her then about it. Okay? I'd rather talk to her in person than call her. You're sure you can keep her safe?"

"Sure. I've got somebody practically sitting on her doorstep."

"Who?"

"Jonathan." This was good. Jonathan was an ex-Boston cop who used to work organized crime. He had had a whole lot more experience with violence than most of the local officers.

"Jesus Christ, Adam. It sure is a dicey world out there."

"Take it to heart, sweetheart," Adam replied. "You skirt around the edges of it all the time."

I hung up the phone and just looked at it for a minute. Adam was right. I got over my head more often than I knew. Probably the main difference was this time I knew it.

I turned back toward Toby's office. My head was spinning. One thing at a time. Camille was all right for now, and I still had to get Ginger out of the middle of this thing with Willy. If Ginger ran into Willy, she'd look like Camille did after the abduction. Come to think of it, so would I.

I stopped in the hall. I was upset by what Adam had told me. Camille's perp was an active serial killer who had hung around the area and had every reason in the world to want Camille dead. She was, after all, the only living witness. But I didn't want to convey any upset to Toby. What I was trying to do with him was not all that easy to pull off. I wanted Toby to take exactly the kind of case he screened out.

Toby's caseload—not that he had much of one—was full of the walking wounded. He took celebrity cases, cases referred by other chairmen. He took cases where children of wealthy donors worried about which medical school they'd get into. He took cases where surgeons were tired of medicine and considering a career change. He did not take indigent women who cut their vaginas and would come in on emergency three times a week and make his life hell with one crisis after another. It had been a long time since Toby got up in the middle of the night.

All of which was a terrible shame. Because for all Toby's faults, he was actually a gifted therapist. Clients didn't seem to threaten him in the same way that colleagues outside therapy did, and he lost that narcissistic, need-to-be-a-big-guy edge he carried elsewhere. Without it, he was surprisingly astute and compassionate.

I had heard Toby present cases and had seen clients whom he had treated in a previous counseling. They were clearly the better for the time with him. It angered me all the more that Toby had a gift and wasted it on people so functional they would get better talking to a rock.

I waited a minute and tried to get myself together, then walked up to Toby's secretary. She looked surprised to see me; I was not a frequent visitor to Toby's office—as in, usually I had to be dragged there.

"What's Toby's schedule like today?" I asked. "I need to see him about a client who's in crisis."

She looked at her schedule book. The door to Toby's office was partly ajar, not enough for a visitor to see Toby's desk but enough that Toby could hear whoever was at his secretary's desk. I heard his desk chair scrape on the floor, and then he said, "Michael, come on in."

It occurred to me that maybe Toby wasn't as busy as I

thought. Maybe he sat there eating bonbons while the rest of us ran around like little worker bees. It made me feel better for what I was about to do.

Toby opened the door wide, but his smile was even wider. It made me realize just how unhappy he usually was to see me. I had never gotten a smile anywhere near that wattage out of Toby before.

"I spoke to Lucy," he said as he ushered me to a seat. "She is terribly relieved at that young man's confession. She says it's made all the difference."

"Tell her to forget the apology bit," I said. "It won't mean a damn thing."

"Oh, I don't think she's still considering that," Toby said, laughing. "The confession was enough. That and the fact that it looks like he's going to be thrown out of school. I wouldn't worry about her asking for an apology."

"Good." And it was good. Fake apologies just muddy the water. They put pressure on the victim to say, "That's all right," as though the guy had accidentally stepped on her toe instead of brutally raping her.

"What can I do for you?" he said, and for once I think he meant it.

"Actually," I said, "I need help on a case."

Toby looked surprised and immediately a little pleased. If he could help me out on a case, he wouldn't owe me. And that meant he wouldn't end up in the embarrassing position of having to back me some day when the press was down his throat about me—as had happened before.

"I screwed up a case," I said bluntly. "You know, Toby, I am not that big a fan of analytic theory, but I think there are times when those of us who have moved away from it miss the boat."

Toby nodded vigorously and started to say something, but I

started up again quickly. I didn't want Toby to get off on a diatribe about how analytic theory had been maligned.

"I had a case where I was focusing mainly on the abuse issues," I went on. "And I ignored an increasingly symbiotic transference reaction that eventually reached psychotic proportions."

I hadn't talked that way in a long time, and I just hoped I could remember the language. It was like trying to speak Greek that you learned in high school. Marv would have done a better job on the lingo, but he wasn't manipulative enough to pull this off.

"That's very unfortunate," Toby replied gravely.

"Yes," I agreed. "I became a complete part object, and the client lost all reality testing. Her superego only functioned in a sadistic way, and her ego functioning—never strong at the best of times—became overwhelmed with id impulses." I realized I couldn't remember which particular analytic school Toby belonged to. Was he part of the ego-analytic folks? If so, I'd better cool it on the id. The id was out of favor with those guys.

I looked up. Toby was still nodding, and he had leaned back in his chair and put his fingertips together. Whatever school he was, I must be close enough.

"The client—Ginger—began to cross boundaries. Essentially she stalked me—although I didn't know the full extent of it at the time. I did know she was crossing boundaries enough that I transferred her to Marv in hopes that she might find more stability with a father figure rather than a mother figure." Toby raised his eyebrows. It was unusual to transfer a client.

"But I did not confront her about the boundary crossing—which I now think was an error." This was actually the only thing I'd said thus far that was wholly true. "She transferred readily to Marv—after all, I was only a part object to her—but it turned out the sex of the therapist was insignificant."

Toby gave a slight smile as if to say, "Obviously, dummy," although he wouldn't have phrased it that way. He would have taken ten minutes to say it, but it would have come down to the same thing.

"The client—Ginger—simply put Marv and me together as mother and father figures and is now crossing boundaries with both of us. She has us allied in her mind and feels abandoned and rejected by our so-called alliance."

Toby sighed as if to say, "Amateurs should not mess with these difficult cases." It was okay by me if he said it, except I didn't want to spend the time for him to get it out, so I kept going.

"I really think she needs a more experienced therapist than either of us. I think she needs someone who will set the strictest possible limits on any boundary crossing, and, of course, that's something analytic therapists have always excelled at."

I'd say. Analytic therapists are known for crossing the street to avoid saying "hello" to a client. Fortunately, Toby wasn't *that* orthodox.

Not everything I said was a lie. Analytic jargon aside, Toby was what Ginger needed. She'd exploit any sort of interpersonal exchange, and Toby wouldn't give her anything to hang on to. And whatever else I thought about Toby, he wouldn't tolerate any boundary crossing.

Too, he had the best access of anyone in the building to hospitalization—which Ginger needed periodically. No matter how crowded the inpatient unit was, amazingly, there was always room for the chairman's clients.

"Well," Toby said. "Of course, if I could be of any help . . ."

"I'm sure you could," I said. "Would you consider taking her?"

"Of course," Toby said, as though there had never been a question. Right. As though every day of the week you could get the chairman to take a case from hell—particularly when it was a case where someone might actually kill him or herself: There were potential lawsuits when people killed themselves.

"It's a very difficult case," I said. "She's periodically suicidal."

"I'm happy to help." Well, what could he say after agreeing? What? She's suicidal? I've changed my mind. On the other hand, now he couldn't say he hadn't been warned.

I left quickly, and on the way out I made an appointment for Ginger with his secretary for the next day. I wanted to get out of there and nail this down before Toby came to his senses.

So why did Toby take a case that ordinarily wouldn't get past the secretary? He did it because I told him what a big, important guy he was and how much wiser he was than the rest of us lowly mortals. Give me a boa in the backyard anytime over this narcissistic stuff. It makes people blinder than a bat.

On the way out I thought about it. Toby would buy a dead horse any day. Not because he couldn't stand being alone or he needed anything concrete. He'd buy it because narcissists don't exist without a mirror around. It's not because they love themselves so much. It's because the only time they can see themselves, the only time they feel they have a self, is when they see themselves in the mirror of somebody else's regard. They are whatever the mirror says they are. They have the least sense of self of anybody on the planet.

Toby had paid dearly for that look in the mirror I gave him today. The sad irony of it was, to him it would be worth it.

As I passed Melissa's desk, she said, "Carlotta called. She wants you to call her back. She's at work."

I sat down at my desk and immediately dialed her number. Thank God for women friends. The friendship with Carlotta had always been a haven. I got a small knot in my stomach every time I called Adam: Both of my x chromosomes would start chirping, and I could hardly think with all that dithering about. Talking to Toby was like talking to somebody who saw me as . . . well, a part object . . . somebody who existed only to meet his narcissistic needs. Then there was Marv's betrayal, which just made me appreciate Carlotta all the more today.

Whatever it was, Carlotta and I had differences that made yin and yang look like clones, but who cared? I was at my most warm and fuzzy when she came on the phone.

"Michael," she said dryly. "You are a pain in the butt."

194

"Excuse me? This is what I get for dropping everything to call you back right away?"

"You have cost me more fucking sleep this week."

"Like what? The thing with Willy?" Ginger was still in my mind, and for a moment I was confused about what Carlotta knew and what she didn't.

"Of course, the thing with Willy. What else? There's something else?"

"I'm being chased by the entire Russian navy," I said solemnly.

"This could be true," she said. "Listen, I haven't told Adam yet. That's what I've been obsessing over. I spent the entire week trying to figure out whether to tell Adam that Willy's here—up close and personal enough for you to throw me out of my house."

"Uh-oh," I said. I had completely forgotten she had threatened to tell him. Threatened, hell. Promised was more like it.

"So?" I said. There wasn't any point in arguing. She had decided something.

"I kept thinking you were probably right. It wouldn't do any good, and it would just cause friction between you and Adam. He can't protect you if you won't let him. Besides a fight with Adam would just make it less likely you would call him if you need him."

"Exactly," I said.

"But I decided to tell him."

"What?" I said. "After all this? You were right the first time."

"Yes and no," she said. "I finally decided—it's not that it will do you a damn bit of good if you're determined to get yourself killed—it's that I am not going to have an answer when we're both looking down at your dead body, and he says, 'You knew he was here? And you didn't call me?'"

"I am just not going to live the rest of my life wondering if it would have made a difference. So, I'm having dinner with him tomorrow tonight to talk about it. You want to come?"

"I do not think so." As in how many wild horses would it take? I was pissed, but there was nothing I could do about it. I was not going to control Carlotta. "Look, Carlotta. Do what you need to do. I don't think it's going to help, but, you know, what can I say? In the end, you're going to do what you want to do."

"And so," she said, "are you."

Marv came in and told me he had set up a meeting with Ginger for later in the afternoon. We were planning on seeing her together to present a united front. I had insisted. I was afraid Marv would do the apology thing on his knees if I wasn't there.

I would have just enough time to see Camille at my private practice office and get back. Usually I didn't see private clients when I was at Psychiatry. But sometimes clients were in too much crisis to wait a week between appointments, and for those folks, I sometimes chased back and forth.

As I approached my private practice office, I realized what a mess I was in. How could I go into that office and talk to Camille knowing that Willy might be listening to every word? How could I *not* tell that woman that somebody had some way of listening in?

On the other hand, the thought of telling her a second sadist was running loose, this one listening to her therapy sessions, would put her into orbit. If she wasn't paranoid now, she'd be then. It would shatter any sense of safety and destroy our relationship. What was I supposed to do?

And if this was true for Camille, it was true for all my clients. I had had a full day last Friday, and the fact was, I'd known that Willy *could* be bugging me the whole time. But, I reasoned, I had checked. I had swept the room for bugs between every single client.

That didn't help last time, a little voice inside me said. You swept before the lying little twerp rapist, and Willy had still bugged him.

I swallowed hard. For the first time in my life, somebody could bring me up on ethics charges and be right.

It could be argued—maybe it would be—that I should have closed my practice immediately the moment I had a hint someone might be bugging me. Not a bad argument. But what was I supposed to do with all the folks I saw? I didn't have a caseload of surgeons considering career changes. I had a caseload of traumatized people. Camille was in worse shape than the rest, but nobody on my caseload could be classified as a functional person who would get better talking to a rock.

I could see it now. "Roberta, I know your father tyrannized your life as a child, made you fill in fifteen-minute time sheets for weeks when he was away on business trips, and sexually abused you for eight years, but I need to tell you that a powerful, malevolent male could be listening to your every word. You think you're safe? Not even here.

"Yes, Kiwi, I know your husband is beating the shit out of you, but somebody might be listening to this conversation who is far worse than he is. Somebody might be listening who likes to torture women and children. Would you like to hear some of the things he has described doing to them?"

So I couldn't tell them. But I could have said I was sick and closed my practice down. Or something. The more I thought about it the more I realized I should have done something and now had to do something. But first I had to see Camille. There wasn't anything I could do about the problem this second.

I swept the office again for bugs. It was probably stupid. I had never caught anything with Danny's little bug-sweeping device. But it was the only thing I could do to feel safer, so I did it. I was just finishing when Keeter and Camille showed up, I mean Camille and Keeter. Somehow Keeter always got my attention first. She curled up in her usual spot, on the floor between me and Camille. I couldn't help remembering how she had looked crouched to jump when I walked into Camille's house. Remind me not to crowd this dog. I wrenched my attention away from Keeter and looked at Camille.

I was always surprised at how bad she looked. This morning her hands were shaking and her eyes had a hollow look. I had seen that look before. It meant people were living someplace where nobody should even visit.

I thought briefly of Auschwitz and the descriptions I had read of the blank look that people got as they became more depleted and felt more hopeless. Other inmates learned to recognize that look. It usually meant the person was going to just quit eating and die.

And yet. Although Camille had long ago lost all her emotional fat reserves and had been using up muscle and bone, there was still something left. It wouldn't last forever. Nobody in the known universe was even close to invincible. If something didn't change, sooner or later, the flashbacks or the perp or whatever it was would grind her to a pulp. But she was a marathoner, and somehow I didn't think she was completely beaten yet.

"How are you?" I said gently.

"I'm okay," she said, "I think. Did you talk to the police?"

"I did," I said, "and Chief Bowman wants very much to help you. He called the Boston police to find out more about what happened. Camille, did you ever hear anything more about this guy or any other attacks on anybody else after you left Boston?"

"No," she said. "I never spoke to them again."

"You never read the newspapers or anything?"

"No," she said. "The newspapers are too upsetting."

I noticed she didn't ask me why I asked. She didn't want to know.

"You need to know that Chief Bowman has a very tough, experienced cop watching your house right now. He used to work organized crime in Boston, and I don't think even if the perp is back he can get past this guy."

"He can get past anybody," she said forlornly.

"We don't know that," I said. "Last time he picked on you, he picked on an unarmed woman. He didn't pick on anybody with a guard dog and a cop standing watch."

Camille didn't say anything, but I could tell she wasn't reassured. In her mind, he was larger than life.

"I know this is hard on you," I said, "but I need to know some things about the guy who attacked you. Do you think you can talk about him?"

I hated doing this. It wasn't supposed to be my job to play junior cop. I was supposed to be a therapist. And yet, there were times when I had to use a little common sense. If there was a serial killer after Camille, she wasn't going to be around for therapy if he wasn't caught. And it was going to be a whole lot harder for her to talk to Adam than to me.

"Maybe I could talk a little," she said. "I took extra Haldol this morning."

"You never saw his face, right?" She nodded. "Did he remind you of anybody you knew? Did he sound or move like somebody you knew?"

"No," she said. "He was a stranger."

"How tall was he?"

Camille's hands were shaking worse, and she started twisting a Kleenex, but she kept going. "Small," she said so faintly I almost couldn't hear her. "Not much taller than me."

"How big?"

"Thin . . . wiry . . . and very strong."

"Camille." She had started to drift away when she said "strong."

"Camille, how old was he? And then I promise I won't ask any more questions about him."

Camille focused on the Kleenex she was twisting. "Young," she said. "I don't know how old. . . . His voice was young."

"That's all," I said. "No more questions about him."

That was all I could ask anyway. I couldn't really ask her any questions about whether he reminded her of Chris. I couldn't take the chance she was suggestible and would put the two of them together just because I said it. I couldn't even ask her in the same *session* to describe Chris. I'd have to leave that for another time and ask her to describe several people so she wouldn't know what I was driving at.

But for the first time we had some kind of description of the perp, and the cops in Boston could match that against Chris or anybody else they had in mind. I'd tell Adam about it, and when he met with her maybe he could get a few more details.

Camille agreed to meet with him, but I didn't want to do it today. She could only talk about this a little at a time. We'd done all we could on it today, and Adam would get more information if we waited until tomorrow. It also gave me another excuse to check in with her.

I walked her out after the session and watched her leave. I just had a bad feeling about this. It had changed everything when I realized there might really be someone out there who was still after her. I was still shaken up from Adam's description of what this guy had done to the next two women he got ahold of. Would I have realized he was back sooner if that son-of-a-bitch Willy hadn't been on my tail? Yes, I would have.

That was the problem with people like Willy. They could affect you without laying on a finger. I had started worrying and fretting and orienting everything around Willy from the moment he showed up. In the meantime I couldn't see what was right in front of me. Camille had to ask me how it could be a flashback if it was about the future and not the past. Duh. The poor lady was in the fight of her life, and the only help she had was from an unethical therapist with—currently—the IQ of a gerbil.

20

When Ginger walked in the next morning, Marv and I were sitting quietly on opposite sides of the room. I had suggested we sit on the couch together and hold hands, but Marv didn't appreciate my sense of humor.

Ginger looked tense, and well she might. Marv had only told her on the phone that we needed to talk to her together and that it was important. He hadn't said what about, but Ginger knew it couldn't be good.

She sat down warily and looked from one of us to the other. I began, as Marv and I had agreed. "I want to thank you for coming in and being willing to see us together. Ordinarily we wouldn't meet with you together—if I were the client, I'd feel outnumbered—but this time we thought it was important that you talk with both of us."

Ginger was too anxious to wait. "Why?" she said quickly, although it was pretty obvious that was exactly what I was planning on telling her.

"Give me a second, Ginger. I need to go back first. When

I transferred you, I told you the truth. I told you that I thought a male therapist might be able to help you more than I could. Partly that had to do with the fact that you lost your boundaries with me and were miserable when I wasn't around, and we talked about that part.

"But we didn't talk about the fact that you crossed my boundaries and intruded on my private life. That alone was enough to terminate the therapy. In a way, it already had." Ginger looked surprised. She glanced at Marv for reassurance, but he didn't respond.

"What I'm trying to say is that for a therapist to do a good job, she has to keep her own thoughts and feelings out of the therapy as much as possible. When you become a player in the therapist's private life, she—or he—loses objectivity. The therapist starts responding to you from her or his point of view, rather than simply focusing on yours.

"And I have to tell you honestly, Ginger, having someone over and over again intrude on time that's supposed to be private kicks up a lot of bad feelings in the therapist. All that has to be put aside to be neutral and objective and supportive. If the intrusions go on long enough, the day comes when the therapist just has too many bad feelings to keep them out of the therapy. I lost faith that I could help you, not *only* because you had lost your boundaries with me, but because you were stepping on mine.

"I should have told you all that. I didn't because you were going through such a hard time that it seemed like it would just be another rejection. But by not telling you, in a way, I set you up to lose Marv too. Because you started doing the same thing with him that you did with me.

"Do you understand what I mean?"

"Sure," Ginger said angrily. "You're telling me Marv's kicking me out too."

"Not exactly," I said. "It's true that you've crossed too many boundaries with Marv to keep seeing him, and it's true you've been stalking me again . . ." I used the term deliberately, and Ginger exploded.

"I did not stalk you. I was helping you. Marv told me about that guy."

"Ginger, what guy? There's always a guy getting out of jail. I've worked with six trillion offenders. There's always somebody mad at me. It's not your job to take care of me. All you can do by stalking me is lose your own supports."

"I was just trying to help." Ginger started crying.

"I'm sorry, Ginger, but it doesn't help. It doesn't help to have somebody on a cross-country jumping course scaring my horse. It doesn't help to have somebody standing in the woods staring at my house."

Ginger started crying harder and lay down on her side on the couch. She pulled up her knees and started rocking.

"I'm sorry, Ginger, but I'm not going to do you any favors if I set you up to do this again."

Marv held his hand up to stop me. "Ginger," he said softly, "How are you feeling right now?"

"I feel like shit," Ginger said. "I feel like total shit. This has happened to me all my life. No matter what I do, I'm always wrong. I've never been able to do anything right. I should just die."

I gave Marv a look. The look said, "Don't get her going or she will lock into that for the next ten light-years." It was true. Ginger was winding up. When she felt desperate, she got manipulative as hell. And she had that strange business where if she could make us feel bad, she felt good. It was as if depressed affect was some kind of ball that got passed back and forth. Ginger wouldn't have to feel her own emotions if she could just give them to us.

I wasn't biting. Transferring her feelings and glomming on to us wasn't going to help Ginger. And it was going to make me want to throttle her.

"Ginger," I said. "You're still assuming we're going to throw you out."

"You are," she said. "I know you are."

"Actually," I said, "we're not. We are transferring you, but it is to the most experienced therapist in the department."

Ginger paused but didn't speak. She was still lying on her side.

"It's true," I said. "We both feel you need someone with more experience than both of us. So sit up, if you can, because you need to hear about this and make a decision about whether you want to try it."

"Who is it?" Ginger said. Then she sat up slowly.

"The Chairman of Psychiatry," I said. "Dr. Toby Cantwell. He's been in the field longer than either Marv or me, and he's, well, he's something special. Wouldn't you agree, Marv?"

I shouldn't have said it. I could tell by the look on Marv's face that he thought I was being flippant. The truth was, I wanted to say something positive about Toby, but I was so conflicted about him, everything I thought of was double-edged. Which was stupid, because Ginger would only see the therapeutic side of Toby, which I didn't have any concerns about.

Marv turned to Ginger. "He really has had more experience than anyone else in the department. He can't fix things *for* you, Ginger, any more than we can, but if anybody can help, I suspect he can."

Ginger said, "He'll probably just kick me out too," and slumped back in her seat.

"He might," I said. "And that's why we're having this meeting. Ginger, you really need to understand this. Dr.

Cantwell isn't going to tolerate your crossing his boundaries any more than Marv and I will. And he won't tolerate your crossing ours either. So here's the deal.

"Tomorrow, at four o'clock, you have your first meeting with Dr. Cantwell. Hopefully, it will go well, and it will be the beginning of some healing for you.

"But remember this, if you cross anybody's boundaries—if you hide in my woods, if you start doing drive-bys at Marv's, if you start calling Dr. Cantwell's house—then the next Tuesday at four o'clock, someone else will sit in his office. And I won't take you back and neither will Marv."

The room fell silent. It was a harsh thing to say. It was really an ugly thing to say. Ginger was completely still. She was genuinely afraid of loss, and I had just deliberately threatened her with it. Maybe it wasn't ethical. All I knew was that being threatened with loss wasn't nearly the tragedy in Ginger's life that running into Willy would be. And hiding in my woods was the easiest way to run into Willy.

I wouldn't talk about other things after that. I kept coming back to the decision she had to make. If she wanted to see Toby, she could not stalk *any* of us. If she couldn't do that, she'd have to go elsewhere for therapy.

It would work, I thought. For a while. But it wouldn't last. Ginger would behave herself for a few weeks or months, and then she'd start up again. What I had done was just buy a little time. But I had a feeling this would all be over by the time Ginger started in again. Either I'd find Willy before then, or he'd find me.

21

The phone rang around eleven. I was already in bed and not inclined to answer it, but when I heard Adam's voice on the answering machine I changed my mind. Adam said Camille was freaking out—screaming again—and Jonathan was absolutely positive no one else was in the house. He didn't tell me how Jonathan knew for sure no one had been hiding in there before he got there, but my guess was he had taken a look around while Camille was in therapy.

In any case, Jonathan insisted no one had entered since he got there, and—however he knew—he was sure no one was in there already—so there was no way around the conclusion that this time, anyway, whatever was going on was in Camille's head.

I agreed to drive in. I didn't really want to, and I didn't usually do that kind of thing. If I came in every time Camille got upset, I might as well pull up a camper on her lawn, but I could hardly say no. Small town police forces don't have enough people to do a twenty-four-hour stakeout, and I knew what a drain it was on Adam's resources to do this. So when he asked for help, I just said, "On my way."

But why? I wondered on the way in. Adam had seen lots of people upset and freaking out. Why was he dragging me in? I picked up the car phone and called him. I was getting used to the damn car phone. Worse, I was getting dependent on it, which, of course, was the problem with owning. You don't really own anything; things own you.

He picked it up on the first ring. "Adam," I said, "I'm on my way in, and I don't want you to misunderstand this. I don't mind going in, but I am curious why you thought it was important for me to see her tonight."

He didn't hesitate. "Somebody has to check out the screaming. Jonathan was concerned enough that he called me at home. He says it sounds completely out-of-control, and, already, the station is getting calls from the neighbors.

"Jonathan thinks nobody else could have gotten in there, but the whole thing is bothering him enough that he wants to go in and check it out, anyway. I think he's concerned she's going to hang herself, or maybe that damn dog we ran into last time is going to shoot her while Jonathan's standing outside twiddling his thumbs.

"I told him to hold off. You know a strange man can't just show up at her door, and there's no point in my going: She's never even met me. You're the only one she knows."

"Not a problem," I said. I couldn't argue with his thinking. One of Adam's strengths was that he thought things through under pressure. He didn't just rush in like some people I knew. "I'll go see what's going on."

Ten to one Camille was just horribly upset. In suicide assessment you always have to figure out the difference in "perturbation" and "lethality." Some of the people who are the most upset aren't always serious about dying, and some of the people who are serious about dying are deadly calm. But

Jonathan didn't know Camille well enough to read her. And if they didn't check it out and something happened, everybody involved would be traumatized. Not to mention that Camille might be dead.

I pulled into her driveway and rolled down the window. I couldn't hear anything. The yelling had stopped. That doesn't mean anything, I reminded myself. It stopped last time too, and Camille was sitting in the house popping Haldol and still insisting she heard the perp. But silence is creepier than noise, and I found my heartbeat quickening. There was always the chance someone like Camille would hang herself or something, and the thought that I could be the one to find her unnerved the hell out of me.

I got out of the car and stared at the house. The lights were on, and there was no sign anything was wrong. Keeter wasn't barking. But that didn't mean anything. She had been trained to stay silent and ambush an intruder. Remind me, I thought one more time, not to crowd this dog.

I looked toward the park. No sign of Jonathan. Well, he was out there somewhere, but it looked like I wasn't going to get a welcoming committee.

I walked up to the doorway and knocked, but I didn't wait for a reply. "Camille," I said. "It's Michael. Are you all right?" How many times was I going to walk up to her silent house after a report of screaming? But even if it was a thousand, I'd bet each and every time I'd still be afraid something really bad had happened to her.

"Michael," a faint voice answered very close to the door. I let my breath out. Whatever was going on, she was definitely alive.

"Could you open the door, Camille?" I asked. "It really is me, and I'm alone."

Camille opened the door a crack and peered out. Then she closed it and pulled the chain off. She opened it wide, and I walked in. I immediately looked for Keeter. There she was, crouched on the floor, ready to spring. She didn't look that much friendlier than last time.

"Uh, do you think you could do something about Keeter?" I asked. Camille glanced at her and then made a hand signal. Keeter reluctantly got up and walked over to her, but she kept her eye on me the whole time.

"He was here," Camille whispered. She looked like she was barely able to hold it together. Her pupils were dilated, and her eyes were open so wide I could almost see the whites all the way around. Uh-oh. It was beginning to look like paranoia after all. The only times I had ever seen the whites all around the eyes was in paranoids.

"Camille," I said. "Let's sit down and talk about it."

She took me to the living room, and I sat down, but Camille didn't. She was so agitated she couldn't. She rocked back and forth from one foot to the other. She looked like she might start pacing.

"How do you know he was here?" I asked.

"I heard him." She was still whispering. "He said he was coming for me soon. He said I'd die this time. He said . . . he . . ."

"Whoa, Camille, I know you thought he was here, but it couldn't have been real. There's a police officer outside named Jonathan, and he's been here all afternoon. He says no one could have gotten in. Do you want to talk to him?"

"No," she said quickly. "He's outside?" She went to the window and looked through the blinds. I had the bad feeling she was getting Jonathan and her attacker confused.

"Camille," I said. "The *police* are outside. The perp isn't."

"I know," she said turning around and looking all around the room. "He's here." Even though I knew he wasn't, the hair started to stand up on the back of my neck.

"Your mind is playing tricks on you," I said firmly. "He can't be here."

"He never comes out when you're here," she said. "He always waits. Will you stay? Please?"

"I can only stay for a while," I said. Oh, Jesus, what were the ethics of this? I was not only at a client's house involved in her private life, I couldn't get out.

"Please, Michael. Please don't leave me alone with him. Please don't." She had turned to face me, and her voice slid into pleading as she spoke.

It was painful to hear her beg, but the fear was so strong I doubt she even noticed she was begging. What, I wondered again, were the ethics of staying? On the other hand, what were the ethics of leaving?

"I would be all right," she said, "if you stayed—just for tonight. I could maybe even sleep. . . . I can't sleep here alone. . . ." Her voice trailed off.

What were my options? I could hospitalize her. I had no doubt they'd admit her in her present state, but where would that lead? Nowhere. She'd end up owing a ton of money to the hospital. We'd have another six-hour fight over Keeter, and Camille would be out tomorrow.

She had no friends or family I could call. It was too late to find a private duty nurse. There were no volunteer organizations I could think of to call, plus I wouldn't put a volunteer in with someone who might be paranoid. Paranoids are not too stable.

On the other hand, staying at a client's house is so unethical they hadn't bothered to put it in the code of ethics. It is one of those "duh" items. But what choice did I have? She wouldn't make it through the night alone in this state. And she wasn't Ginger. I didn't think she'd start manipulating around this.

"All right. I'll stay tonight," I said carefully. "I will sleep on the couch and leave early in the morning. And tomorrow we will make arrangements for a private nurse to stay with you — agreed?" Camille nodded vigorously. But then if I'd said, "I'll stay if you'll jump out of a ten-story window tomorrow," she'd also have agreed.

"Camille, you really need to understand this. I will not do this again."

"I know," she said. "I won't ask." And I believed her.

I sighed. I did not want to be there. I wanted to be home. I needed some time away from the world each and every day. Not to mention that I was acutely uncomfortable spending the night in a client's house. But there was no point in bitching, I was stuck.

I called Adam to tell him. He was apologetic for putting me in that position. I had my own apologies to make. It was beginning to look like the perp was in Camille's head after all.

I went out to the car and took off my fanny pack and locked it in the trunk. I'd been carrying it nonstop lately, but I wasn't going to go to sleep in Camille's house and leave a loaded gun lying around. The risks of a loaded gun around Camille outweighed the benefits. I didn't even want to think how I'd feel if she killed herself with my gun. Not to mention that if she got ahold of it in the night and had a major flashback, she could just as easily decide I was the perp and shoot me.

I got my travel bag and went back in. I found my toothbrush and my nightshirt, but decided I'd sleep in my clothes. It was bad enough to be in a client's house; I was not going to run around in my pj's. I spread out the blankets Camille provided on the couch.

My one fear was that Camille was so wired she would stay awake all night and keep me up. Once the nervous system goes on red alert like hers had, it doesn't usually settle down very fast. But after Camille knew I was staying, she started losing steam.

Her energy drained quickly, and she soon lost all of her agitation. Once she let go of the fear-energy, there didn't seem to be anything else holding her up. I told her firmly to go to bed—and take Keeter with her. I'd be in the living room on the couch, and I promised not to go anywhere.

Camille insisted on leaving the door open to her room, which I wasn't too happy about. I had fantasies of waking up and finding I was nose to nose with a snarling rottweiler. It would have been nice if the couch had had a top bunk.

It didn't take long before I was drifting off. I wondered sleepily if Adam had called off Jonathan. If this one was in Camille's head, probably the other ones were too. Everything seemed turned upside down lately. I was trying to protect myself from Willy, but I had almost shot a client instead, and I'd yet to see Willy, who was hovering out there somewhere in Never-Never Land. I was sleeping at a client's house; try to explain that to Ginger who—dear God—I hoped wouldn't drive by. Marv and I had punched holes the size of golf balls in our friendship. How easy would it be to repair that? In the meantime, the only way I could get near Adam was to bring him a police problem. I didn't want Adam *in* his police uniform; I wanted him *out* of it.

I could start with the top buttons. One at a time. As the buttons opened I could run my fingers through the soft, curly hair on his chest. Somewhere around that taut stomach I'd run out of hair—briefly. As I kept going lower his breathing would change. I loved the way it deepened as his . . . interest . . . grew. I was smiling as I drifted off.

I was dreaming that I was facing ethics charges in the World Court in the Hague. The prosecutor was walking toward me when suddenly, he turned into Willy. He got very close to me and started whispering, almost hissing, in my face.

I woke in the dark, disoriented and confused with my heart rate doing 80 miles an hour. It took me a minute to realize where I was. It took me another minute to get the dream out of my head. I could still hear him whispering and another sound too, a sort of whimpering.

I couldn't get the whispering to stop. Jesus, what a dream. I sat up and looked around. And then I stopped breathing. I was wide awake, and I could still hear a man whispering, almost hissing. The whimpering was Camille.

I hit the deck and crawled around behind the couch while I tried to figure things out. I was wide awake now, but still confused. At first I couldn't even tell where the voice was coming from—and I couldn't begin to figure out how he had gotten in, with Keeter on the inside and Jonathan on the outside. Maybe Jonathan had left after I called Adam.

I tried to remember where I'd put my fanny pack and realized I had left it in the car. Great. I'd been carrying my gun to the bathroom lately, but I hadn't brought it into Camille's house.

Where was the goddamn phone? I had used it once. I remembered it was cordless. So where had I put it? I couldn't remember. The room was dark now, and nothing looked familiar. Oh, shit. I had handed the phone back to Camille. I didn't have a clue where it was, and I couldn't see Jack shit.

I could yell. If Jonathan was still outside, he'd hear me. But if the perp was in here, Jonathan probably wasn't out there. And what a chance to take. If Jonathan wasn't outside, calling him might turn out badly. Jesus, the perp had probably walked right by me while I was asleep. Had he seen me? Did he know I was here? If not, where did he think that car came from?

Keeter, you bitch. Go after the bastard. She must know him. That has to be it. I stopped and listened again. I could try to make it to the car and get the car phone, but I didn't even remember if it would work without the car being turned on, and I'd have to leave Camille alone.

First, I had to find out where he was. I started crawling toward Camille's room. The sound was coming from in there. I crawled forward expecting any minute to find a gun the size of a canon pointed at my head, but the voice just kept going. What was he saying? I was close enough to hear, and I dropped down to listen.

"Ah, your clitoris—what a juicy little morsel. I'll give you a choice. A lighted cigarette? A scalpel? That might be best for you. Once I cut it off, it won't hurt anymore. Except, of course for the gaping wound. Maybe pliers. But I'd like to save those for your nipples. You'll have to choose which instrument. If you don't choose, I'll just cut off your fingers, one joint at a time, until you change your mind."

Oh, boy. Verbal torture. Camille started to wail. The perp's voice didn't change at all. But that was what had always struck me about sadists. They talk about torture like everybody else talks about going to the grocery store. Sadists all have that strange flat lack of feeling in their voices.

The sound from Camille was rising, and it began to drown out the perp. Soon she'd be screaming incoherently. Who could blame her? A big part of me wanted to scream too and head for the front door. Maybe I should. If I could get to a phone in time, Adam might just catch the son-of-a-bitch.

I was almost at the door to Camille's room. I crawled to the wall next to it and looked around the corner into her room. I wanted to see where he was first. My eyes had adapted to the dark, and I looked around. I could see Camille sitting up in bed with her hands on her cheeks. Even in the dark I could see she was shaking. I could see Keeter lying beside the bed, but I couldn't see the perp. Where was he hiding? The room wasn't that big.

I paused trying to figure out which way to go. I took a deep breath and started crawling slowly forward. I could barely hear him talking under Camille's wailing. I crawled forward, inches at a time, and looked all around the room. I could hear him, but I couldn't see him. I inched toward the closet, but stopped when I realized the voice wasn't coming from there.

Finally, I got it. I really got it. I stood up and walked over to the lights and flipped them on. Camille didn't even notice. Keeter did, and she looked at me like maybe she'd finally found the source of the problem. I walked back into the living room and turned on the lights there. There wasn't anybody in either room, but the voice just kept going.

I found the phone and called Adam at home. He answered immediately. "Adam," I said. "I'm at Camille's. Can you hear me?"

"Barely," he said. Camille was sobbing and screaming. She was in a full-blown flashback and was begging the perp not to hurt her anymore.

"I think you'd better get over here," I said. "I've figured out the problem. There's no perp here, but there is a voice. There is definitely a voice."

"On my way," he said.

I walked back into Camille's room. I wasn't going to look for the tape recorder. Everything was evidence now, and I knew enough to keep my mitts off. "Camille," I said, "it's Michael." I walked around the side of the bed farthest from Keeter and held out my hand. "Come on, we're leaving." It would have been easier if I could have shut the goddamn recording off.

"Camille," I said, again. "It's Michael, we're leaving." She turned toward me. "Don't let him hurt me, please," she whimpered. "I won't," I said. In the distance I could hear the sirens starting.

"We're leaving. Let's go."

"But . . . he . . ."

"You're not tied," I said loudly to drown out that incessant voice. "You don't have any tape on. It's over. Let's go. We're going over to Harvey's house." I held out my hand again.

This time Camille slowly took it. She was half in this world and half in another. Keeter came around my side of the bed and looked at me suspiciously. No wonder she wasn't any help. What's a dog supposed to do with a tape recorder?

Camille got up slowly, and I put my arm around her and walked her out of the room. Tears were running down her cheeks, and I could feel her shoulders heave with convulsive sobs, but she had stopped screaming. The whole thing reminded me of somebody Adam had walked out of a gym not so long ago—me.

The voice got fainter as we moved through the living room. I opened the front door in time to see the red lights coming down the street. Adam lived a little farther out, and the police cars had beaten him in. Harvey came out of his house, and I asked him to take Camille to his house, I'd be right back. I walked back into Camille's house just as the police cars were pulling up. I just wanted to hear that voice one time without anybody screaming. I thought I knew it somehow. I walked into the bedroom and listened.

Son-of-a-bitch, I thought, when I realized who it was. Son-of-a-bitch.

22

By the next day, it was all over. The police found the tape recorder that the son-of-a-bitch had hidden in the bed. It was not a simple business: It was attached to a device that caused it to start randomly and rewind automatically when the tape was over. Since Camille was the only one there, she was the only one who ever heard it.

It was a custom job, not the kind of thing you could go out to Radio Shack and buy. It took a clever fellow to set it up for random play, but that was hardly a surprise. Willy was always a clever fellow.

Adam put out an APB on Willy on the strength of my recognizing his voice. But since he could easily have hit the road by now—leaving me to wonder and Camille to suffer—we all knew it might take a while to track him down, if ever.

Camille was staying at Harvey and his wife's house for a few days. She hadn't wanted to go back home alone, and Harvey and Lenore had gallantly offered her a place. I suspected they would shortly regret their kindness or impulsiveness. It is more than a little difficult to deal with someone suffering from PTSD, and Harvey didn't much like dogs.

In the meantime the police were going to continue quietly watching Camille's house. Willy's equipment was there. Maybe he'd come back to check it or remove it or whatever.

I had gone home shortly after Adam arrived. He knew about Willy getting out of prison, and he knew all about Camille, so there was nothing I *had* to tell him that night. I did have a whole lot more to tell him—Willy and the e-mail and the bugging of my office and all that. But it would be better, I thought, to tell him in the privacy of his office in the morning.

I didn't relish the exchange—I had promised to tell Adam if Willy contacted me, and I hadn't done it—but I was too damn tired to get into it in the middle of the night. Tomorrow, I decided. I would tell him tomorrow. That would still be in time to head off Carlotta and in plenty of time for whatever help it would give in catching Willy.

But when morning came, I hung around for a while. I would tell him; I had to. But first I needed a little time to recharge my own batteries.

I made some coffee and headed for the deck. It was a crisp spring morning, and I put on the bathrobe Carlotta had given me for Christmas. It was made from Turkish terry cloth and was luxuriously thick and soft. It wasn't the sort of thing I would ever have bought for myself: mostly I sleep in T-shirts and avoid single-purpose items like the plague.

But Carlotta had known me better than I knew myself. It was a licking-your-wounds robe, and I frequently had wounds to lick. It was the thing to wear when you missed the big shot at the buzzer, when you lost the case you should have won, or when a kid you fought for went back to an abusing parent—although there wasn't enough terry cloth in the world to help that. It was what I instinctively reached for today, when I had to face the fact that coming to see me had made Camille worse.

Camille had come into my life with active PTSD from running into one of nature's little aberrations: a full-blown, card-carrying, soul-dead sadist. She had been in awful shape, but not nearly as bad as she was now. If she hadn't met me, Willy would never have stalked her and harassed her and she would never have had the many flashbacks he had caused. She had deteriorated to the max, and that wouldn't have happened without his help. And the problem was, he would never have crossed her threshold if she hadn't crossed mine.

If I tried to tell Carlotta or Adam how miserable I felt about bringing Camille a gift like Willy — not that I was going to — all I'd get back was that it wasn't my fault. As if that helped. People are dolts, myself included.

For years, I hadn't understood why rape victims kept insisting it was their fault. If they hadn't been walking down the street at seven o'clock at night, if they hadn't worn a skirt above the knee, if they hadn't been wearing high heels, it never would have happened.

I finally got it. What would I rather believe — that I had some control and could keep it from happening again by changing a hemline? Or that it could happen anytime, anyplace, no matter what I did? Helplessness is never a plus.

And I also felt helpless. I *was* helpless in this case. I had never intended to let Willy loose on Camille. I hadn't even realized it was a possibility. And that just made everything worse. If they didn't catch Willy, he would inflict a sense of helplessness on me I'd have trouble living with. He could come back and do something — something new and nasty — to anyone I knew, anyone I cared about, anyone I treated.

I really did have to talk to Adam. Maybe he could figure out some clue from Willy's e-mail, about how he got access to my office. If there was anything at all in Willy's behavior that would help catch him, I needed to be sure Adam had it. If Adam didn't catch Willy, sooner or later Willy would strip away any sense of efficacy I had. And I didn't even want to think about the amount of destruction he'd leave in his wake.

I got up reluctantly. There was something soothing in the robe and the stream and the sunlight, and the rest of the day wasn't going to measure up. I'd have to call Adam from the office and arrange a time to talk about this. Necessary but painful. There was the small issue of betraying his trust by lying to him. But first, Camille was coming in, and I had to get there in time to sweep the room for bugs before she came.

I drove in preoccupied with the strange way things work. Hemingway was no fool. Nobody is an island no matter how much they want to be. What would it take? I had moved to an isolated house in the country, given up on any kind of normal social life, thrown away most of my possessions, and I was still a sitting duck.

I knew what it took. You had to not give a shit about any other human being if you wanted to be invulnerable to the kind of thing Willy had pulled. Son-of-a-bitch had just set the price higher than I could pay.

I got out of the car and reluctantly took off the fanny pack. As long as Willy was out there I still wanted to wear it nonstop, but I had a few rules about guns. I never took one into my office because I saw children there. Children and guns are a bad combination. I had counseled adults who had dead children because they had hidden their guns in one locked drawer and their bullets in a different one and their kids still got into them. I put the fanny pack in the trunk and closed it, feeling nude and vulnerable without it.

I walked in, took the bug detector out of the drawer, and scanned the room with renewed vigor. The last thing I wanted to do at this point was to tip Willy off that we knew what he was up to. But again I found nothing, nothing, and more nothing.

I looked at the scanner. There was one possibility I hadn't even thought about. What if the damn thing was broken?

Oh, Jesus, what a mess that would be. I sat down and tried to think. There were other possibilities. I hadn't heard from Willy since the e-mail about that lying little twerp. For all I knew, he could be a thousand miles away. He'd scared the bejesus out of me and left his little device with Camille. No doubt he had hung around to savor her deterioration for a while, but for how long? I really didn't have any way of knowing if he was even still around. Playing a few minutes at a time, a few times a day, his recorder would run for weeks without needing new batteries.

The scanner could be working fine. Willy could just be gone.

That, of course, was the worst-case scenario I had been mulling over all morning. He could be running blitzkrieg campaigns, wreaking havoc and then disappearing. If he stayed away for months or years until everything died down, he could resurface safely and start all over again. If he kept doing that, he could make me miserable for years and years without getting caught. Or worse, he could lull me into thinking all he was going to do was harass me.

As I remembered, Alexander the Great did something like that with some elephants once upon a time. He had marched up and down the river at random times in the night until the enemy quit even getting up to see the parade. Then one night he crossed the river.

I stared at the phone. I should call Adam. I had left myself enough time to go by and talk to Adam. This was harder than I thought. Maybe betraying Adam's trust was kind of a big deal to me, and I had well and truly done that. Who said you couldn't develop new skills in your forties. First, lying, now procrastination. Pretty soon I'd be into passive aggression—which had always eluded me before.

The phone rang, and I jumped. If it was anybody but Adam I was going to be relieved.

"Michael, do you have time to see us today?"

"Lorraine?" Lorraine was a single mom with three small boys. She tended only to call in a crisis, and then she needed to be seen that second. In between, there was no point in setting appointments: She canceled and failed to show and left messages that everything was fine.

In Lorraine's world, problems were ignored until they couldn't be. I'd made my peace with the fact that I wasn't going to change her disorganized and sometimes abusive parenting style, but maybe I could keep the situation as stable as possible—at least I could try to keep her from killing any of her offspring.

As if reading my mind, Lorraine added, "So help me, God, I'm going to kill the little bastard this time."

"How about right now?" I said looking at my watch. Camille wasn't due for an hour, and Lorraine didn't live far.

"The sooner the better," she said and hung up.

Thank you, Lorraine. It was a short reprieve, but maybe it would give me time to figure out why I was so upset about fessing up to Adam. And it was a situation where I would have postponed talking to him even if I had wanted to.

To my surprise, Lorraine showed up with her eldest, six-year-old Daniel, in tow. Usually it was Damion, her two-year-old, or Donald, her three-year-old, who had fought or broken something or disappeared or whatever. Lorraine was one of those moms who thought it was cute to start all her children's names with the same letter.

"He's a goddamn pervert," she said, completely ignoring

223

Daniel, who looked more dejected than I had ever seen him. He had reluctantly followed his mother into the waiting room and stood by the door as if ready to bolt.

"Whoa," I said. "Let's let Daniel sit here in the waiting room and play for a minute while we talk." This was not a mother I wanted to see *with* the child. Lorraine's idea of talking to her child was to heap emotional abuse on his head. "But one thing I know," I said looking at Daniel. "Daniel is not a pervert."

Daniel looked slightly relieved. Jesus, the self-fulfilling prophecies people lay on their children. I gathered up some Play-Doh and Magic Markers and paper and set Daniel up in the waiting room. I smiled at him. "Your mama is upset," I said, "and she says things that aren't true when she's upset. I know you're not a pervert"—whatever Daniel thought that was. "Let me talk with her for a few minutes, and we'll figure things out." I walked back into my office and closed the door calmly. Lorraine was sitting on the couch, looking so angry she was one step short of one of her fits-of-screaming-rage attacks.

"Goddamn it, Michael," she said. "Every time I try to do something nice for them, they spoil it. They've broken every fucking toy they own. So why do I bother? Don't think my son-of-a-bitching father ever bought a goddamn thing for me. But do they appreciate a thing I do? I was so pleased he hadn't broken this one. What a joke!"

She reached into a bag and brought out something that looked like a miniature radar dish attached to a handle that looked like a joystick. There were wires hanging down and earphones. She threw it on the couch.

"Slow down," I said sitting down very slowly. I move slowly and I talk slowly when people are upset. People respond to body English more than they know. The temptation is almost overwhelming to match their agitated tempo, but that just makes things worse. "I don't have a clue what you're talking about, but one thing I know for sure, if you keep calling Daniel a pervert, sooner or later he's going to believe you."

"So it's my fault if he turns into a pervert?" she said. "Why is everything always my fault?" Lorraine sounded like a petulant eight-year-old, which in some ways she was.

"Lorraine, calm down," I said gently. "All I'm saying is your children listen to you more than you know. Tell the truth. Somewhere in your soul, don't you still believe you're what your father said you were?"

"What's that got to do with it?" she said.

"Everything," I said. "Do you want Daniel to carry around the idea he's a pervert? No matter what he's done, he's still six years old, for Christ's sake."

"He's a six-year-old pervert," she said. "You know, they suck me in every time. I should have known. Do you know why he hadn't broken this toy? Do you know why? Because he'd discovered he could peep on the neighbors with it, that's why."

"Peep on the neighbors?" I said, surprised. It was certainly a new behavior for Daniel, as far as I knew.

"Yes, peep on the neighbors. You know how our houses are so close—well, you don't, but if my neighbor sneezes I get a cold. Anyway, Daniel's window is just a few feet from our neighbor's bedroom window."

"And he was peeping on him?"

"Yes, he was. I came in to check on him. To tell you the truth, he was too quiet. Usually, he's calling me every two seconds. He wants water. He wants a story. He has to go to the bathroom. He's scared. He acts just like a big baby. But the last few nights, he's gone to bed just like that. No water, no nothing.

"The first couple of nights I was so tired, I was just grateful. I mean, Damion and Donald were still up every two seconds, so it wasn't like I got to sit down. Then I began to wonder.

Daniel hadn't seemed sick, but I started thinking maybe he was. I went in to check on him, and there he was, sitting at the window in the dark, peeping on the neighbors."

"Lorraine, let me ask you some questions, okay? To try and sort out what's going on. Have you ever caught Daniel doing anything sexual?"

"Sure. He used to put his bottle on his you-know-what and rock on it when he went to sleep."

"When he was a toddler, right?"

"Well, he hasn't had one since then."

"Most kids play with themselves."

"Not mine."

"You've got to trust me a little bit, Lorraine. There's a big difference in kids doing things you don't like and being a pervert. Does Daniel play with himself around other children or in school or anything like that?"

"Oh, no. I'd have beat the shit out of him if he'd done anything like that."

"Has he done anything sexual with other kids that you know about?"

"My God, no."

"Has anything happened, anything at all to make you concerned about Daniel and sex?"

"You mean before this?"

"Yes."

"No, but this is bad enough."

"Actually, to be honest with you—and I say this knowing you'll find it hard to believe—it isn't."

"It isn't? This isn't bad enough? What are you talking about? If the neighbors had caught him, he could have been arrested."

"Not at six, he couldn't. Lorraine, kids are curious about sex. You may not like it, but it's true. Weren't you? Don't you remember being curious about sex as a kid?"

"Me? I knew more than I ever wanted to know about sex by the time I was six, thanks to my son-of-a-bitching father."

"Well, Daniel doesn't—thanks to the fact that he's had better parenting than you did. He's just curious."

"Well, he shouldn't have been doing it." Some of the wind had gone out of Lorraine's sails, but in her mind she couldn't back down.

"True enough. But normal kids do a lot of things they shouldn't do. It doesn't make them perverts. Look, it's good news. Right? What, you want to be raising a pervert? Or you'd rather be raising a normal kid who gets into stuff he shouldn't?"

There was silence. I probably didn't entirely persuade her, but on the other hand at least she calmed down. Later, she even looked a little sheepish when she faced Daniel in the waiting room. Lorraine called her children every name in the book when she was upset, but when she calmed down, she was usually sorry. There were even times she apologized, which wasn't nearly as good as not doing it in the first place.

I didn't get that much time with Daniel; I spent most of my time calming Lorraine down and getting her to see that, maybe, she was a bit sensitive about sex, and, just maybe, it had more to do with her father than Daniel. All I could really do for Daniel was to reassure him. By the time they left, they were in better shape than when they came, but it wouldn't last.

As Lorraine opened the door to leave, Camille came in with Keeter. Lorraine and Daniel backed up and gave Keeter a wide berth. I had to smile. Ordinarily Daniel was overly friendly with animals, but this was one time his mother didn't have to tell him not to pet a strange dog. Daniel had better sense than his mother gave him credit for.

I wasn't sure what to expect with Camille. We hadn't had much chance to talk last night. Was she relieved to know that it was Willy and not the kidnapper who was after her, or would it frighten her all the more that there were *two* sadists out there? It didn't help, of course, that Willy hadn't been caught.

Camille came in and started to sit down. Daniel's toy was still on the couch, and she handed it to me before she sat down. I put it on the floor beside me. It was probably all right that they left it. I didn't think Daniel was going to get to play with it for a while, and it would just remind Lorraine of his "pervertedness."

Keeter took up her usual stance, lying between me and Camille, although she did look bored, which I took as a positive comment on our relationship.

"How do you feel?" I asked, looking closely at Camille. She didn't really look any better: same dark circles under her eyes, same fearful glancing at the windows. I realized I was holding my breath while I waited for her answer.

"I don't know," she said, slowly. "I guess I'm relieved you believe me. Nothing else has really changed. I knew he was out there."

"You mean Willy?" I asked.

"Yes," she said. "I never had a name before. I think that helps a little."

I paused a minute. What was wrong with this picture? "Camille, I'm confused," I admitted. "Are you talking about Willy or the guy who kidnapped you?"

Now Camille looked confused. "What do you mean? It's the same. Didn't you know that?"

I most certainly did not know that, and there was something very wrong with that idea. Why did she think they were the same person? I glanced down as I thought and noticed the toy on the floor. Hell of a thing. How did he peep with that thing, anyway? Was it infrared? Then I froze. Was I seeing what I thought I was?

I reached over and picked it up slowly. There was the radar-looking dish with the joystick. And there were wires. I followed them to a set of earphones and put them on. I turned the dish around and pointed it at Keeter. I clicked the joystick, and suddenly the sound of Keeter licking her paw filled my earphones. I stood up slowly and did it again. Keeter had stopped licking her paw and looked up at me curiously. In the earphones, her breathing sounded like the ocean's roar. Daniel hadn't been peeping; he had been eavesdropping.

Camille was staring at me, but it didn't seem important. I walked around behind my chair and tried the toy again. Nothing. "Line-of-sight," I said out loud. "Son-of-a-bitch."

No wonder. No wonder I couldn't find a bug. I headed straight for the windows and looked up. There was nothing facing the side window, but the front windows were across the street from a church, and there was one window that looked straight down, line-of-sight, on my window.

I pointed the toy up to the window and squeezed the button. Nothing. Maybe nobody was up there now. Or maybe I just had a toy version of this thing, and the range wasn't that far. But if there was a toy version of this thing, there was a real version of this thing. "Son-of-a-bitch," was all I could say. I had wondered about Willy planting a tape and just leaving it. It wasn't like Willy not to stay around for the suffering. Well, he had.

I headed for the door. "I've got to go," I managed to say, and then I caught myself at the door and stopped. I suddenly had the feeling of hands around my throat so distinctly I could hardly breathe. The last time I had run off on my own, it had turned out badly. Who says I can't learn? All it takes is strangling me.

I turned around. I needed to get my fanny pack—but I realized I couldn't. The fanny pack was in the car trunk. If I went outside and took it out of the car trunk, Willy could see me. The goddamn car was sitting in the driveway in full sight of the church. Getting a fanny pack out of a car trunk in the middle of a therapy session would tip off somebody a lot dumber than Willy.

I took a deep breath: I'd just have to push through this. I turned around—I needed to tell Camille something to explain my crazy behavior—when I caught sight of the window. I walked over and pulled the shades down. Line-of-sight. All I had needed to do was pull the shades down. Willy had never teased me about Danny because the shades had been down and he hadn't been able to listen in. He never knew he'd been there.

I picked up the cordless phone and handed it to Camille. "I'm sorry, Camille," I said. "I really have to go, but I'll be back. If I'm not back, if you hear anything, call 911." Camille looked totally appalled. She just looked at me. I waited, but she didn't speak. I turned and headed for the door.

She found her voice. "Wait," she said. "He's out there, isn't he?"

"Yes," I said.

"You're going looking for him," she said with pure disbelief in her voice.

"Yes."

There was silence, and I started to move again when Camille spoke. "Take Keeter," she said. "Don't go alone." I turned, and she was holding out the lead. Her chin and her hand were both quivering, but still she held it out. Jesus, the courage that took.

I looked at Keeter. She looked like a big comfort right now. I crossed the room and took the lead. Keeter stood up and looked at Camille and looked at me. Would she go with me?

"Keeter," I said forcefully, "I don't have time to screw around, so let's go." I started to move, but Keeter didn't. She just stood there looking at Camille. Camille made a hand signal, and Keeter turned and trotted after me, looking excited. The leash fell slack as she automatically heeled. Clearly, something was up, and Keeter seemed to like it more than just sitting around.

I ran from the waiting room into the living part of Carlotta's house and out the back door. Keeter trotted beside me quietly. I crossed several backyards and then took a chance and crossed the street half a block down from my office. I walked through backyards all the way and came up to the back door of the church across the street from my office. Keeter was still heeling even though I hadn't asked her to. She seemed focused and intent, but she had a look that said lunch was about to be served.

The back door of the church was unlocked, and I just walked in. The building was silent. Weekdays, probably there weren't a lot of people around. I crossed the main chapel to the front of the church and found the stairs going up. I went up to the second floor and walked into what looked like the minister's office. I was glad he wasn't there. It was easier not having to explain, and besides, I didn't want anybody to know someone had been spying on my clients.

I looked out the window in his office, but the shrubs that partially covered my office windows blocked the view. Why didn't I think to notice how far up that window was? I headed back for the stairs and went up to the third floor.

Then I found it: a large room overlooking my office with nothing in it but some cardboard storage boxes. The light in the room was dim, the blind on the one window was pulled most of the way down, and the lights were off. I walked over to the window and knelt down to see under the blind. I didn't touch anything. This was a crime scene, and I didn't want to contaminate evidence.

But even peeping under the blind I could tell it was a perfect line-of-sight bead on my office window. And it looked like you could hang out here forever and no one was likely to know.

The room was empty. So maybe Willy knew the police were after him and he had fled. Whatever. But this was it. The son-of-a-bitch had sat in this empty, dark room and listened in on God knows how many therapy sessions. And all my sweeping for bugs had done exactly nothing because there had never been a bug to sweep for in the first place. What was he going to do, harass all my clients, or did he just pick Camille because she was the most vulnerable? Jesus, what had I done to my clients by keeping my practice open? Had he recorded them?

I walked around the room looking for signs of Willy and trying to sort things out. Wendy and the lost boys. I was wrong. He hadn't been taunting me with kids he was going to molest. Wendy took care of her siblings and the lost boys. Peter Pan had showed up to lead everybody off to fantasyland. No doubt, he had cast me as Wendy, taking care of my grown-up charges, while he saw himself as Peter Pan, trying to lure them away—although his idea of fantasyland was a little different from Peter Pan's.

I had dropped the lead to let Keeter look around. She was sniffing around the boxes, and I noticed the hair on the back of her neck was standing up. She was smelling something and seemed to recognize it. Probably she recognized Willy's smell from Camille's bedroom. He had to get in there sometime to plant the tape recorder. His smell would have still been there when Keeter got back, and she wouldn't have liked it: an intruder in her space.

Keeter walked behind some boxes stacked in front of the window, and I lost sight of her. No doubt that was where Willy had sat or knelt or something, since it was directly in front of the window.

I decided to join her to see if I could find evidence someone

had been there—the dust on the windowsill might be dis-
turbed—when I heard sounds on the stairs. Oh, my God. Let it
be the minister. But I knew it wasn't. I knew instantly it was
Willy. He was just late, that was all, but he was coming to
listen in.

There was time. I could hide. But I couldn't. I couldn't stand
crouching down waiting to be caught. I just stood there: What
else could I do?

Willy's shadow preceded him, which didn't help my nerves
any. He came around the corner with something that looked
like a large camera bag slung over his shoulder. He looked
startled when he saw me, and then he grinned. He put both
his arms on the sides of the door, pretty much filling the door
frame.

Neither of us spoke for a moment in the dim light. Funny, I
didn't realize he was so big. I knew he was portly, but I
thought he was medium-sized. Belatedly I realized that an
average male was still taller than me at five-seven. And being
a wide-body counts when there is only one door.

"Well, well, well," he said. "Clever girl. I do underrate you at
times. You must grant it was quite an aesthetic little number.
A rather elegant way to get to you, don't you think? I set
myself a challenge: What kind of havoc could I wreak without
laying a finger on anyone?"

Willy dropped his arms from the door frame and patted his
portly belly. It was an oddly incongruous gesture: it seemed so
normal. His tone—his gestures—he could have been discuss-
ing the weather, only he wasn't.

"I see you came alone. How nice. I was just thinking of you
and how we might continue our little tête-à-tête in a more
intimate way. To be honest, I was tiring of all these silly
technological toys. Too esoteric. Too . . . bloodless, shall we
say. How thoughtful of you to solve my little dilemma."

"Give it up, Willy," I said firmly. "The police know all about you. We found your tape recording. They're waiting for you now at Camille's." My voice sounded better than I expected. Not great, but at least I didn't squeak.

"Beside the point," Willy answered. "Given we're not there." If he hadn't known they were looking for him, he covered it well.

"Fortunately," he went on, "my motto is 'Be prepared,' a hangover from my days as a scout leader." He opened the bag over his shoulder, his eyes never leaving me. He carefully took out what looked like a larger version of the toy radar dish and put it aside on the top of a box. He reached back into the bag.

"Did you know you can torture someone in complete silence? Oh, yes. It's just a little more complicated. You have to be careful with the gags and all that. Not that it's as satisfying as actually hearing the moaning. I personally prefer the way the moaning deepens as the pain grows. But one does what one can." He sighed, then he reached into the bag and pulled out a small .45 with a silencer.

Involuntarily, I took a step backward. Oh, shit. I should have made my move immediately. Great, the first time in my life I hesitate and think about something, and it is exactly the wrong thing to do. I should have run into him as he was coming around the corner. Willy may have underrated me a little, but I sure as hell had underrated him a lot.

He reached back into the bag. Slowly, he pulled things out: a large bowie knife, precut lengths of rope, a gag, duct tape, and then some things that seemed even worse—a lighter, a scalpel, a pair of pliers, and some instrument-looking things I didn't recognize. He did it all so carefully it was almost hypnotic, pulling each one out and laying it precisely, just so, on a cardboard box he used as a table. He spaced them carefully, evenly apart from each other. I'd heard of torture kits, read about them, but I had never seen one and certainly never dreamed one would be used on me.

Strange what goes through your mind at bad times. I thought of Faulkner's story of the man who asked for a last drink of water before being executed and kept pretending to drink long after the water was gone. Some part of me wanted Willy to keep pulling things out of his bag forever, no matter how grotesque, because push wouldn't come to shove until he stopped. He pulled out handcuffs, which hit me harder than anything—I can't stand to be confined—and then he stopped.

"Willy," I said, with whatever dignity I could summon. "Don't be ridiculous. All I have to do is scream."

"I wouldn't do that," Willy said. "Because then I will be forced to put a bullet through your throat, which I can do before you finish even one. I'll be out of here long before anybody figures out where the sound came from. But you will not be out of here. You will be lying on the floor gargling and gasping for air for quite some time, dying very slowly."

Oh, shit. But wait a minute. Where was Keeter? I had forgotten all about her in the hypnosis of the torture kit. Where the hell was Keeter? I had a goddamn maniac attack dog somewhere behind me, behind the boxes where Willy couldn't see her, and she hadn't made a peep. They were supposed to growl or bark or something. They were supposed to attack people who threatened you with guns. What was she doing, cowering with her paws over her head?

There was no way I could turn around and look over the boxes without tipping off Willy. And whether Keeter could help or not, I didn't want to give her away; Willy would just put a bullet in her brain if he saw her. I covered my face with my hands for a second as though trying to collect myself and glanced as far behind me on each side as I could see.

There in the dim light on the side of the boxes on my left

was Keeter. She had crept up silently on her belly without making a sound. Of course, that was how she had been trained.

Keeter was waiting, just like she always did, for the perp to enter the building and close the door. I'd as soon she didn't wait. I didn't know when Willy was going to close the door. I didn't know if Willy was going to close the door. Actually it was fine with me if she attacked right now.

It occurred to me a little late I should have asked Camille what the signal was for "attack." It was like bringing a gun without knowing how to get the safety off. I'd have to rely on Keeter's judgment because I couldn't tell her anything.

"Willy," I said, just to keep him focused on me. "What is the point of all this? Do you really think you can torture someone in a church building on a main street with no one knowing?"

"I know I can," he replied calmly.

"It's not going to happen, Willy. You can shoot me or not shoot me, but you're not going to handcuff me, period."

Willy laughed. "I don't think you understand, Michael. You are living the last pain-free seconds of your life. When I get tired of the anticipation I will simply put a bullet in each of your kneecaps. You will go down instantly, and while you are writhing in pain I will indeed handcuff you. The rest simply depends on my imagination. But I will be in complete and utter control."

Even from where I stood, even in the dim light, I could see that his eyes were starting to shine. "Oh, yes," he said. "That's never happened to you, has it? No one has ever had absolute and total control of you, able to do anything they choose, make you suffer, even take your life away.

"I doubt you appreciate the high that comes with controlling someone like that. It's better than crack, better than cocaine. Well, from the doer's point of view, of course."

The image was so gruesome I tried to block it out of my

mind. What was Keeter up to? I tried to think. If she couldn't respond to me, I needed to respond to her. What was she waiting for? I put my hand on my forehead as though upset by Willy's plan—which I was—and glanced at Keeter. She was absolutely still and crouched. She looked like a spring compressed to the max. Her eyes never left Willy's face. Keeter, old girl, he's not going to close the door until he shoots me, so get on with it.

I measured the distance with my eye. He was too far away from her. He wasn't crowding her. That was the other thing that would make her go, if he crowded her.

There must be something that would draw him closer—something that would make Willy take a chance. What could I sell him that he'd want to buy enough to come closer without kneecapping me first? He already had everything he wanted: the setting, the control, the victim.

I held out my wrists handcuff distance apart. "I don't think you can do it, Willy," I said. "Shoot someone that you know from a distance maybe. But up close and personal? Put the handcuffs on my wrists and hurt me? You and I have talked for years. We've been friends of a sort. You wouldn't be human if you could ignore all that."

Willy practically sputtered. "My dear child. Surely you don't believe what you're saying. You can't be some airheaded Pollyanna who thinks I'm just a kindhearted, misunderstood soul?"

"I'm willing to bet my life on it, Willy. If you're right, you don't have to bother with kneecapping me: I'm willing to let you cuff me. But if you're wrong and you can't do it, then you go out and face the music for what you've done playing games with Camille. Deal?"

Willy hesitated. If good-hearted folk frequently don't know what to make of people who are bitter-hearted evil, then vice versa is also true. Willy wouldn't know whether to believe me or not. But he wanted to. He wanted to because betraying a trust was more exciting to him than winning a fight. Willy would get an erection just thinking about the look in my eyes when I realized he was going to do exactly what he said.

I glanced down again quickly. Keeter hadn't moved a muscle. She looked like she would wait in that crouched position forever. I looked up and saw the handcuffs flying toward me. "You put them on," he said.

I caught them and threw them back. "Not on your life. Easy to stand over there and give orders. No, you have to come close enough to see the look in my eyes. That's what you're avoiding, isn't it, Willy?"

Willy was salivating by now. He hesitated a moment longer and then moved forward slowly. "No tricks," he said.

"Well, you've got the gun and the knife and you outweigh me by about a hundred pounds. I'm not sure what more you want. But if it makes you feel better . . ." I slowly lifted my hands in the air. I was hoping that might mean something to Keeter. I wished I knew something about how she was trained.

Willy paused and then kept moving forward slowly. He was focusing intently on me, looking, no doubt, for a kick or a hidden weapon. I shut up. I didn't want to confuse Keeter with friendly sounding conversation. Willy was eight feet away, maybe seven—how far was Keeter's territory? When was he too close?

He stopped again. Willy had decided he had come close enough. And goddamn it, Keeter hadn't. What was the distance between where he was and where she felt crowded? Was I going to get shot over a couple of feet? Why was he so goddamn leery of me, anyway; I have an honest face.

I held out my hands again. Willy was way too far to reach them. "You can't do it, Willy, so let's just go. Deep down, I've always had faith in you. I've always known there was something decent in you despite all the rotten stuff you've done. Maybe it was no accident you chose a church to listen from."

Willy couldn't help himself. The thought of destroying the trusting look I held up to him was too much. He took one more step, and I saw a blur move to my left, a completely soundless blur, moving through the air toward Willy, heading for throat-height. For a second I saw the stunned look on Willy's face, and then I heard the gun go off. In the next instance Willy was down with Keeter on top of him.

This time I didn't hesitate. I flew through the door and down the stairs. I hit the front of the church door on the run and tore across the street without looking. I burst into my office and grabbed the keys for the trunk. Camille was sitting at the desk with the phone in her hand. She was shaking, but she was still functioning. "Dial 911," was all I said, and turned to leave.

"Where's Keeter?" Camille called after me. I looked down, and there was blood on my shirt. It had to be Keeter's.

"I'll be back," I said, and headed out the door. I threw open the trunk and grabbed my fanny pack. I didn't even put it on. I just started running across the street and pulled the gun out on the way.

I got back upstairs before the sirens started. Willy was still down. Keeter had missed his throat but had caught his shoulder blade. From the looks of it she had crushed the bone and then bit him a few more times for luck before she got too weak.

Willy was sweating and crying, and his shoulder was bleeding pretty freely. Keeter had him pinned under her. She was bleeding too—how badly was hard to say without moving her. Her eyes were shut, and her body wasn't moving. Willy was in too much pain to try to get her off—she weighed easily over a hundred pounds. "Keeter?" I said, but she gave no response.

"Get her off," Willy said. Beads of sweat were popping out on his forehead, and he looked like he might be going into shock, which, oddly enough, didn't bother me in the slightest.

I was just sorry she missed his throat. I didn't bother to answer him, but headed back down the stairs, this time to get Camille. She was probably the only person who could do anything for Keeter.

I didn't even think about doing anything for Willy except calling the police. I personally wasn't in the mood to help Willy at all. On the contrary, I thought after we got Keeter off his chest, we ought to drive a stake through his heart.

23

The sirens came closer as I took off my blouse. I didn't care about standing around in my underwear; Keeter was bleeding badly. Camille and I tried to bind up her side as best we could to try and stop it. Then we tried to push her off Willy, but it wasn't easy. Camille said she weighed almost one twenty, and there was so much blood on the floor that Camille and I were slipping around in it. We worked as gently as we could.

Keeter was semiconscious but determined not to let Willy up, so mostly she wasn't cooperating. Whenever she was awake enough to recognize Camille, she'd listen to her and let us move her a little. We finally got her off Willy just as we heard footsteps on the stairs. Moments later Adam burst around the corner with two officers. He took a glance at Willy and asked, "Have you called an ambulance?"

"No," I said. Actually, I hadn't even thought of it. He pulled out his walkie-talkie and spoke into it, then knelt down beside Willy. Willy's eyes were closed, and his color didn't look good. Adam pulled back his eyelids to look at his eyes, then took his pulse. Willy's breathing was rapid and shallow, and I'd be willing to bet his pulse was fluttering. "He's in shock," he said and pulled off his jacket and covered him up with it. Then he started trying to bind up the wound.

In the distance we heard sirens again. "Go downstairs," he said to one of the officers who just seemed to be standing around, "and direct the ambulance."

It was very odd seeing somebody in as much trouble as Willy was and having no impulse to help him. It was worse than that; I was hoping he'd die. I'd felt the same way about Ted Bundy. I thought he had forfeited his right to be among us, and, for my money, so had Willy.

I found myself resenting Adam trying to save him, but I kept my mouth shut. People who've been exposed to torture kits aren't objective; they aren't even rational. And Adam wouldn't stop doing his job no matter what I said.

We had done all we could for Keeter. Now we needed to get her to a vet. I looked up at the one officer who was still standing around. "We need some help," I said. "We need to get her to a vet."

"You," Adam said firmly, "are not going anywhere. Officer Barrett will help your friend get the dog to the vet."

I started to argue, but then stopped. Camille was functioning better than I'd ever seen her. Maybe it was a good thing for her to go deal with the vet on her own. "Call on the way," was all I said. "Let them know what they've got coming in."

Luckily Officer Barrett looked like he was one of those weight-lifting-type cops. He picked up Keeter easily and headed off with Camille.

The ambulance crew arrived a few minutes later, and after a period of scrambling and IVs and shots, Willy was put on a stretcher and the medics took off rushing down the stairs, leaving Adam and I standing around in the dim room. We were both covered with blood from our knees down from kneeling in the stuff.

Adam said to the one officer left, "Secure this scene and call for the state crime lab to come out. I'm going to take Dr. Stone's statement." He was not exactly warm. He was more like totally and completely pissed off, and my guess was, at me.

"Can we go to my office?" I said. I just wanted to get out of there and away from all memories of how close I'd come to losing my kneecaps and God knows what else.

"No," Adam said formally, "I want to keep an eye on things here. But," he added, seeming to relent slightly, "we can go to another room."

We found another room to talk in, and as the blood dried on our pants, I came clean with the story of Willy. It wasn't a pretty story. All Adam had asked of me was that I tell him if Willy contacted me, and I had not only not done that, I had bald-faced lied to him. Even last night I hadn't told him the whole story.

The more I talked about Willy and what he'd been up to, the more Adam's jaw set and the more his lips got thin and tight. He didn't say anything though. He just wrote down what I said and asked some questions, but he had a layer of ice around him that would have sunk the Titanic. I hadn't been very hopeful for my relationship with Adam before. I was pretty sure I knew where it stood now.

I started to tell him I was planning on coming clean that afternoon, but I didn't. It just sounded too weak. Too little, too late.

Besides, the truth was I didn't really know why involving Adam had been so hard for me. Disjointed images came to mind: swimming alone at night at fifteen on the inland waterway, where running into snakes wasn't even all that uncommon. Driving cars at 120 miles an hour at sixteen and waiting on every curve to see whether fate took a shot or not. I always seemed to have to walk up right to the edge of something, and I could never take anybody with me. The only honest thing I *could* have said to Adam was, "I don't know what this is all about, Adam, but it's old."

I didn't say it. I just kept plowing through the story. I finally got through all of it, but I was getting very cold and very tired. The adrenaline was long gone, and I felt like I'd been dropped off a cliff. Adam finally seemed to notice I wasn't doing well, and he stood up. "That's it for now," he said. "There're going to be some problems with this, but now isn't the time to talk about them."

I didn't know what he meant, but I was too tired to care. It was still morning, but I felt like it was midnight and I'd crossed the Sahara before dawn.

I started to get up when he said, "Give me a minute. I'll be right back." He went away, and when he returned he said, "Carlotta's on her way over. I'd like you to wait here until she comes." He didn't sound quite as stiff as before.

I started to protest. I get a knee-jerk reaction when people tell me what to do, but then I realized it didn't sound so bad. I was beat. "Okay," I said, and Adam raised his eyebrows. I think he realized, then, just how wiped I was.

He looked at me a minute longer, and I had the feeling maybe some part of him wanted to put his arms around me. Maybe some part of me wanted to put my arms around him. But he didn't and I didn't. I was feeling like a shit for lying to him, and I didn't even know why I did it.

And Adam? I don't know what he was feeling. He just shook his head and said, "Jesus, Michael, you're a work of art," and then he was gone. I guess that meant he was still mad.

24

I was out of it the rest of the day, and that night I slept for twelve million years. I stayed at Carlotta's and had some of the worst nightmares of my life—all to do with pliers and scalpels and handcuffs. Nonetheless I kept sleeping, and when I woke up, it was eleven o'clock the next day and Carlotta was there with coffee. "Don't you work, anymore?" I said. I had gotten some of my testiness back overnight.

"You're better," she said, relieved. "Adam said you were cooperative, so I knew you were in trouble."

"Bitch, bitch, bitch," I said. "Shut up and eat your porridge." It was a revisionist version of the three bears, and Carlotta knew the joke. She laughed.

"Adam called. He wants you to stop by the station at your earliest convenience."

"Why?" I said cynically. "Has some fool set bail for Willy?" I sat bolt upright. "How is Keeter? Is she all right?"

"Adam said she was."

I slumped down, relieved. "That is one smart dog," I said, "and one tough dog. I suppose Willy's alive too?"

"I'm afraid so," Carlotta said. "I'm not going to ask you about it now," she went on. "I think Adam's going to put you through enough, but someday I'd like to know what utter and complete stupidity you've been involved in."

"Deal," I replied, just relieved not to be on the hot seat again.

I finally made it down to see Adam, although I didn't rush. It was mid-afternoon before I started out, and he had called again. I didn't want to see Adam. I hate to see people who are right to be mad at me. How can you get righteously indignant with a friend to whom you lied through your teeth?

On the other hand, what was I supposed to do about it— grovel? Probably, he was expecting an apology. Well, fuck that. It wouldn't do any good, anyway. If it happened again, I'd probably play it the same way, and Adam knew that. I muttered all the way to the station and walked in like a sullen adolescent. I was in the wrong and resentful as hell that I was feeling guilty.

Adam looked less furious than the day before and more resigned. "Well," he said without preamble after he had shut the door to his office, "what do you want him charged with?"

"What do I want him charged with? Try kidnapping and attempted murder."

"I can do that," he said slowly, "but you have to realize the implications."

"What implications?"

"You're going to have to bring out what Willy was doing in that room and what you were doing there. I don't know how comfortable you're going to be with putting in the paper that Willy has been listening in on your therapy sessions."

I was silent. I hadn't thought about that. I'd made up my mind last night I was going to have to tell all my clients a sadistic sex offender might have listened in on their therapy sessions and just might know their most intimate secrets, but it hadn't occurred to me that it would also get put in the newspaper. "Did you get a search warrant for his house?" I asked.

"Yep," he said.

"Was he taping?"

"Yep," he said.

"How many are there?"

"I don't know whether there are multiple sessions on the tapes, but there are a dozen or more tapes. He was working as a janitor at the church, and he had plenty of access."

"Oh, Jesus," I said. "Will they get admitted into evidence?"

"I would think so," Adam said. "The prosecution would certainly want them—they're proof positive why he was there—and the search was legal: i's dotted and t's crossed. Even if you talked them out of it, the defense would probably try to get them admitted. Anything that would embarrass local folk would put pressure on the prosecution to settle the case. I'm assuming there're some things on the tapes you don't want made public?"

"You might say that," I said. I had affairs and alcohol problems and people who hated their spouses and people who were in love with their friends' husbands. I had spouses of batterers who were making secret plans to leave them, and I had people who were gay and their own spouses didn't know it.

"I don't think my clients would want their business made public," I said slowly. "Not to mention that there is a big question about whether it was ethical for me to keep my practice open once I even had a hint somebody might be listening in on the sessions. If those tapes are admitted into evidence, I have a feeling I'll be looking at lawsuits and ethics charges."

"Uh-huh," Adam said, and I realized he had thought of this already.

"So what am I supposed to do? Let Willy walk? What about the stuff with Camille?"

"Criminal threatening, breaking and entering," Adam said. "That's the worst we can throw at him. It won't keep him in very long. Although there is one thing. . . ."

"What?" I said. Why is nothing ever simple?

"Camille said last night that he was the one who kidnapped her before."

"You sound skeptical," I said, not mentioning that I was too.

"I am," he said. "It's too much of a coincidence. I'm willing to buy—well, he obviously tried to play on her fears for who knows what sick reasons—but for somebody he kidnapped years ago when he didn't even live in her part of the country to end up as your client—I'm having trouble with it, although it's true he wasn't in prison then, so I suppose it's possible."

I had a whole lot of trouble with it, and I had even more reason. Camille had described her kidnapper to me. Like Willy, he had been into rape and torture, but the physical description she'd given me hadn't fit Willy at all. She had described him as young and slight—which Willy hadn't been for decades.

"I talked to the police again who handled her case in Boston," Adam went on. "She refused to have an internal exam at the time, so they couldn't get evidence for DNA testing. But they did get DNA testing on the murder they had later. I'm sending Willy's DNA in for testing, but I'd be willing to bet there isn't going to be a match.

"There's a thing called suggestibility, Michael. Now don't get upset. You know it and I know it. I know you think it's misused about 90 percent of the time in child sexual abuse cases, but on the other hand—a woman as posttraumatic as

Camille Robbins with Willy's voice being piped into her bedroom night after night describing rape and torture and claiming he's the kidnapper. I have to ask: What are the chances she's gotten the two confused?"

Pretty good, I thought, but I didn't say so.

"On the other hand, Michael, I've got a case that's hard to ignore. We've got his tapes from her house. There's no issue of a search warrant. It was Camille's house, and she gave permission. We've got other similar tapes in our perfectly legal search of his premises. He's clearly been emotionally torturing her, and she swears up and down that he's the same man who kidnapped and tortured her before. He says so himself on the tapes.

"The only evidence Willy could have to the contrary would have come from her therapy sessions. That's the first time she was ever able to talk about the abduction.

"The problem for Willy is that even if Camille said anything on tape that exonerated him, he'll never be able to use it. The tapes were illegally obtained, and I seriously doubt that his attorneys would even try to have evidence admitted of additional crimes the jury wouldn't know about—assuming you don't charge him with anything.

"So I'm asking you. I'm not asking *what* she said in the therapy sessions. I'm just asking you, how stable is this woman? How suggestible? Do you have any reason from your sessions to doubt Camille Robbins when she says that Alex B. Willy is the man who kidnapped and tortured her?"

I looked up at Adam's face and studied it for a moment. In for a penny, in for a pound, I thought. "None at all," I said. "Coincidences happen."

Adam looked thoughtfully at me for a long moment. "Michael . . . ," he started, and then lapsed into silence. His face was full of indecision.

I held up my sweet, lying little face for his scrutiny. "If she says he's the one," I said calmly, "that's good enough for me, and I know her better than you do." I fell silent, too, but look all he wanted, Adam wasn't going to find any indecision in my face, not a single, solitary fair-is-fair-he-didn't-do-it-so-put-him-on-the-streets subatomic particle.

25

Nothing happened right away. Willy was too injured even to be arraigned. But he got better, and a few weeks later they arraigned him, and he found out what he was facing.

I suppose I was expecting the call. I didn't have to go, but I decided to. Partly I needed to face Willy again for my own reasons, maybe to be sure I could. But there was some kind of closure that I needed, too, although I couldn't really say why.

I went down to the visiting room of the county jail and for once was glad for the glass wall separating us. I might be ready to face Willy, but I wasn't ready to be in a room alone with him, at least not without Keeter. Willy's neck and shoulder were bandaged, and he had lost weight, but he was definitely alive, unfortunately, which I was still sorry for. I guess I'm not the forgiving type. I got it honestly. Mama always said, "When you've got your foot on a rattlesnake's neck is not the time to get religion."

I sat down, folded my arms, and said nothing at all. This was Willy's show, and maybe I came most of all to see how he would play it.

"Good morning, Dr. Stone," Willy said. "I trust you have recovered from my little games. I'm sure you are aware I would never have really . . ."

"Don't insult me, Mr. Willy," I said.

"Surely you don't think . . . ," Willy started.

I stood up to go. "Well, now," he said hastily, "do sit down. We'll just move on. We may differ on whether I was really serious or not, but that isn't the issue," he added quickly. "Ah . . . there seems to be some kind of misunderstanding."

"Really?" I said.

"I believe you know what I'm talking about," Willy said. "I admit to playing a few games with Ms. Robbin's head, but it should be obvious to any moron that I wasn't the one who raped and tortured her."

"Tell it to the judge," I said. "You'll get your day in court."

"I don't think it's going to get that far," Willy said. "Not if you're who you say you are."

"Oh?"

"Well, this is where we get to find out, Dr. Stone, if you're any different than I am." Willy shifted in his seat and warmed to the topic. Clearly, he had rehearsed what he was going to say. "Oh, I know you don't have my particular aesthetic interests, but in regard to the larger issues—truth and justice and those ideals you profess to believe in—well, do you or don't you?

"Because if you do, you can't let an innocent man go to prison for something he didn't do. And you know that Camille's description of her assailant didn't match me until I started playing my little games with her—and I was just playing games with her."

"Mr. Willy," I replied calmly, "you set yourself up, not I. You tortured that poor woman until she couldn't separate you and the other perp. Who am I to get between you and the fate you set up so carefully for yourself?"

"You can't be serious," Willy said. "So am I to take it that justice and the law are fine so long as they fit your agenda?"

"You talk like they're the same," I said. "The law and justice may sleep together occasionally, but it's not like they have an ongoing relationship. I'm a much bigger fan of justice than I am the law."

"Don't rely on semantics, Dr. Stone. Sending me to jail for a crime I didn't commit is flouting the law, and it's hardly justice."

"Between your going free for a crime you did commit and going to jail for a crime you didn't commit, I figure the law isn't going to be served either way. And yes, in my opinion, justice *will* be served if you head straight for prison. The bottom line is this, Mr. Willy: I don't pay for no dead horses."

"What's that supposed to mean?" Willy asked.

"It means your whining to me about justice is a little like a cancer cell asking for fair play. Let me put it this way. I am not the sanest human being I know, but I've got enough of my mind intact not to buy what you sell. Actually I just figured out what you sell. You sell the idea that there is no real nastiness in the world.

"The problem is that there is: There is downright evil in the world, and you, sir, are a fair example of it. People who buy dead horses can't really deal with malevolence. But it's there. You meant to hurt me, and you meant to hurt Camille. You get a kick out of other people's pain."

Willy was silent. For some reason, he didn't seem prepared for this. Or maybe there was no good answer to this. Maybe he only had one thing to sell, and you bought it or you didn't.

"I've thought about this. If I interfered with your going to jail in any way, then for the next twenty years, I'd have to wonder if every face I passed on the street was going to be your next victim. I won't do it. I won't help you add more notches to your belt. You're going down for the count, Mr. Willy—and that's who I say I am."

EPILOGUE

I didn't hear from Adam for a while. Hard to blame him, but I found to my annoyance I missed him. Men are habit-forming: They ought to come with warning labels. Carlotta kept telling me to call him, but what was I supposed to say? The truth was, I probably wasn't going to change a whole lot, and if he couldn't live with my craziness, I couldn't blame him. I had, after all, thrown him out of my house for trying to help me. Then I lied to his face, probably several times actually.

But he did call, finally, and he said he wanted to talk. Could he come over? "Not tonight," I heard myself saying. "Tonight is the night I get over my phobia of b-ball courts. I've got to play basketball again, or I'm going to lose my mind."

Adam knew all about the guy who tried to strangle me in a gym—he was the one who rescued me—and he knew, too, I hadn't been able to go to a gym alone since then. I had planned to go to the gym tonight—I wasn't *exactly* lying—but I did hear a little voice inside my head saying, "Well, it doesn't have to be *tonight,* turkey." I ignored it. I had a bad feeling about what Adam wanted to say, and I really didn't want to hear it.

I hung up and looked at the phone. I just wasn't in the mood for an emotional bloodbath. If Adam was gone, he was gone. No point in holding a funeral service. Some people just want to talk things to death, and I'm not one of them.

But when I entered the gym, I found, to my surprise, that Adam was there shooting by himself. I went over and sat down on the bench for a moment just watching him. I should have been pissed off. I sure as hell hadn't asked him to come and keep me company. I was pissed off, sort of, but I had to admit I was mostly just relieved. The silent gym—once upon a time my favorite place in the world—didn't look too good to me these days. Adam waved but didn't speak. Probably he wasn't too sure of his reception.

He looked awfully good. Mostly, playing ball, I don't really notice. When I was a five-seven, one-hundred-pound thirteen-year-old, the gym was absolutely the only place in the universe I didn't feel awkward. People are sexless on a basketball court. They're fast or they're slow. They fake a lot, or they just power their way through. They have the economy in their moves of the well-coached, or they have all the superfluous mannerisms of the self-taught, but whatever it is, they aren't male or female.

So, it was odd, but Adam looked awfully good tonight. He was doing layups, and as he drove, the muscles in his thighs changed definition. I had noticed Adam's thighs before. They never looked bad. He had that kind of basketball long and lean muscle, not that bunchy weight-lifting leg muscle I didn't personally care for. I had had some experience with Adam's thighs up close and personal, and, yes, they were very nice indeed.

But I don't know why I was thinking about it with basketball to play. I finished tying my shoes and walked out onto the court with my ball. "Baby-sitting?" I said. My voice surprised me with its sarcasm. Habit, I guess.

"It's a free country," he replied. "Just working on my shot."

I didn't comment. I just started methodically warming up. Five under the basket on one side, five in front, five on the other side. Me and Bill Bradley. I moved a couple of feet out and started it all over again. There was no sound except the balls bouncing and the net swishing. Thank God Adam knew enough not to ruin the place with useless chatter. I caught my ball and turned to Adam. "I'm sorry I lied to you," I said. In the aftermath of catching Willy, it was the one thing I hadn't been able to say. I tried to tone down the grumpiness in my voice, but I only partly succeeded.

"It's okay," he said. "It goes with the territory."

I turned to shoot, but stopped and turned back to Adam. "What? Now you're saying I'm a chronic liar?"

"You're a predictable liar," he said.

Predictable. I didn't seem to have a comeback to that, so I started shooting again. His voice had this sound in it like he knew me or something. No, more like he knew me, fault lines and all—and he wasn't heading for the nearest exit.

Was that intimacy, I wondered? Not the free fall letting go followed by the I'm-out-of-here-buddy-and-besides-you-have-a-wife-so-don't-try-to-hold-onto-my-shirt kind of thing, which was the closest I had come to intimacy. I was good at the kind of intimacy that came with a safety harness.

I went back to shooting. I was working in a circle from one side to another, foul line distance from the basket. This was easy territory, and I didn't miss much. My range extended to the top of the key, and after that I'd start to get into trouble.

"Horse?" he said.

"In a moment," I replied. Jesus. Does he think he can

interrupt my warm-up just like that? He wouldn't have done that to Bill Bradley. Adam seemed full of energy. He was putting more energy into his warm-up than most people put into their games.

Horse was the best idea—it was a straight shooting contest— but personally, I preferred one-on-one. We'd get around to that eventually, although we both knew I didn't stand a chance against Adam one-on-one. He had maybe sixty pounds on me and six inches. I did okay on offense with him, but you just can't defend against that kind of height.

I headed for the limits of my range to finish my warm-up. I started in the corner and to my delight was on. I sank three in a row and moved a couple of feet over and started again. Joy is when the ball just drops for you. It all seems so easy when it works. I was getting my legs under the shot, and the ball was just rolling off my fingertips straight and true. It had a lazy backspin and an arc you could die for. I could feel my mood lift with every shot.

Adam had stopped shooting and was just watching me. I faked and went up again. No sense just shooting without the move before it. You don't get to stand there in a game and just shoot. Adam walked over and stood under the basket. He started catching the ball as it swished through and throwing it back. I dribbled twice and put the ball up again, working carefully around the half-circle. I had caught the wave or something: Everything I threw up was going in. I came in closer and tried a fade-away jumper just for the hell of it.

I saw Adam smiling at me and missed the shot. I turned my back on him and dribbled a couple of times before I wheeled around. What was that smile? He had looked like a male Mona Lisa. The Cheshire cat? Whatever he was thinking, he hadn't said it.

I started to feel self-conscious and missed two more. "One-on-one?" I said, more to stop Adam from looking at me as much as anything. That smile just hadn't been a good-buddies-hit-each-other-on-the-shoulder *basketball* smile. I began to wonder if there was a way of leaving the gym tonight with a far better memory than the one of someone trying to kill me. Would it help with my PTSD—theoretically speaking? Would Adam contribute to a scientific experiment? I laughed out loud.

"What is it?" Adam said.

"Nothing," I said. "I'm losing it."

"One-on-one?" Adam asked. "Not horse?" I should have said horse. Horse was the great equalizer. One person shot, and if it went in, the other person had to make the identical shot or get a letter. If someone got all five letters, he or she was out. You didn't have to be tall or wide; you just had to know how to shoot. I should love horse, and I like it all right, but nothing gets the adrenaline flowing like one-on-one, in-your-face contact ball.

Adam walked up with the ball and handed it to me. True to the ethics of pick-up ball, he knew better than to just throw it to me: I might take a shot before he had a chance to get into position. Would I do that? Yes, I would.

Adam went into a defensive crouch. He was playing very close to me, which wasn't exactly a surprise. Adam was no dummy, and my outside shot was falling. I'd have to drive on him to back him off or I wouldn't get a single outside shot, but it was hell to drive one-on-one with someone like Adam. Sure, I could fake him and get a step on him, but he'd catch up before I got to the basket.

I faked left and drove right. I got a step on him, and as he accelerated to catch up I stopped, faked in the direction I had been heading, and pivoted back for a left hook. It wasn't a good idea to throw up something I had not tried one single time in warm-up, but because of that, it was the only shot Adam wouldn't be expecting. Yes, and because of that, it was also the only shot I couldn't make. The ball went long and bounced around between the rim and the backboard.

I tried to follow my shot, of course, but Adam had already spun to block me out. He had his hands behind him to keep tabs on me, and I was trapped behind him. I could feel the heat of his body as we stood like two spoons, Adam in front and me behind, waiting for the ball to quit bouncing and come down. Adam was pushing back to keep me out, and I, of course, was trying to push him under the rim so I could get the ball over his head.

It was the usual jostling and pushing under the boards, so I don't know why it bothered me. But I was having trouble concentrating. Adam's hand was on my hip, and I could feel the warmth of it right through my shorts. I was acutely aware of the feeling of his back on my breasts. The ball came down, and I could feel the power in his body surge as he jumped for it.

He dribbled to the top of the key, and I followed. I had barely got in my defensive stance when he headed right back for the basket with the smallest of fakes. Arrogant bastard. I guess he felt he got enough speed he didn't need to bother to fake. I scrambled to keep up and managed to reach in and knock the ball away. Okay, so the NBA might have called it a foul, but in pick-up ball, no blood, no foul.

In any case, Adam didn't call a foul. He just laughed and retrieved the ball. To my surprise, he headed right back in again. He pivoted with his back to the basket and started edging in backward.

It was something Adam rarely did with me. Sure, he could score that way, but proving he had enough height to outscore me under the basket wasn't much of a challenge. If I didn't know better, I'd say Adam was enjoying getting me under the boards. Maybe he hadn't faked before because he wanted me to keep up with him. He kept edging backward, and I, of course, braced against him trying to keep him out. My hips were wedged against his backside, and I don't know who was fouling whom but there was a lot of contact.

Ordinarily this is not a problem. Ordinarily I don't even notice this kind of thing in your average rough-and-tumble game of pick-up ball, but Adam's body was starting to get warm and moist from playing, and his breathing was getting deeper, and I was getting in over my head, which I found very confusing because it was so bizarre. Bizarre to be noticing this kind of thing on a basketball court. He wasn't helping any; he didn't seem to be in any hurry to shoot, but just kept dribbling backward back and forth across the lane.

"Three seconds," I said. In a real game you can't spend more than three seconds in the lane on offense. It's specifically to keep people from parking there, but I had never heard of anyone calling it in a pick-up game.

"Three seconds?" he said. "Now we're calling three seconds? Okay." And he wheeled into a fade-away jumper. 1-0 Adam.

"Losers keepers," I said, meaning if you made your shot, the other person got the ball. I didn't usually play that way, but if I didn't, I could spend all night under the boards with Adam, and I wanted to concentrate on the game. It was sacrilege to be concentrating on anything but basketball in a basketball game.

"Hold it," he said and took off his shirt. Oh, Jesus. Adam did a little weight-lifting, and he didn't have the usual skinny, caved-in chest of the average workaholic middle-aged weekend ballplayer. He had a very nice chest and God-given shoulders. So now he was wearing nothing but a pair of short-shorts. I had a fleeting thought of what it would be like to pull those shorts down, but I banished it. At least I tried to banish it and concentrate on the game. Just kneel down and slowly inch-by-inch pull those shorts down.

I had on a halter top under my T-shirt, and ordinarily, I

would have taken the opportunity to take off my T-shirt, but I decided not to. I wasn't feeling any too sure of myself.

Adam caught me looking at him. "You look good," I said lightly. "I see you're keeping up with the exercise." I tried to sound detached. Just a noninvolved observer. I started dribbling as Adam walked up. He went into his defensive stance, and I faked a drive and started to go up for a shot, but Adam grabbed the front of my T-shirt and spoiled the shot.

"Hey," I said, trying to sound annoyed. "What are you doing? We're playing b-ball, for Christ's sakes." But Adam didn't let go. He just stood there holding my shirt. Silence fell in the gym. I didn't know exactly what to do. I didn't even know exactly what I wanted to do. Then Adam started slowly pulling me toward him, gently but insistently. When I was inches from him, he released my shirt and hooked his thumbs in the corners of my waistband.

"It isn't a foul unless you call it," he said. Great minds think alike. He started to slowly pull down my shorts, looking in my eyes all the while. I had a lot of time to call it. I mean, I could have called it, and I knew his fingers would have instantly sprung back. But there was that scientific experiment I'd wanted to do. It's important to support science.

I could feel the shorts slipping down inch by inch.